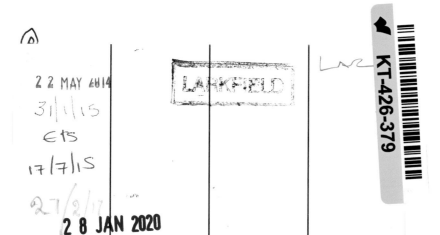

Please return on or before the latest date above.
You can renew online at *www.kent.gov.uk/libs*
or by telephone 08458 247 200

3/14

THE UNKNOWN BRIDESMAID

FORSTER. M

CUSTOMER SERVICE EXCELLENCE

Libraries & Archives

00884\DTP\RN\07.07   LIB 7

THE UNKNOWN BRIDESMAID

THE UNKNOWN BRIDESMAID

MARGARET FORSTER

LARGE PRINT

Oxford

First published in Great Britain 2013
by
Chatto & Windus
One of the Publishers in The Random House Group Ltd.

Published in Large Print 2013 by ISIS Publishing Ltd.,
7 Centremead, Osney Mead, Oxford OX2 0ES
by arrangement with
Chatto & Windus
One of the Publishers in The Random House Group Ltd.

CIP data is available for this title from the British Library

ISBN 978–0–7531–9212–2 (hb)
ISBN 978–0–7531–9213–9 (pb)

Printed and bound in Great Britain by
T. J. International Ltd., Padstow, Cornwall

For Gertrud Philippine Watson

CHAPTER
ONE

Julia gave the child the doll, and waited. There was a toy cradle in the room, and a toy pram, the old-fashioned sort, not a buggy. Beside the cradle and the pram was a neat pile of miniature blankets, and sheets, and pillows. No duvets. Julia made a mental note to include a duvet in the choice of bedlinen. Most children today would be used to duvets, not sheets and blankets. Sheets and blankets might confuse them.

The child, a girl of eight, small for her age, thin and quite frail-looking, though she had been examined and pronounced perfectly healthy, held the doll in both hands, gripping it round its shoulders. She looked at it without any apparent interest. It was a baby doll, with a bald head, and blue eyes which could close if the doll was tilted in a certain way. It was dressed in a Babygro, a blue one, and underneath it wore a paper nappy. After a minute or so, the girl looked up at Julia, and frowned. She put the doll down, and folded her arms.

Quietly, without speaking, Julia picked the doll up and gave it a cuddle, patting it on its back as though it were a real baby. Then she went to the toy pram and put the doll into it. The girl began to show some interest, but this interest was more in Julia's action than in doll or pram. Carefully, Julia tucked the sheets and blankets round the doll until only its head, with its closed eyes, was visible. Then she pushed the pram backwards and forwards, edging it nearer and nearer to the girl, and then finally letting it come to rest right beside her. The girl immediately pushed the pram away, quite violently.

Julia was eight when the invitation to be a bridesmaid came from her cousin Iris. It was a great surprise to Julia's mother as well as to Julia herself. Iris's mother and Julia's mother were sisters, but they were not close. Julia's mother had always felt that Maureen, her older sister, treated her with disdain. She'd felt this all her life, and so had been happy, once she had married and moved away from Manchester, where they were both born, to keep her distance. But a wedding changed things. Julia's mother understood that her sister would want the gathering together of her family, if just to match the gathering on the bridegroom's side. The bridegroom was a major in the army and his father was an MP. Maureen couldn't match that but she could at least have her sister and niece at her side.

But, though she understood this, Julia's mother did not immediately accept the invitation for Julia to be a bridesmaid; she waited three days, and then she rang her sister up, saying she doubted whether Julia could accept because of the expense involved. There would be the dress, the shoes, the flowers, and she had no money to spare for any of those things. She reminded her sister that she was a widow on a small, a very small, pension.

2

Her sister was furious, but she tried to keep the anger at Julia's mother boasting of her poverty (which is how she regarded it) out of her voice. She reminded herself that her sister had had a hard time, and was indeed quite poor, whereas she herself was comparatively well off, and ought to be magnanimous. She said her sister was not to worry about the expense. She said that of course she would pay for Julia's outfit and everything that went with it. She had always intended to and should have made this clear. If Julia's measurements were sent, a dress would be made and shoes bought.

Julia's mother still made a fuss about expense. She and Julia were to stay with Maureen, so the cost of a hotel was not involved, but a train ticket to Manchester would be pricey. Then there was the expense of getting to the station in the first place. The buses from their village were rare, and at awkward times, so a taxi would be needed. On and on Julia's mother went, moaning about money, doing sums on scraps of paper, looking in her bank book and emptying loose change out of various tin boxes marked "gas" and "rent". Julia, always a good and obedient child, held her breath and waited. Meanwhile, a swatch of material arrived in the post, sent by Maureen to show Julia the colour and texture of the dress being made for her. It was not pink. That was the first disappointment. Julia had always assumed the dress would be pink. Instead, it was not exactly white but a kind of cream. And it was not soft or silky. This scrap of material felt like cotton, or even — "Good heavens," said Julia's mother — rayon. "If it's rayon," she warned Julia, "it will crease instantly."

3

A taxi to the station was not in the end needed. Julia's mother had told everyone about the coming wedding, dropping the name of the bridegroom's family ever so casually, and she and Julia were offered a lift by the village shopkeeper's daughter who was going into Penrith that day. But nobody met them at the other end. Manchester station was, to Julia, terrifying. She held her mother's hand tightly. "I don't know what to do," her mother kept saying, which didn't help Julia's fear. "Maureen said we'd be met." Clearly, some arrangement had gone wrong. After a good fifteen minutes of standing stock-still on the platform where they had alighted, Julia's mother told her they would have to get a bus. She had a vague memory of a bus which went to the end of Maureen's road, but had no idea where the bus stop could be found. "We will have to ask," she said, in tones of horror. What, Julia wondered, was so terrible about asking where to find a bus stop? But her mother's agitation had communicated itself to her so completely that this wondering did not help. The noise in the station, the shrieking of the trains as they arrived and departed, and the surging crowds of hurrying people, made Julia terrified.

That was her recollection. Aged eight. Terrified, over something so unthreatening.

The girl's mother was waiting in the adjoining room. One look at the woman's face and it was obvious that she had recently done a lot of weeping. Her eyes were red and the dark shadows underneath them appeared

4

shiny, as though they were damp. Her hair, thin hair, bedraggled, had been pushed back behind her ears, but little tendrils had escaped and clung to her cheeks.

"Well?" she said to Julia, making no movement towards her child, who stood in front of her mother, waiting. There was no gesture of affection. She didn't, Julia noted, even look at the girl. It was as though she were not standing there, entirely submissive. "Well?" she said again, her voice rising higher this time on the question.

Julia smiled, and sat down. "I think Honor might be thirsty," she said. "It was rather warm in my room. I'll just get her a glass of water. I won't be a moment."

It would have been useful to have a two-way mirror in that room, but there had never been any money for that helpful device, and Julia was not sure if she herself would have agreed with the spying element. Useful, though, in a situation like this. But re-entering the room, carrying water for Honor, Julia was pretty certain nothing significant had happened during the two minutes she'd been absent. Mrs Brooks hadn't folded her daughter in her arms, or in any way tried to connect with her. Both mother and child were in exactly the same positions, their faces wearing exactly the same expressions, both of them tense and silent.

"Well?" Mrs Brooks said, this time neither challenging, nor impatient, but resigned.

"Sit down, Honor," Julia said gently. "Drink this. You look hot. You must be thirsty. Mrs Brooks, would you like some tea or coffee?"

Mrs Brooks shook her head. "Let's get on with it," she said. "Let's have it straight, for God's sake."

Julia looked at her. She looked into the mother's eyes steadily, unblinkingly, keeping her expression entirely blank, no frown, no slight smile, waiting. Honor drank the water greedily, in three big swallowings which were heard distinctly.

Mrs Brooks closed her eyes and sighed. "What happens now?" she asked.

The bridesmaid's dress didn't fit. Julia's mother was almost delighted by this. There was no dismay in her voice as she said to her sister Maureen, "The dress doesn't fit, it's been made too small!" Her tone was one of peculiar triumph.

"Or Julia has grown since you sent those measurements," said Maureen, adding, "if they were accurate in the first place."

Julia stood miserably in the too tight dress while the sisters argued, each insulting the other in every word said. Julia tried not to listen. She wondered if she was allowed to take the dress off now it had been demonstrated that it didn't fit her. There was a mirror in the bedroom where this unsuccessful fitting took place, a full-length oval-shaped mirror on a wooden stand. Julia could see herself only partially because the mirror was slightly swivelled, making the lower half of her body invisible. It was a little like looking in a fairground mirror. She felt she was distorted, though she didn't know if this was the fault of the tight dress or the mirror. Whatever the reason, she felt miserable, standing there waiting to see what would happen when her mother and aunt stopped arguing. It never occurred to her to give her own opinion.

Then Iris came in. Oh, she was so pretty!

"Julia!" Iris said, laughing, holding her arms out. "How you've grown! What a big girl you are!"

Julia blushed deeply. She'd forgotten what her cousin looked like, all that long blonde hair, so smooth and sleek, and the big blue eyes and the round face with the neat little nose, and the perfect skin with cheeks so pink, glowing with health and happiness. Julia couldn't credit that her Aunt Maureen was this girl's mother. Where had Iris's prettiness come from? And then Iris saved her.

"Mummy," she said, "Julia's dress doesn't fit. Phone Mrs Batey right now and get her round here to see what she can do. I can't have my best bridesmaid in a dress that doesn't fit. Poor love, look at her, it's a shame."

Mrs Batey came. She was in a huff, suspicious that the dress not fitting would be blamed on her dressmaking skills, but Iris handled her expertly. Mrs Batey, Iris cooed, was clever. Mrs Batey could see ways of managing things which no other dressmaker could. What Mrs Batey saw was that all the dress needed was the side seams let out. The waist dropped, and the hem let down. There was time, just, to do all this (at a price), and for Iris, Mrs Batey would do anything.

During the next few days, before the wedding, Julia saw how everyone was in thrall to her cousin Iris. She was both loved and admired. Her own mother,

Maureen, adored her. Julia could not have said how she knew this, but know it she did. So did Julia's mother. "Sun rises and sets with Iris," she complained, though why this had to be a complaint Julia could not fathom. "Spoiled, she's been spoiled from the day she was born. There could be a shock coming." A shock? Julia was alarmed and worried, and asked her mother what would this shock be, would the lovely Iris be hurt? The reply to this was far too enigmatic for an eight-year-old. Julia didn't get the full significance of "She'll have to come down to earth with a bump once she's married". A bump didn't sound too dangerous. Iris could surely survive it.

Julia had flowers in her hair, which pleased her enormously, cornflowers and daisies, cunningly wreathed together and attached to a velvet band. They made up for the dress being off-white and quite plain. And she had a posy, too, tied with blue ribbon. "You're as pretty as a picture," Iris said. It was Iris who was the picture. Even Julia's mother was silenced by the vision of Iris in her bridal gown. The dress was simple, nothing meringue-like or frothy, cut on the bias, the satin draping perfectly round Iris's slender figure. "How do I look?" Iris asked. "Lovely," was the chorus, and again, "Lovely, *lovely*." Then Maureen began to cry, and barely stopped for the rest of the day. Tears of happiness, tears of joy, or so she said, but even Julia could tell these were tears of loss and pain. They were "so close", this mother and daughter, or so Julia heard guests constantly saying to each other throughout the wedding reception. Never been such a close mother and daughter. They were more like sisters, someone said, which Julia thought perfectly ridiculous. Did that person have eyes? Could she not see what Maureen looked like, what Iris looked like? Sisters?

Honor had required extra care after her difficult birth. That, of course, might explain a lot (the difficult birth). And the fact that Honor was a girl and not a boy. It had emerged early on that Honor "should have been" a son, not a daughter. Julia hadn't asked why Mrs Brooks had wanted a son, why she cared about the sex of her first baby. It was not, after all, relevant. Mrs Brooks herself, it had also emerged, was one of three sisters, the middle one, also "meant" to be a boy. "I was never forgiven," she had told Julia dramatically. Julia had smiled politely and skilfully steered her back along the path she wanted her to go along. So, she had said, tell me about Honor as a baby. This was also a tale of woe. Honor was difficult, didn't feed properly, cried most of the time, took ages to regain her birth weight, couldn't hold her head up until she was three months old, maybe more, and really Honor's development had gone on like that, difficult, right from the start.

Julia asked, at one point, who Honor showed affection to.

"Affection?" Mrs Brooks echoed, as though affection were a disease.

"Does she have a pet, perhaps?" Julia pressed. "Or a soft toy she cuddles?"

"She's been given plenty of soft toys," Mrs Brooks said, sounding angry, "she hasn't been deprived of soft toys, I can tell you that. She's had teddy bears and every stuffed animal you can name, a whole zoo of them."

Julia nodded, and politely asked again if Honor had shown affection for any of them and was there a particular toy she took to bed?

"She's ten," her mother said, "she's too old to take toys to bed, for goodness sake."

Julia nodded again, and made a note. "What about relatives?" she suggested. "Her aunts? Your sisters or cousins? Does she have cousins she's fond of?"

"No," said Mrs Brooks.

"No to aunts, or No to cousins, or both?" Julia said. "No to both," she said, and did not elaborate.

Considering how defensive she always was, Julia was surprised no justification for this lack of contact followed. The subject was considered closed, but Julia wouldn't agree to this. "Friends?" she queried. "Is Honor fond of any school friend, or has she been until recently?"

"She's never been keen on friends," Mrs Brooks said, but this time sounding almost apologetic and not aggressive. "I've tried," she went on, "I've invited children in her class to come and play after school, though Honor didn't want me to, but it wasn't a success."

"How many times did you try?" Julia asked, injecting as much sympathy as possible into the question.

"Once," she said, "then I took the hint. What was the point if Honor wasn't interested? It just made me look silly when *I* had to play with the other child."

"What did you play?" Julia asked quickly.

"What?" Mrs Brooks was annoyed again.

"What did you play with the other child?"

"Heavens, you expect me to remember that?"

"Why?" said Julia gently. "Was it a long time ago, this one play date?"

There was a distinct pause, a real hesitation. Something was being weighed up, but Julia didn't know what. It was time, perhaps, to ask this woman more about herself. She liked talking about herself. Julia had already heard how she had had the most unfortunate of upbringings, which involved a great deal of detail, in the telling, about her parents' divorce and how this had affected her. But time was short. She couldn't let Mrs Brooks get going on her own troubles.

"I think," said Julia, "I need to talk to Honor's teacher."

The wedding was on a Monday, which scandalised Julia's mother. "A Monday!" she kept exclaiming, as though this day of the week had some in-built taint attached to it. But Monday it had to be, for reasons Julia never understood except that they were to do with the bridegroom's next tour of duty with his regiment and his father arriving back only on the Sunday night — it was all complicated. However, a Monday it was, a wet Monday. More horror from Julia's mother when the curtains were opened that morning and the weather revealed. Julia herself felt miserable just looking out on the lashing rain and wild wind stripping the trees of leaves. In her mind, the very word "wedding" was equated somehow with sunshine and blue skies. How could there be a wedding in this storm?

Iris, though, just laughed. The rain and wind did not dismay her at all. "Rain on your wedding day means good luck," she said firmly. Julia's mother asked where she'd got that bit of wisdom from, but Iris laughed some more and didn't reply. "You *are* an old misery, Auntie," she said mockingly. Julia held her breath. It was true. Her mother was an old misery, but only Iris dared to say so. The peculiar thing was that instead of being insulted, or reacting with anger, Julia's mother merely nodded her head and tightened her lips. Anyway, the rain didn't last and the wind died down long before the time of the wedding. By 2 p.m. the sun was beginning to struggle through the clouds and though there were puddles all along the path to the church they looked pretty, like little lakes, glinting in the suddenly sharp light.

Julia skirted these puddles carefully, not wanting to damage her beautiful white satin shoes. She progressed on tiptoe, holding up the skirt of her dress, and arrived at the church door triumphant. The other two bridesmaids, the bridegroom's sisters Sylvie and Pat, were not so careful. They were much older than Julia and their dresses (she noticed at once, and with envy) were more elaborate, full-skirted and frilly on top, whereas Julia's dress was plain and simple, not a frill or flounce to it. But the sisters were nice girls who made a fuss of Julia. She must walk in front of them, they insisted, and right behind the bride. "You look so sweet," they said, and Julia blushed and smiled. Her mother was nowhere near. She was already sitting in her place. I am so sweet, Julia repeated to herself in her head, so sweet, so sweet. She stood with the other bridesmaids waiting for Iris to arrive and felt happy and light-hearted. Then the car with Iris and her father arrived and there was such excitement in the air, such a lot of bustle, with ushers darting forward to open doors, and the music beginning, and at that moment Julia heard a whisper and felt something slipped into the hand not holding her posy. "Give it to Iris," the whisper said, "it's a secret, afterwards."

There was a pocket in her dress, in a side seam. "I've made you a pocket," Mrs Batey had said, "to keep a hanky in case you need it." And a handkerchief was indeed safely tucked away there, an embroidered handkerchief her mother had given her at Christmas, embroidered with her name in purple silk thread. Julia looked quickly at what was in her hand — a small, square box wrapped in tissue paper, tied with a ribbon — and slipped it into her pocket. Her heart raced a little fast. The whisper had been Reginald's, the bridegroom's. She'd only met him once, the day before, and had been intimidated by him. He was tall and strong-looking and he'd been wearing dark clothes and looked, to Julia, sinister. She didn't say a word to him, and all he said to her was hello. But now he was in his soldier's uniform. Julia could see him, standing waiting in front of the altar as Iris slowly advanced on her father's arm. He didn't smile. He held himself rigidly, at attention it seemed, and Julia shivered a little at the sight of him, though she didn't know why.

Julia didn't tell her mother about Reginald's whisper, or about the little box he'd given her. He'd said it was a secret, and her understanding of "secret" was that she must keep it to herself. But she would have liked to consult her mother about exactly what "afterwards" meant. After the wedding was over? After the wedding breakfast? After Reginald had gone off with his regiment? She worried about when to give the box to Iris. There was no chance in the church afterwards. Too many people, all thronging round the bride, and then bride and bridegroom were whisked off in a car to the church hall. There, Julia was seated next to her mother at the top table, with Iris four places to her left, in the centre. There were speeches, and applause, and a lot of laughter, though Julia failed to understand why people were laughing, especially at the best man's speech. "Rude, no need for it," her mother muttered.

Then there was the photograph, a time of maximum confusion, with the photographer making a great fuss about who was to stand where. Julia was first of all told to sit at Iris's feet but then told to stand next to one of the other bridesmaids, so that she was at the end of the row. This didn't suit the photographer either. He said the "composition" was wrong, and the "proportions". Once more, Julia was put in front of the bridal couple but this time slightly in the centre, with the other two bridesmaids flanking the bride and bridegroom. Other group photographs were taken, with more and more people in them, and in the final one Julia was squeezed right at the end, almost out of the picture. She was tired by then and found it hard to smile, as instructed, or even to say "cheese".

Later, at school, she boasted about being a bridesmaid, describing her dress in a way that was not exactly a lie but was rather imaginative.

"Honor doesn't participate," the teacher told Julia, "not in any way. She doesn't volunteer any opinions. If I ask her some direct question, she just shrugs. She can't be coaxed into expressing herself."

It was a fee-paying school, the children wearing a neat uniform: blue-and-white-checked shirts, plain dark blue skirts or trousers, and a blue blazer with a white dove crest on the pocket. The school had been founded in the late sixties when a dove was the symbol of peaceful protest against the Vietnam War. Parents liked the idea of this, and they liked the uniform. Mrs Brooks said Honor couldn't have been at a nicer school, what with the uniform and the small classes and the strict discipline. The fees were high, but she believed anything worth having comes at a price. It was obvious. You get what you pay for. But Honor had not made the best of the opportunities being at such a model school gave her. She hadn't liked school from day one and had made a fuss about going every single morning from then on. What was there not to like? her mother had asked, of course she had, but Honor gave no reason, just repeated, so annoyingly, that she hated school and did not want to go. Told that the law said she had to, she said she hated the law too. Which, said Mrs Brooks, was such a stupid thing to say, so childish. "But she is a child," Julia had said pointedly.

There was something about the tidy, quiet school which Julia found a little disturbing. She'd once been a teacher herself, and no school she'd ever taught in had been as unnaturally quiet as this one. The school building was an Edwardian double-fronted house, set in its own grounds. These grounds were not extensive, consisting as they did of a lawn either side of the driveway and a larger lawn at the back with some climbing apparatus at the end of it. There were no playing fields or anything like that, but then the children were aged five to eleven and not in need of football and rugby pitches and the like. There was a school bus, painted in the blue and white school colours, which took the children to the park and to a swimming pool in a local leisure centre. Their every need, the prospectus claimed, was catered for. But entering the school, Julia was struck by how the building appeared to dominate the children. The rooms were quite dark, and high-ceilinged, and though the furniture was modern and brightly coloured it was dwarfed by the space it occupied. The corridors, and the staircase, had lots of the children's artwork pinned on the walls but, again, the dark oak of the banisters, and the dark brown of the carpet on the broad stairs, seemed to fight, and win, a battle with the colourful paintings. The children looked out of place, especially the younger ones.

Honor's teacher was called Miss Cass. Julia was introduced to her by the headmaster, a Dr Richards (she assumed he was a doctor of philosophy, but in that she was wrong). "This is Miss Cass," he said. No Christian name was given, and Julia didn't ask for one, though she gave her own. Dr Richards said he would leave them to "chat" about Honor Brooks, but he reminded Julia that Miss Cass only had fifteen minutes to spare. Julia said she was grateful to be spared them. They were left together, Julia and Miss Cass, in a small room next to the headmaster's study (he'd referred to it as a study, not an office). There were two leather armchairs facing each other with a coffee table between them, upon which rested a copy of the school prospectus. Miss Cass hadn't yet sat down nor had she invited Julia to do so. Thinking that to stand for the allotted fifteen minutes was absurd, Julia took the lead, though she felt she shouldn't have. "Shall we make ourselves comfortable?" she said, smiling, and promptly sat down herself. Miss Cass hesitated, and then perched on the very edge of the seat of the other armchair.

Julia explained who she was and why she had come to ask Miss Cass about Honor, and then Miss Cass told her about Honor never responding to anything at all in class. Julia worded her response, to what Miss Cass said, carefully. "So you think Honor is shy?" she said.

Miss Cass looked surprised. "No," she said, "I wouldn't call her shy."

"What would you call her, then?" Julia asked.

There was a long pause while Miss Cass thought, and frowned. Disappointingly, she then said she was unable to describe accurately Honor's attitude, but she

17

repeated again, quite emphatically, that the girl certainly did not give the impression of shyness. Julia switched tack. She asked the teacher if Honor was a satisfactory pupil in other ways, was her schoolwork good, was she obedient? Miss Cass said Honor's work was average, that she didn't lag behind but nor was she outstanding in any way. She wasn't *dis*obedient but there was always a certain reluctance about following instructions. She would do everything slowly and slightly resentfully. The minute Miss Cass had used the word "resentfully", she took it back. "What I mean," she said, "is that Honor never seems to enjoy cooperating." Then she looked anxious, as though about to retract even that innocuous statement, so Julia quickly said she thought she understood what Miss Cass meant. "Do you have any of Honor's written work available for me to see?" she asked. Miss Cass said she had an exercise book containing work of Honor's which she was currently marking, but she would have to ask Dr Richards for permission to show it to Julia. Julia nodded, and said she would ask herself after their fifteen minutes were up.

They almost were. Miss Cass had taken so long replying to Julia's simple questions that the time passed quickly. Julia looked at her watch. "One final thing," she said, "have you met Honor's mother?" There was an immediate change in the teacher's attitude. This was something she was happy to discuss. Mrs Brooks came in every day demanding to see Honor's form teacher and every day she had a list of complaints about how her daughter had allegedly been treated. Miss Cass was astonished at the list of what Mrs Brooks called "assaults" which Honor was supposed to have suffered. She was said to have been pinched, scratched, pushed and to have had her hair pulled so viciously that she now had small bald spots all over her scalp where hairs had actually been yanked out. This was bullying, Mrs Brooks claimed, of the worst kind. Honor was defenceless against the ganging up that was going on. She didn't pay the fees she did to have her daughter treated like this.

Now the fifteen minutes were definitely up, but Miss Cass had warmed to her subject and indignation made her forget the time. It was Julia who reminded her. She stood up, held out her hand, and thanked the teacher for being so helpful. Miss Cass, though, hadn't finished. She was eager to emphasise that Mrs Brooks was mistaken. Far from Honor being bullied, she was the bully, and Dr Richards had spoken to her after this tirade from the mother had been reported to him. Miss Cass had been so upset by the allegations, horrified that she might have missed observing Honor being tormented, and she had carried out a full investigation. The most trustworthy children in her form had assured her that no one bullied Honor Brooks. They were all much too frightened of her.

Dr Richards said yes, Julia could look at Honor's English exercise book, but in his presence, in his study. Julia didn't mind in the least where she looked at it, or in whose presence, but she was amused at Dr Richards' self-importance and suspicious nature. The exercise book was produced by Miss Cass and laid on Dr

Richards' desk. "Might I pick it up?" Julia solemnly asked.

"Of course," Dr Richards said, suddenly apparently aware of Julia perhaps mocking him, and pushed it towards her.

Nothing written there was particularly revealing. Honor's writing was neat. Her sentences were, for the most part, properly punctuated. The content of the various pieces of work was unremarkable, though there was one essay entitled "My Saturdays" which offered a glimpse into Honor's life. "On Saturdays," it began, "I see my cousin."

But her mother had said Honor had no cousins.

Julia and her mother went straight home after the wedding, though they had been invited to stay. Going straight home meant catching an evening train, the last one that stopped at Penrith. Julia fell asleep as soon as she was seated and slept the whole way. Her mother had to shake her awake ten minutes before the train arrived at Penrith. It only halted there for a couple of minutes and so she and her mother had to be standing ready at the door. Julia swayed with fatigue and half fell out of the train. Her mother dragged her along the underpass and out into the dark windy night, and pushed her into the taxi she'd arranged to pick them up. Julia slept again, and had to be shaken awake when at last they reached home. She had no memory of climbing the stairs and getting undressed and into bed but when she woke up and saw where she was she realised she must have done. If it had not been for the bridesmaid's dress draped over a chair the whole wedding would have seemed a dream.

It took Julia a long time to remember the present for Iris which Reginald had given her, and when she did she panicked in case she had lost it. But no, it was still in the pocket of her dress, the wrapping paper intact except that the tiny bit of white ribbon tied round it had come loose from its bow. Julia retied it carefully. Then she held the little package in her hand and wondered what she should do with it. She ought to have given it, as instructed, to Iris "afterwards". But there had been no opportunity straight after the church ceremony and then at the reception Iris was surrounded by people, and Julia resolved to wait. Reginald had said his present was a secret and so it could not be given in front of others, or that was how Julia reasoned. She would slip it to Iris when the two of them were alone. But they never were, and the truth was that Julia, during the meal and the speeches, eventually forgot what she'd been entrusted to do. It was hard to admit it to herself, but it was true, she simply forgot until the following morning, and then was overcome with guilt.

She didn't dare tell her mother. It was not just that her mother would make a fuss but that Reginald had said his present was a secret, and a secret it must remain. Julia felt quite clear about that. Forgetting to give her cousin the gift was one thing, betraying Reginald's trust another. But how could she get the present to Iris? Iris had gone off with her new husband anyway and when she and Reginald came back from their short honeymoon (only forty-eight hours) they wouldn't be at her parents' house for long. After that, Julia had no idea what their address would be. Tears came into her eyes just thinking of the impossibility of getting the present to Iris. What would Reginald think? He would think Julia had either lost it or stolen it. Then Julia really did cry.

Her mother heard her. She came into Julia's bedroom and said this was what she'd expected. The travelling, the wedding, the rich food had all been too much, and this was the result she'd anticipated: "hysterics". She didn't once ask why her daughter was crying because in her opinion she knew the answer. She told Julia to wash her face and come down to the kitchen and get some wholesome food into her and then, together, they would take a brisk walk to the village shop and that would sort her out. "And hang that dress up," Julia's mother said, "and put it on a padded hanger. You won't ever wear it again, but I might be able to make something useful out of it." As soon as her mother left the room, Julia again checked the pocket of the dress. Reginald's present was still there. She took it out and put it into the drawer holding her underwear, tucking it right at the bottom, covered by a vest she rarely wore.

Should she post it? But she only had her Aunt Maureen's address, and her aunt might open any package that arrived. The worry was making her feel sick. Downstairs, forced to nibble at the toast her mother provided, she risked asking the question to which she already felt she knew the answer.

22

"When will we see Iris again?"

Her mother laughed, that scornful laugh of hers containing no merriment whatsoever. "See Iris again? Well, she doesn't visit us, does she? Oh no, we have to visit them. That's how it's always been, we get *summoned* when it's convenient. It took a funeral to bring them here, remember that?"

Julia only remembered it vaguely. She'd been barely five when her father was killed, how could she be expected to remember? A lot of people crying in their house, that was all she thought she remembered. She didn't remember her father himself all that distinctly. There were several photographs of him round the house but these didn't summon up any real memories.

Julia managed to finish the toast and the boiled egg put in front of her, and then risked another question.

"When do you think we will be summoned again?" She kept her voice low and light so as not to enrage her mother more than was necessary.

But her mother was instantly provoked to attack. "Why are you suddenly so keen on that lot? What's that family to you? What do you think you are to them? Iris might have asked you to be her bridesmaid, but has she ever shown any real interest in you? Even after your father was killed? Has she ever sent you anything for your birthday or a little something for your Christmas stocking? No, she has not. I'd be ashamed if I were them, ashamed."

There was a long silence. Julia didn't dare to point out to her mother that this tirade was not a reply to her question. The best thing to do was keep quiet and hope that eventually her mother would realise she hadn't answered and would go into another reply which might be more informative.

"Summoned?" she queried after a good few minutes. "Summoned, did you say?"

"You said it," Julia said, her tone cautious, the accusation of being cheeky hovering in the air. "You said we only see Iris when Aunt Maureen summons us."

Julia's mother nodded, inexplicably pleased with this explanation. "Well then, there you are. We'll get summoned if there's another wedding or a funeral."

Julia sat thinking about this. How could there be another wedding when Iris was an only child, just as she was, and she was already now married? And who would a funeral be for? Who was likely to die? But then her own father hadn't been likely to die. He'd had an accident involving a chainsaw which had slipped (Julia had been spared the details). She'd heard him described by people as having been the strongest, most fit man they'd ever known. So maybe Aunt Maureen or Uncle Tom would have an accident of some sort and there would be a funeral and she and her mother would be summoned and she would see Iris again and give her Reginald's present.

Julia agonised over what to do for another three days, then decided she would have to tell her mother. It was silly to wait for a funeral and a summons that might not come for years. Reginald would have found out by now that Iris had not been given the secret present and he would want to know what Julia had done with it. Over breakfast Julia tried to catch her mother's attention.

"Mum," she said, and at that moment the telephone rang.

"Get that, Julia," her mother said, "though I don't know who can be ringing at this time of the morning."

Julia obediently answered the phone. It was her Uncle Tom, his voice hoarse, as though he had a terrible cold. He told her he needed to speak to her mother. Julia relayed this message, and saw a peculiar expression cross her mother's face as she dried her hands and turned from the sink to go over to the alcove where the phone rested. Julia had never seen this look on her mother's face before and couldn't quite interpret it. Excitement was there, and eagerness, but also something else. Dread? Julia didn't know.

After that, things happened quickly. Julia was told to pack her nightdress and a change of underclothes in a bag, and then put her coat on and stand at the window watching for the taxi.

"Where are we going?" she asked.

"Manchester, to your aunt and uncle's, now hurry up."

Julia fairly skipped up the stairs, delighted to be returning to Manchester. All the problems about Reginald's present would be solved. She put the present in her bag and resolved to slip it into Iris's room as soon as she got to her aunt's house. She'd remembered her aunt say that Iris would be returning, after the brief honeymoon, before going to live in the married quarters of Reginald's regiment. She had a lot of stuff to sort out and take, and Uncle Tom was going to drive her there. Julia was smiling and humming with relief as she put her coat on and took up her position at the window.

"Take that silly grin off your face," her mother snapped, "we're going to a house of mourning."

Julia put off writing her report on Honor Brooks for as long as possible. There seemed so much doubt about so many aspects of the case and she hadn't been able to resolve them to her own satisfaction never mind to other people's. Honor was an enigma. Her mother, on the other hand, was not. There was no need to wonder what part she had played in all this, or what she thought about Honor. She was absolutely sure that her daughter was guilty and had fully intended to do what she had done. She wanted Honor "dealt with", as she put it. "There must be places where they treat girls like Honor," she said, and added, "she isn't safe, mixing with normal children, I mean the other children aren't safe, not after what she's done."

But that was the point: what had Honor done? The baby was dead. That was indisputable. Honor had been the last person known to have touched her. That was admitted by her. She went into the baby's room because she heard her crying and she picked her up, trying to comfort her, and she cuddled her. Cuddled? The word and its meaning had been gone over and over. How hard had the three-week-old baby been cuddled? How had Honor held her? Over her shoulder? Tight to her chest? And for how long? Till she stopped

26

crying, at any rate. Then Honor put the baby back in the cradle and went downstairs where her mother and her friend, the baby's mother, were talking. "Is the baby asleep now?" the friend, the mother, had asked, and Honor had not replied. She walked straight out into the garden and kicked a tennis ball lying on the grass. This was made much of by Mrs Brooks. The ignoring of the enquiry about whether the baby was asleep and then the kicking of the ball were in her opinion proof of guilt.

In all Julia's experience, she had never come across any mother who did not attempt at least some sort of defence of her child. Most mothers were aggressively defensive, no matter how damning the evidence. It troubled Julia a great deal that Mrs Brooks was so antagonistic towards her own daughter. Why? Where were the seeds of this buried?

She resolved to have one final interview with Honor.

Today, Honor was wearing a strange assortment of garments whereas previously she had been in her school uniform. Julia studied them. Nothing remarkable about the jeans, except that they seemed too big for the child, but the frilly apricot-coloured dress worn over a long-sleeved red T-shirt was startling. The colours clashed. The scarlet fighting with the almost-orange, and the material of the dress, gauze-like, looked odd stretched over the cotton T-shirt. Maybe, Julia thought, I am out of touch with what eight-year-old girls choose to wear. It crossed her mind that her mother must have allowed Honor to do just that, "choose" her own clothes. Surely she herself would never have selected this outfit?

To mention the clothes or not . . . Julia hesitated. Best not to make too much of them, probably. She invited Honor to sit on the large beanbag, telling her how comfortable it was to settle into. Other children enjoyed hurling themselves onto the bright blue canvas, but Honor treated it as though it were a straight-backed wooden chair, lowering herself carefully onto it, refusing to surrender her body to it. Her arms were braced either side, her hands clutching the canvas. She looked awkward, ill at ease, so much so that Julia felt she had to ask her if she would prefer to sit on an ordinary chair. Honor said she was OK. There was a defiance in her expression which Julia read as a refusal to give in to the idea of moving. She was going to sit where she'd been told to sit however uncomfortable she was. It meant some kind of victory, though over what Julia wasn't sure.

It was half-term, hence no school uniform. Even though Honor had not been at school since the baby died, she had always been wearing this uniform until now. Her mother said it made the home schooling seem more school-like if Honor wore her uniform, and Julia agreed she could see that this might be true. But this week was the official half-term, and so Honor's tutor had been told not to come though she had been willing to.

Julia wondered, aloud, what Honor had been doing this week.

Honor shrugged. "Nothing," she said.

Julia said that must be very boring for her.

Honor shrugged again, and said, "Don't mind."

"You don't mind being bored?" Julia asked, keeping disbelief out of her tone. "That's interesting. When I'm bored, I mind it. I want something to do, or something to happen."

Honor neither shrugged nor spoke. She just stared at Julia, and waited.

The day the baby died was a Saturday. Leila Brooks and Honor had arrived at around two in the afternoon. Leila's friend, the mother of the baby, had made coffee for Leila and given Honor some apple juice. She'd also provided cupcakes, apologising for not having baked them herself. They were iced, a selection of pink, yellow and chocolate. Leila declined a cupcake but Honor had two and would have accepted a third if her mother had not admonished her for greed. All this detail — the time of arrival at the friend's house, the cupcakes, etc. — had been gone over many times. None of it was important except that attention to detail helped to recreate the atmosphere of the afternoon and through doing that there was the hope that the truth of exactly what had happened might emerge. But it had not emerged. There was no clear medical evidence that the baby had been in any provable way harmed by Honor. She had been the last person to touch the baby, a fact freely admitted, so there had not been any real need for forensic tests to confirm this, though they had been carried out anyway. It was the baby's mother who was convinced that Honor had harmed the baby. Mrs Brooks had come to believe this too. They thought

Honor had smothered the baby, pressed her so tightly to her chest or shoulder that she had been asphyxiated. But there was no evidence of this. It was a cot death.

Julia had a hospital appointment. She resolved to spend the time sitting in the clinic profitably. She would sit with her eyes closed, thinking about Honor Brooks and what she should write in her report. Forcing herself to concentrate hard would make the waiting more tolerable.

Right, she told herself, once she was seated in the corridor between a large man who had a plaster covering his left cheek, which he kept touching, and a pregnant young woman who was turning the pages of a magazine, turning them noisily and quickly, appearing to pay no attention to the contents — right, *concentrate.*

CHAPTER
TWO

Claire smiled, all the time. Julia found herself smiling back, as one does. The child had the sort of face which was made for smiling, her cheeks plump, the face itself broad, her complexion pink-and-white. A pleasant, amiable face, a pleasure to look at. But the expression upon it, in spite of the smile, was bland. There was no sincere happiness there, though the smile tried to give the impression that there was. The eyes, perhaps? Did they give away what the smile tried to cover up? Julia wondered about this. The eyes were slightly hooded, odd in such a young girl. Julia wasn't sure whether this was because Claire was tired, or it was just that the upper lids of her eyes were formed that way.

She sat comfortably on the beanbag, hands clasped in front of her, on her lap. She'd arranged her skirt carefully. Julia had seen her do it. She'd smoothed the material so that it covered her knees, and patted down the folds either side. She looked, Julia thought, like one of the original illustrations for *Alice's Adventures in Wonderland*. Her dress had a sash, and she wore a velvet headband on her long, fair hair. Old-fashioned. Her socks, knee-high socks, were white, and her shoes, Mary-Jane style, were black patent leather. Julia wondered what other children thought of Claire's attire. Looking at the notes, she thought it unlikely that the girl moved in circles where these clothes were normal.

"So, Claire," Julia said, "how old are you?" She knew precisely how old Claire was, but this harmless question was as good an opening as any. Claire replied that she was eight and a half. Her smile grew even broader, and she started to fiddle with her hair, taking hold of one piece and twirling it round her finger. It looked a winsome gesture, but Julia wasn't sure if this was intentional. Was the girl, after all, nervous? It would be understandable if she was. A lot had happened in her young life recently. Probably it had not been fully explained to her why she was here. Some children challenged Julia straight away, asking quite truculently who she was and why she was questioning them. Julia rather liked that kind of spirited approach. It meant things moved on quickly. But Claire was not one of those children. She was not going to challenge Julia in any way. This was going to be a slow business.

Claire was good at smiling but not at talking, and not at revealing her true feelings.

This time, they were met at Manchester station. Uncle Tom, dressed in a black suit and wearing a black tie, was waiting on the platform. "Tom," Julia's mother said, and put her hand on his shoulder. Tom didn't speak. He shook his head and sighed and picked up their bags. Slowly, the three of them walked through the thundering noise of the station, none of them speaking, but then, Julia thought, they wouldn't have been able to hear each other anyway.

In the car, it could have been different, but no one spoke there either. Uncle Tom drove carefully through the rain-lashed streets, the noise of his squeaky windscreen wipers the only sound. It was a long drive. Outside the garage of his house, he stopped the car, just short of its doors, and said Julia and her mother had best get out here because space was tight in the garage. "Don't ring the bell," he said, "she'll have been watching for you coming." He was right. The front door was open, and Aunt Maureen was standing there. Julia didn't know what she had expected but it was not what she saw. Aunt Maureen's face had changed almost beyond recognition. Her eyes were slits set in ugly red circles, and her mouth looked strange, its lips clenched together. She ushered them out of the rain and into the house, and then stood with her back against the front door, as though bracing herself. "Tea, Maureen," Julia's mother said firmly. "It would be nice to have some proper tea after that train muck." Julia felt faintly ashamed. Shouldn't her mother have said something different?

It was ages until they saw Iris. Tea was brewed and drunk and Aunt Maureen talked, though saying repeatedly that she couldn't talk. Julia kept her head down and listened. She didn't make the mistake of asking any questions though there were lots of things she didn't understand. Her mother didn't ask any either. By the time Aunt Maureen had made a second pot of tea, though the first pot was not yet emptied and neither Julia's mother nor Uncle Tom had finished what was in their cups, Julia had picked up that Reginald had been shot by a sniper while he was on patrol. There was mention of three letters, "I" and "R" and "A", which Julia realised were significant but she didn't know what they stood for. Her mother seemed to, though, and Uncle Tom certainly did. The three letters IRA were, he said "murdering bastards". Nobody objected to this description. Julia said the two words to herself over and over, excited by them. "I don't know why," her mother said, "we don't just leave Ireland to the Irish and get out of there, let them fight it out among themselves."

Eventually, Aunt Maureen led the way upstairs to Iris's room. They went up in single file, Julia the last. She fingered the secret present in her pocket, determined that whatever happened she would leave it in Iris's room even if she couldn't manage to give it to Iris herself. It made her agitated, thinking of Reginald dead and his present ungiven. Had he asked Iris about it while they were on their all-too-short honeymoon? Had he died reproaching Julia? She felt she might be sick, just imagining this, imagining his face as he told Iris he had given the youngest bridesmaid a present for her, and where was it?

Iris was in bed. The curtains were pulled tight shut but the material was not thick and there was some dim daylight in the room. The bedcovers were right up to Iris's chin. For a moment, Julia thought Iris, too, might now be dead. Her heart began to thud and she tightened her grip on the little package in her pocket. Her mother went up to the bed and looked down at

34

Iris. "Come on now, Iris," she said, "this is no good. You have to eat, you have to get up, or you'll make yourself ill, and what good would that do?" Iris didn't reply. Aunt Maureen opened the curtains a bit, so that Julia saw Iris's face properly. She hadn't been crying. That surprised Julia. Iris was very pale but there were no traces of tears on her cheeks and her eyes were not tear-filled. She was staring at the ceiling, seeming mesmerised by the dangling lampshade. "Julia," her mother said, her voice sounding indecently loud, "sit with Iris while Aunt Maureen and I make Iris a nice snack. We'll bring it up on a tray." Julia was horrified. She dreaded being left alone with this frightening new Iris, so still and silent, but her mother left the room quickly, pulling her sister with her.

The time to give Iris Reginald's present had come. Clearing her throat, Julia went up to the bed, on her tiptoes, and whispered, "Iris, this is something Reginald gave me for you." She held out the present, but Iris didn't take it. She just went on staring at the ceiling. Julia wondered if grief, or shock, had perhaps made her cousin deaf. She went even nearer, and repeated what she had just said, adding that she was sorry she hadn't been able to deliver the present earlier. Iris took not the slightest notice of her. Cautiously, Julia put the present on the pillow, beside Iris's head. Iris ignored it. Julia wondered if she should offer to unwrap it, but decided not to. She went on standing nervously by the bed, acutely aware of the rain splattering against the window, and of the sound of a kettle boiling hysterically in the kitchen below, a shriek that seemed to go on forever before it stopped abruptly.

There was something she should say to Iris, something she had the uneasy feeling her mother should have said. Sorry? No, that wasn't right. Sorry wouldn't do. Nothing would do, which was perhaps why her mother hadn't attempted any words of comfort. All the feeling in Julia rose up in her throat, an awful disturbance coming from her stomach and threatening to make her vomit. The pressure of wanting to say something and not knowing what to say, or how to say it, made her whimper with panic. It was lucky that her mother returned then, carrying a tray upon which rested a cup of tea, gently steaming, and a slice of toast, cut into triangles. "Come on, Iris," her mother said. "Put a pillow behind her head, another pillow to prop her up," her mother instructed her sister. "Just do it." Aunt Maureen obeyed, struggling to do what she had been ordered to do, and the present rolled off the first pillow and onto the floor. It made no noise. The floor was carpeted and the present was light. Nobody except Julia saw it happen. She drew no attention to it. She let it lie there, almost under the bed. Iris, when eventually she got out of bed, which Julia reasoned she was bound to do, would find it. If she didn't, Aunt Maureen would, when she next hoovered the carpet.

The point was the present had finally been given to Iris even if she had no interest in it. The responsibility was no longer Julia's.

"What did you do then, Claire?" asked Julia. Claire widened her eyes, intensified her smile, and said she couldn't remember exactly. "Try," Julia urged. "You got off the train with your mother, and you were carrying a bag. Is that correct?" Claire nodded. "Was it heavy?" Claire shook her head. "What was in it?" Claire said she didn't know, she hadn't looked inside the bag, she'd just been handed it by her mother who had told her to carry it because she herself had too much to carry. Julia (who knew the answers of course) asked Claire if the bag was a plastic carrier bag, or made of material of some sort — canvas? leather? — and whether it was zipped closed, if it was that sort of bag, or remained open. Claire said it was not a plastic bag, she was sure of that, and it did have a zip, which was pulled tight across the top. She added that the bag had long handles and that it had touched the ground sometimes and she had had to lift it higher.

The bag had been stolen. It didn't belong to Claire's mother at all. The mother claimed to have picked up this bag in mistake for her own, which was of a similar size and design. She had so much luggage and got muddled and was worried that she and Claire wouldn't get off the train in time, hence the confusion. It was all feasible. The bag was an expensive one, but lots of imitations of it existed and could be bought cheaply. But no cheap versions had subsequently been found on that train. Someone could have found it, and taken it home and kept it, but the woman from whom the expensive bag had been stolen said there was no other bag like it when she had put it on the luggage rack.

None of this was of concern to Julia. Her job was to ascertain how much responsibility Claire had for the theft of this bag. Nobody seemed sure. The child was only eight. Her mother had handed her a bag and told her to carry it. She had obeyed. But why had she not said "This is not your bag, Mum"? Was she unobservant? Did she truly not notice? And she had said the bag was not heavy but it must have been, considering what it contained. Most children would have felt the weight and complained about it, surely. Claire had carried it all the way through the station, keeping pace with her hurrying mother without difficulty in spite of the weight of the bag. And then they were stopped, Claire and her mother. The real owner of the bag had run through the crowds searching for her bag being carried by someone else, and she had caught Claire by the arm and shouted, "You've got my bag!" Claire had smiled, looked at her mother, and dropped the bag.

"Do you and your mum travel much?" Julia asked Claire. Claire hesitated, but only for a second, then nodded. "Do you always have a lot of luggage?" More nods. "And where do you go, Claire, with all this luggage?"

Claire shrugged, the smile never shifting. "Places," she said.

"To visit relatives?"

Nod.

"Your grandparents?"

Claire said, "Sometimes."

"Aunts? Cousins? Friends?" Julia prompted.

"Sometimes."

Julia asked if Claire enjoyed this travelling, knowing Claire would probably stick to "sometimes", as she did.

"Your mum is very lucky to have a strong girl like you to help carry her bags," Julia said, and then, gently, "Don't you get tired of carrying heavy bags?"

"They aren't always heavy," Claire said, and then her smile faltered for the first time. "I mean," she corrected, "that bag wasn't heavy."

Julia looked at her, and remained silent for a moment or two. The owner of the bag had made a scene, clinging onto Claire and shouting for the police. Claire's arm still bore faint marks from how firmly she had been gripped. "Does your arm hurt?" Julia asked. "Does it still hurt, where the woman got hold of you?" Claire said no, it didn't. "Did it hurt at the time?" Claire said no, it didn't, not really. "But you must have got a shock," Julia suggested, "you must have been a little frightened?" Claire, her smile wavering only slightly, said no, she hadn't been shocked. "Has this happened before?" Julia asked. Claire hesitated. She looked at Julia searchingly, and Julia knew the girl was trying to work out how much Julia knew. She didn't want to be caught out if Julia had the evidence that this picking up of the "wrong" bag, and what happened subsequently, was familiar, that there was a pattern of similar incidents. So Claire did the wisest thing. She kept quiet.

There was no need for Julia to see Claire's mother, but she would like to have done. The woman had two convictions for shoplifting, but Claire had not been involved in either episode. She'd been with her mother, though, in a buggy, and the buggy was where her mother had hidden the goods. At a year and eighteen months old, respectively, Claire could not have been party to either theft. She wouldn't even have been aware of the sweater tucked underneath the removable pad on the seat of the buggy, or of the necklace and earrings nestling in the closed-up hood. Claire, then, had no responsibility whatsoever for her mother's shoplifting. But since then? Almost certainly, the girl had aided and abetted, under instructions from her mother. There were many ways in which the shoplifting and the bag-snatching could have been represented to her. Julia thought about them all.

"It was a good bag, Claire, wasn't it?" she said. "It costs a lot of money, that sort of bag, doesn't it?" Claire was back to shrugging. "Do you like shopping?" Julia asked. Surprisingly, Claire said, not really.

"Why not?" Julia pressed.

"No money to buy anything," Claire said, "so it's boring."

"But you had money to spend last week, didn't you? Did you enjoy shopping then? Did you enjoy spending it?"

Claire nodded, but her smile faded. Julia was not going to ask where the money had come from. Claire, she knew, was expecting her to ask this, but she had no need to ask it.

"Do you ever do any baking, Claire?" she suddenly asked instead. "Do you make cakes, or buns, that kind of thing?"

Claire said, sometimes. "Who taught you how to do it?" Claire said, her grandma. "Not your mother?" No, her mother hadn't time. "What has your mother taught you?" Julia asked. Claire, for the first time, frowned, then said, lots of things. Julia asked for an example, and one was given: how to pack. Julia could hardly suppress a laugh.

"Well, Claire," she said, "I think you and I understand each other very well. Nothing was your fault but if it happens again it will be, won't it? So you'll have to be very careful. It will be hard, but you have to take responsibility for yourself from now on. Your mother knows that too. You say you didn't get a shock, but she did. You weren't to blame, whatever you thought you were doing." Julia smiled at Claire encouragingly, but now Claire was not smiling at all. Her face was contorted with resentment.

"Can I go now?" she asked.

Julia nodded. Claire stood up, smoothed her dress down, and walked out of the room without looking at Julia again and without saying goodbye. She banged the door behind her.

Julia felt slightly shaken. Claire was a tough character, by no means defenceless against her mother's will and power. She was only eight, but seemed more like eighteen in her understanding.

Aunt Maureen taught Julia how to make scones. Julia had watched her own mother make scones many times, but had not been allowed to try to make them herself. "When you're older, I'll teach you," her mother said.

But Maureen thought Julia was more than old enough. "Eight," she exclaimed, "eight, and you've never done any baking!" She said this in the hearing of Julia's mother who, because of the circumstances, because of Maureen being in such a state about Iris, did not react as she would normally have done. She just smiled, which was retaliation enough, and graciously left the kitchen saying she would leave Maureen and Julia to it while she went upstairs to try to "liven Iris up".

Livening Iris up was a much harder task than making scones. Julia herself had been sent, regularly, to try to get her cousin to respond to something, anything. "A young face will cheer her up," her mother told her. It did not. Iris stared at the ceiling, same as ever, and didn't reply to anything Julia asked. The question she repeatedly asked was: what was in the little package Reginald had left. "Have you opened the present yet, Iris?" she asked timidly, careful to say "the" present and not "Reginald's", because she'd been told not to mention his name. If anyone did, Iris started weeping again, and she'd only just stopped doing this all the time. But when asked, Iris shook her head. "Where is it?" Julia dared to enquire. Iris nodded towards the cabinet beside her bed. It had a cupboard in it, and a drawer, and there was a lamp on top. Julia eyed the drawer and thought about asking if she could open it and take the present out and unwrap it, but she was afraid of distressing Iris. The risk was too great. So she sighed and yawned and wished she was back at school and not staying at Aunt Maureen's all this time and

42

enduring the boredom of sitting in this bedroom trying to liven up her once extra-lively cousin.

Then, one day, Iris was sick. The next morning, she was sick again. The doctor was sent for, and came, and suddenly Aunt Maureen and Uncle Tom and even Julia's mother were all excited at the "good news". What this news was, Julia didn't know. "You'll know soon enough," her mother said, "it's too early for you to know." Julia was so used to her mother making these kinds of enigmatic statements that she simply accepted them. The good news which she did understand was that they were going home. "Pack your bag, Julia," her mother said, "we're leaving tomorrow. Iris will be fine now she's got something to live for." And it was true, Iris was smiling and talking again, and though very pale she looked better. Her eyes lost the glazed look they'd had for the last four weeks, and though her hair was bedraggled and greasy she had pulled a brush across it and tied it back and was going to wash it in the afternoon.

Home they went. Julia had never imagined she would be so glad to get home. On Monday, she returned to school where her more enlightened friend Sandra immediately divined why Aunt Maureen and Uncle Tom and Julia's mother and Iris herself had all been made happy. "Sick every morning," Sandra queried, "and you don't know what that means, Julia? Honestly, you're hopeless." Apparently it meant a baby. Iris was going to have a baby. "But Reginald is dead," Julia whispered. Sandra said that didn't matter so long as he and Iris had "done it" at least once. Julia went home that day feeling strange. She wanted to discuss what Sandra had suggested with her mother, who would know if Sandra was right, but she couldn't bring herself to broach the subject. She would just have to wait for her mother to tell her about the baby.

This took a long time. It was only when her mother began knitting, and Julia saw the cover of the pattern she was following, that she felt able to ask what her mother was knitting. "What does it look like?" her mother said. Julia said it looked like a baby's jumper. "A matinee jacket," her mother corrected, "for Iris's baby. Maureen can't knit. If I don't knit a few things for the poor child, nobody will." Julia asked when the baby would be born. Her mother made a strange noise, half a snort of what sounded like disapproval (a sound Julia was well acquainted with) and half a laugh of disbelief. "Who knows?" her mother finally said. "Maybe sooner than it should be."

Julia didn't forget about Iris's baby. The little white garments produced by her mother's rapidly clacking needles were a constant reminder. But, all the same, she was taken by surprise when she came home from school one day, a long time after they'd visited Manchester, and her mother told her Iris had given birth to a boy. Julia was immediately disappointed. She'd wanted Iris to have a girl. Unwisely, she said this to her mother who told her how silly she was to have wished Iris had a daughter "in the circumstances". Julia hadn't the faintest idea what these circumstances might be, but was given a clue after she asked what the baby would be called. "Reginald, of course," her mother said.

Again, Julia was disappointed. Reginald seemed to her an embarrassing name to have. Nobody was called Reginald any more. Didn't Iris know that? When Julia told Sandra about the baby's name, Sandra laughed.

They went to pay tribute to little Reggie (as he was always referred to, right from birth) when he was a week old. Julia carried the small case containing all the baby clothes her mother had knitted, each item separately wrapped in tissue paper. "On no account," her mother said, "put that case down, not for an instant. Sit with it on your knee in the taxi and on the train and if you need to go to the toilet give it to me. There's hours and hours of work in there." Julia, as ever, followed instructions. When they arrived at Aunt Maureen's, she still held on to the case. Maureen looked entirely different from the distraught creature she had been all those months ago.

She beamed at Julia and kissed her and said, "You've got a lovely little new cousin."

"First cousin once removed," Julia's mother said sternly, but Maureen ignored her.

They were led up the stairs because Iris was still in bed. Julia heard Maureen say Iris had had a bad time and was still weak because she'd lost a lot of blood and forceps had been used and stitching required. The word "stitching" lodged itself in Julia's mind. She wished Sandra was on hand to explain "stitching", to tell her what had been stitched and what kind of needle and thread was used. It made her nervous about going into the bedroom and seeing Iris. If she'd had a bad time

45

and lost a lot of blood and something or other had been stitched she must look awful. Julia steeled herself.

Iris looked radiant. It was Julia's mother who used this word and Julia took to it at once. It was a beautiful word, making her think of rays of sunshine and warmth, and sparkle. She was pleased with her mother. Iris was sitting up in bed wearing a pretty pink lacy jacket over a white nightdress which had pearl buttons all the way down the front. Her hair was back to its glossy best, and her skin really did look peach-like. She never stopped smiling, though she did once wince as she moved position in the bed, but said it was just a twinge. The baby was asleep in his cradle beside her. They all stood there, round the bed, admiring Iris, admiring the baby. Julia had never seen her mother so soft-faced and gentle-looking. The baby let out a little cry, and Iris leaned over and plucked him from his cradle. He'd looked all right in the cradle, but now that Julia saw him awake she was dismayed. Little Reggie didn't look at all how a baby should look. His eyes were not large and blue like babies' eyes were in picture books. They were just like two little raisins, set above red, wrinkled cheeks. And he had no hair, just a sort of blond down covering his head. The head itself looked to Julia as though it had been squashed. It bulged in certain places and there was a bit that looked bloody and sore.

But her mother and Aunt Maureen cooed over little Reggie, saying what a handsome fellow he was, and that he had his grandfather's nose. Julia stared at the baby's nose, and thought about Uncle Tom's nose, and could

46

see no connection. Iris, to Julia's relief, said it was nonsense. Little Reggie didn't have his grandfather's nose. He was the image of his father — nose, chin, everything about him was like his own father. Aunt Maureen and Julia's mother said nothing, but they looked at each other meaningfully Julia saw the look and interpreted it as the sisters for once agreeing to disagree with Iris but also agreeing to say nothing. Julia was asked if she'd like to hold the baby. She didn't really want to but recognised that she was being honoured and that she should accept, so she did. She sat on the edge of the bed, as instructed, and little Reggie was placed in her arms. He immediately started to howl, his face contorted and his mouth wide open. "Cuddle him, cuddle him!" everyone urged. Julia tried, but she felt awkward and didn't feel she knew how to cuddle a baby. "Dear me," Aunt Maureen said, "you're not going to be a natural mother, Julia."

Julia held the baby out to Iris.

This time, waiting in the clinic, there was a young girl next to her, with a woman, who was probably her mother, beside her. The corridor was not so crowded today. There were four spare chairs, further along, and the main area of the waiting room, where patients checked in, was unusually quiet. The girl and the woman didn't say a word to each other. They didn't have a book or a magazine to look at. It suddenly occurred to Julia that perhaps it was the woman who was here for treatment and not the girl, which she'd for some reason assumed was the case. If it had been the girl, Julia reasoned, surely the woman, the mother, would have been showing some sign of concern, however slight. Then she reprimanded herself. She was deducing things on no evidence whatsoever, in spite of her training. It was perfectly feasible that a girl and her mother would sit in silence, without distraction whoever was the patient.

But Julia did so want to know which one was.

Julia looked at the name: Hera. Names these days were not conventional, and by contemporary standards Hera was not remarkable. The surname was one of those complicated double-barrelled ones which usually turned out to be a clumsy amalgamation of the mother's and the father's surnames. Hera Carpenter-Morrissey. Julia imagined being, say five, and having to learn to write this as your name. Would the child do it every time, or drop the Carpenter bit sometimes and just write Hera C. Morrissey?

"Hera!" Julia said, pulling herself together. Hera, the Greek goddess of stately bearing and regal beauty, but this was not a beautiful child who bore herself regally. She could be an ugly duckling, of course, who would yet turn out to be a beauty, but Julia thought it unlikely. Hera's features were all large and prominent — nose, ears, mouth, teeth. She was nine, but looked much older. Tall for her age, she seemed to try to hide her height by hunching her shoulders. It made Julia uncomfortable just to look at Hera whose proportions were all at odds with each other, fighting for prominence. She was wearing jeans which were too short and her knobbly ankles, sockless, stuck out, their flesh glaringly pale. She was such an unhealthy-looking girl, dull, without any vitality.

"Hera," Julia repeated, clearing her throat, "I suppose everyone asks you about your name, how you came to be called Hera?"

"Yes," said Hera, "they do."

No explanation. If the child didn't want to give one, Julia wasn't going to press her.

"You've got three brothers, Hera, is that correct?"

Hera nodded. Then she pointed at the file on Julia's desk. "It will all be in there," she said. Her tone was not aggressive or rude, just weary.

"Well," Julia said, "I like to check everything myself. Mistakes can happen, as you know."

Hera frowned and said, "What's that supposed to mean?" She imitated Julia's stressing of "as you know" at the end. "What am I supposed to know about mistakes?

Julia didn't pause. "That you know what it's like to make them," she said.

"I didn't make a mistake," Hera said, emphasising "mistake". "I meant it. I meant to do it. I've never pretended it was a mistake. It was my mother who said it was even though I told her it wasn't. It's stupid."

"What's stupid?" Julia asked quickly. "Your mother insisting that what you did was a mistake, or her failure to believe you meant it?"

"Both," said Hera.

They sat in silence for a few minutes, each studying the other. Hera didn't blink. Julia did, several times, which Hera seemed to notice and be pleased by. It was lucky, Julia thought, that they were not engaged in an arm-locking exercise or at this point Hera would have won, my arm would be flat on the table, powerless.

"You hurt your brother," Julia said, in a matter-of-fact tone, "quite considerably, as it turned out."

Hera smiled.

"You find that amusing?" Julia asked, keeping any disapproval out of her voice, trying merely to state it as a fact.

"No," Hera said.

"Then why did you smile?"

"At you," Hera said, "you think you're so clever."

Now there was a change in attitude. This was deliberate insolence, much easier to respond to.

"You hurt your brother," Julia repeated, "you broke his wrist."

"He broke his own wrist," Hera said. "I pushed him to the ground, and he put his arm out and his wrist broke."

Julia paused. "He didn't choose to fall," she said, "you pushed him, so you caused the fall that broke his wrist."

"But all I did was push him," Hera said.

"Hard," Julia said, "very hard, and you're much bigger than him. You pushed with both hands. You pushed so hard he crashed into a chair."

Hera nodded. "I did," she said, "and I meant it. But I didn't break his wrist."

Time for a pause. Julia got up and went to her desk and made a business of consulting the file there, though she perfectly remembered its contents.

50

"This is a waste of time," Hera said, and she too stood up. "Can I go? I mean, I'm going."

"Fine," Julia said, "so long as you realise the consequences."

She was relieved to see that Hera suddenly looked uncertain.

"What consequences?" she asked. "Are you threatening me?"

Such apparent confidence in a young girl, a mere child, but Julia suspected it was not confidence.

"No," she said, "I'm not. Sit down again, Hera." And she sat down again herself. "Right," Julia said, "let's be clear about a few things. This wasn't a squabble between you and your brother. It was part of repeated acts of violence towards him and your other brothers, so something has to be done about your behaviour before you injure someone seriously. You can't go around thumping other children the way you have been doing. That's why you're here. That's why you've been referred to me. Understand?"

This came out rather more sternly than Julia had intended, but it seemed to have some effect. Hera sat down and folded her arms in what Julia deduced was a defensive gesture. She couldn't be certain, but she thought she also detected a faint watering of Hera's prominent eyes. No tears came, but Hera held her head up and stared at the ceiling for a while before looking at Julia.

"Your mother —" Julia began, but Hera interrupted her.

"My mum has nothing to do with it," she said.

"I was going to say," Julia continued, "that your mother seems very troubled by what happened, very unhappy about it."

"I can't help that," Hera said, "it's how she is."

"What, troubled, unhappy?"

"I didn't say that."

"No, but it's what you meant, I think. Your mother cried when she found your brother on the floor, screaming, and you standing over him. She says she cried when she took him to A & E and was told his wrist was broken and would need to be set in plaster. A lot of crying. Were you upset to see your mother crying?"

"It was stupid," Hera said.

Hera's mother had cried in front of Julia. Copiously. Hera, she said, was beyond control. Her rages were frightening and unpredictable. Everyone was frightened of her, even the brother who was a year older (but half a head smaller). Once, Hera had almost strangled this brother. She said she had only been experimenting, to see how easy it would be should she wish to strangle someone. The marks were on his neck for weeks. There was never an apology afterwards. Hera's mother wept as she described her daughter's callous behaviour, saying she had no idea what gave rise to it, why Hera was like this. They were a happy family; there had been no disasters to explain why Hera was as she was, no divorce or death, nothing. She repeated that they were a happy family. Except for Hera.

52

* * *

Julia and her mother stayed at Aunt Maureen's for a week. They had never stayed so long before, except for when Reginald was killed, even though they had often been invited to, because the sisters invariably fell out within twenty-four hours and Julia's mother would announce an abrupt departure back to Penrith. But not this time. Maureen was happy, Iris was happy, and Uncle Tom was happy (not that his happiness had ever had any bearing on anything). The baby was the centre of everyone's attention, his every cry or whimper responded to. Julia's mother was good with him. She walked about the house carrying him and crooning to him in a manner which puzzled Julia. She had never seen her mother so gentle and loving, her usually cross expression quite gone, with only the hard mark between her eyes, the vertical slash on her forehead, to show how ferocious her frown had been for too many years. Julia couldn't understand it.

She couldn't understand the attraction of little Reggie either, and had become tired of pretending she was thrilled to be allowed, occasionally, to hold him. She preferred it when the baby was in his pram, which was an old-fashioned one, a Silver Cross pram with big wheels and a big hood and a rain cover which stretched tightly across it. The placing of the precious baby in this vehicle was a solemn ceremony involving a great deal of adjusting of the interior mattress and covers. Maureen put a pillow there, but Iris took it out, saying pillows were dangerous for small babies. Her mother and Julia's mother raised their eyebrows at each other but

53

neither dared to challenge Iris. On their last day, Julia and her mother were allowed to take little Reggie for a short walk while Iris had a dental appointment and Maureen was getting her hair done. It was clear to Julia that this was an honour, and that her mother appreciated that it was.

They set off slowly, Julia opening the gate so that the Silver Cross pram could glide through without marking its shiny navy-blue sides. The navy blue seemed a contradiction to Julia: if this was a *silver* cross pram, why was it navy blue? Where was the silver? She brought this up with Iris, and was laughed at and told she took things too literally. Once through the gate, her mother turned the pram round and they headed to the park, Julia also holding on to the handle. Two lots of hands gripping the thick handle. Her mother wouldn't let Julia push it on her own until two kerbs had been negotiated and the park entered. Then, on the flat path leading to the duck pond, Julia was given permission to push the pram on her own. It was easy. It hardly took any strength to make the pram move. Julia pushed harder and for a second, only a second, took her hands off the handle to see if the pram would continue to move on its own. Her mother was shocked, and immediately slapped her own hands back on the handle. "Never," she said, "*never* take your hands off the handle. Anything could happen. Really, Julia, you are the limit, the *idea!*"

Julia wasn't given the chance again to push the pram on her own so she gave up and put her hands in her pockets instead. When they got to the duck pond, her mother put the brake on the pram wheels and she and Julia sat on a bench, with the pram's hood up to shield the baby from the sun. They had no bread, so couldn't feed the ducks, which might have relieved the boredom for Julia. Sitting on the bench, swinging her legs, Julia narrowed her eyes and looked at the pram and thought of releasing the brake and giving it a push to see how far it could travel by itself along the cement path. Quite a long way, she reckoned, because there was a slight slope downwards and the pram would gather speed.

The next time they went to see little Reggie he was eight weeks old. He could smile, what everyone said was a real smile and not just wind. Again, Julia was allowed to hold him, under heavy supervision, though she hadn't asked to. She found his face ugly, but of course didn't say so. The tiny bit of hair he'd had had gone and his baldness showed lumps, bulges, all over his head. His eyes hadn't grown any bigger and were now almost lost in rolls of fat. Julia was glad to have him taken from her unwilling arms, and placed in the Silver Cross pram.

There was another outing, to the park, to the duck pond and back. This was as boring an outing as ever, but at least Julia was allowed, once she and her mother were in the park, to push the pram on her own. Her mother of course walked beside her, repeating "Slowly, slowly, Julia", but only Julia's hands were on the handle. It did make her feel quite important to be in charge of the Silver Cross pram and its precious cargo. Again, she had this urge to push the pram away from her to see how far it would go. It gave her an excited feeling in her stomach which was not altogether pleasant. Any moment she felt she might give in to the urge, and she would do it so suddenly, and with such strength, that her mother wouldn't be able to stop her.

"You did that very nicely, Julia," her mother said, when the walk was over and they were turning into Maureen's drive. It was so rarely that her mother praised her in any way, for anything at all, that Julia blushed with pleasure. Her mother told Maureen and Iris that Julia had pushed the pram *beautifully* in the park, though Maureen did slightly spoil the compliment by remarking that it was an easy pram to push, the Rolls-Royce of prams, not like modern-day prams with wheels so small they took a lot of turning. But still. As a reward, Julia was invited to help bathe little Reggie that evening. In the bathroom there was a stand with a plastic bath held within it. Iris ran the water until she announced it was at the correct temperature and then she used a jug to half fill the plastic baby bath. Julia sat with a white towel spread across her knees, as instructed, and watched Iris undress the baby. She was quite shocked at what she saw. Her eyes were riveted on little Reggie's genitals as she tried to make sense of them. Never, in any book with pictures of babies in it, had she seen a naked baby, and never in real life had she seen a boy unclothed. Suddenly, little Reggie became a fascinating object and she watched with a new interest as he was carefully lowered into the bath, with Iris's arm still round him. He yelped at first, but then as his adoring mother gently splashed the warm water over him he seemed to become calm and enjoy the sensation. When Iris had finished, she put the baby onto the waiting towel and Julia wrapped it round him and patted him dry, as directed by Iris. She didn't pat his genitals, but concentrated on his feet. Then Iris took him and put a nappy on him and a vest, and a blue Babygro. All babies were dressed in Babygros now. Neither Iris's mother nor Julia's mother approved of them, partly because each of them had made nightgowns for the baby, but Iris thought they were brilliant.

Julia and her mother stayed the night. It was on the next day, in the afternoon, that little Reggie was put to sleep in the Silver Cross pram which was placed in the garden, at the front, under a pear tree. It was a hot, sunny day but there was plenty of shade under the tree. Julia was told to check that little Reggie was asleep and then come in for tea, leaving the front door open so that any cries could be heard. She stood dutifully beside the pram. "You can rock the pram very, very gently," Iris said, "just enough to send him to sleep." She watched as Julia very, very gently touched the big, broad handle of the pram. The pram hardly moved at all. "Good," said Iris, "you've got the idea." She peered into the dark cavern of the hood of the pram. "Good," she said again, "he's asleep. You don't need to rock him now, Julia. Just play in the garden and listen out for him."

Play. Julia pondered this instruction. What did it mean, "play"? With what? With whom? There wasn't a ball or a skipping rope in sight. There wasn't a swing in this garden either. She wandered round the lawn,

57

stopping at the sundial and trying to work out the time, but couldn't. There was a small pond in one corner, containing a few water lilies. She could, she supposed, throw stones into the pond. Half-heartedly, she picked up a few stones from the path and threw them one by one into the pond, moving further away each time, to make aiming at the water lilies more difficult. Then she heard little Reggie cry. It wasn't a proper cry, more a whimper, but she went back to the pram and rocked it. The whimpering stopped, but she went on rocking the pram, doing it harder. How much rocking would it take to overturn the pram? It was just a passing thought that went through her head. She could see, in her mind's eye, the pram tilting. But it never would. It would need a really, really strong push to upend it, much stronger than any she could give.

Often, she saw pictures like that in her mind. Things happening, quite bad things. They were more often bad things than good things. She never told anyone this, though she would like to have known if everyone had such thoughts.

Half an hour had gone by. Julia didn't need to consult her wristwatch. There was a large wall clock high up in front of her. Its presence always irritated her but getting it removed seemed a job nobody would take on. "It's always been there," other people said, seeming surprised that Julia took exception to it.

"Hera," Julia said, "how would you describe a happy family? What would you say it would consist of?"

58

But Hera was a clever girl and she wasn't falling for this. "Happy?" she queried. "Depends what you mean by happy."

"What do *you* mean by it?" Julia parried.

"I don't," Hera said.

"Don't what?"

"I don't talk about happy families. You did. So you should know what you mean." She smiled, pleased with herself.

Julia nodded. "A happy family, to me," she said slowly, "can be of any size. It doesn't matter how many, or how few, members it has. It doesn't even matter how these people, adults and children, are related to each other, once they've grouped together into a family. But once they have, their happiness depends on how they treat each other. Just one member disregarding the feelings of another can wreck the family — if the rest of the family let it, of course."

Hera yawned ostentatiously.

"I might be boring you, Hera," Julia said, "but I haven't finished yet. I think you don't want your particular family to be happy. Everyone else who belongs to it wants it to be happy, but you don't."

"That's stupid," Hera said, but flatly, without passion.

"You're very fond of that word," Julia said. "Is everyone except you 'stupid'?"

"I didn't say that. But what you're saying about me is stupid. Why would I want to wreck my family? It's stupid."

"What do you want to do, then," said Julia, "behaving as you have been behaving?"

"I can't help how I behave," Hera said.

"Oh, but you can," Julia said, "saying *that* is stupid."

This could go on forever or at least for the rest of the remaining twenty minutes.

"Have you ever been hit, Hera?" Julia asked. "Slapped? Smacked? Pushed around?"

Hera shrugged.

"What does that shrug mean?" Julia asked. "Yes? No? You can't remember?"

"I suppose," Hera said.

"Suppose what?"

"Well, I expect I was smacked when I was little, how should I know?"

"Your mother says you never were."

Hera made a noise of derision, a little "huh" that sounded contemptuous.

"So I shouldn't believe her?" Julia asked.

"Believe what you like," Hera said, "it makes no difference to me."

"Well," Julia said, "it makes a great deal of difference to me. If I believe your mother, and I see no reason not to, you as a young child were never treated as you treat your younger brothers."

"Rick is older," Hera said, smiling triumphantly.

"Yes," said Julia, "but you've hit your younger brothers too, haven't you? But not hard enough for them to break a limb and for you to get found out. That's what you've depended on, isn't it? Not being found out. Making your brothers so afraid of you that they have never said anything. Has that given you pleasure?"

"Don't be stupid," Hera said, angry now.

60

Julia let a pause of a full five minutes fill the room with silence. Hera didn't like silence. It agitated her. She developed all kinds of strategies to combat it, tapping her fingers on the side of her chair, kicking her foot against the cupboard next to her. Julia let this happen, not once telling the girl to stop it. Eventually, it did stop. Hera folded her arms.

"Are we finished?" she asked. "All this talk is silly."

"Not stupid? Silly, but not stupid?" Julia said, risking a smile.

"You know what I mean," Hera said.

"I'm glad you think so," Julia said. "Shall I tell you what I think you mean. Shall I? Are you interested?" Another shrug. "Well, Hera, this is what I think you mean."

There were so many kinds of tiredness. The tiredness she felt now was nothing like the physical exhaustion she remembered feeling when she was a teacher. This kind of new tiredness drained her, but her body was refusing to sleep. The exhaustion was in every limb, in the crevice of every line on her face, and still sleep would not come to rescue and replenish her. It was not that her mind raced. There was no thudding noise of repetitive thoughts in her head. She felt quite calm, but this calmness did not tip her over into the oblivion she craved. Instead, she lay and stared at the ceiling, a blur of white in the semi-dark of the curtained room and she began to count the tiles. They were made of some kind of polystyrene stuff — she had never known the proper name — unpleasant to touch. She knew this because one had fallen off and she'd been surprised how brittle it was. She'd never replaced it. There were ten tiles by ten. The missing tile was luckily in the darkest corner, hardly noticeable.

Hera counted things. Julia had guessed she did when first she saw the girl staring at her own feet with such care, as though obliged to follow markings on the floor. And then, when making a display of ostentatious boredom during Julia's questioning, she was looking so intently, left to right, right to left, along the books on the shelf behind Julia that Julia knew she was counting them. Was this obsessive? Julia, counting her ceiling tiles lazily, didn't think it necessarily so, not in the way it was currently termed as obsessive compulsive disorder. It was a strategy, that was all. Something to do to avoid doing something else — no, that was not right. The tiles above her blurred and a wave of dizziness seemed to sweep through her, delicious, welcome.

In August, the summer little Reggie was born, Julia and her mother moved to Manchester. Julia never understood the reasons for this major upheaval. Nothing was explained and her opinion on whether this move was a good thing or not was never sought. Just one day her mother told her to pack up her things because they were going to Manchester to live.

She would be going to a new school in September, it was all arranged. Her mother had been born and brought up in Manchester and, it appeared, had never wanted to leave and come further north to the country, to where Julia's father was going to work, but she had had no choice.

Saying goodbye to her friends at school wasn't as sad as Julia thought it might be, but then she herself realised that none of these friends mattered much to her, except possibly Sandra. Sandra envied Julia going to Manchester, where she said there would be more "life". Julia wasn't sure what this meant, but nodded sagely. Her teacher gave her a book of poetry, a selection called *Poems of Lakeland,* and hoped she would continue to do as well at her new school as she had done at this one. Julia, she said, showed great promise. Julia repeated this to her mother, who merely commented "Time will tell".

The day they left the house where Julia had been born, and where she'd spent all her nine and a bit years, it rained heavily. She and her mother got soaked just going from the front door, which had to be locked, and into the taxi, and then soaked again, collecting the cases from the taxi and carrying them into the station. All short periods spent in the rain but enough to drench them because this rain was relentless, what Julia's mother called "the wetting sort", sheets of it falling from the dark sky. There was a clap of thunder as they stood on the station platform waiting for the train and her mother said thank goodness we're leaving this place. Julia wondered if this meant that there was no rain and no thunder in Manchester, but she didn't ask. "Best not to ask anything" — the rule of her young life. Best to wait and see what happened.

CHAPTER
THREE

It was a relief, after the tussle with Hera, to have Camilla in front of her. Julia felt grateful. This was not necessarily how work went. A difficult Case could be immediately followed by an even more difficult one. Her mind was still full of Hera. She had not by any means cleared it of the worry that she had not, after all, understood the girl. There was still something missing, which she would have to return to thinking about soon, before the final report was written.

But Camilla Pearson was almost a pleasure to have in front of her. A sweet, shy child, her expression a little anxious, though she was quite composed, sitting perfectly still and attempting a smile. The smile wavered but it was there. She was nine years old, slight of build and very pale. Julia noted shadows under Camilla's eyes, indicating lack of sleep, but the eyes themselves were bright enough, showing no signs of fatigue. Both parents had come with the girl, and sat now in the waiting room. They had seemed anxious about Camilla being seen on her own but had been persuaded of the need for this. Both had given their daughter a hug, and the mother added a kiss before she went into the room with Julia.

64

"Camilla," Julia began, "we're just going to have a chat about a few things, so I can get to know you a bit, OK?"

Camilla nodded, the hesitant smile reappearing.

"I was wondering," Julia said, "how you liked your new school?"

Camilla said it was all right. The "all right" was grudging.

"Did you like your last school?" Julia asked. The nod was enthusiastic. "What was good about it?" Julia encouraged her.

Camilla said she knew everyone there. She'd known them since they were all three in the nursery class. And the school was small, with a garden where they grew things. This new school was big, and there was no garden, and the playground was too hot and noisy and there were too many children and boys played football though they were not supposed to . . . the complaints tumbled out. Julia let them. Camilla had a long list of what was wrong with her new school and enjoyed going over it.

"Is there anything better at this school than at your last one?" Julia asked.

First Camilla shook her head, and then she said that maybe the dinners were a bit better, but that she didn't care about the dinners anyway. Her mother wanted her to have school dinners but she would rather have a packed lunch.

"What would you like in your lunch box?" Julia asked.

Camilla again had a list ready. She would like a cheese sandwich, brown bread and Cheddar cheese, and an apple, a Granny Smith, and a tangerine.

"No crisps, no biscuits?" Julia prompted.

Another energetic shake of the head. "They aren't good for you," Camilla said, "biscuits are full of sugar and rot your teeth, and crisps are rubbish. We did it at my other school."

"It?" queried Julia.

"Diet, what's good for you and what isn't."

Very virtuous, and Camilla knew it. She was pleased with her answer, her expression almost comical in its knowingness.

Julia switched tack. "Your mum works, doesn't she, Camilla? What is it that she does?"

"She's a physiotherapist," Camilla said, "at the hospital where my dad works too. He's an engineer."

Julia asked her if she had been to this hospital, if she'd seen her mother at work. Camilla said once, when there was a day off school, and her mother had taken her with her because there was no one to look after her and she was too young to be left on her own. Julia asked if she'd liked the hospital. No, Camilla hadn't. It was too big and there were smells she didn't like and once they had to walk past a man lying on a trolley, with blood all over him, and it was frightening. She'd sat on a chair watching while her mum got old people out of bed and showed them how to use a sort of walking frame and the old people didn't like it and wanted to get back into bed. Then she and her mum went to another ward where there was a man who had to learn to use his arm again and he groaned and groaned.

There was no stopping Camilla. A chatterbox once started. Julia thought of directions in which the talkativeness could be usefully pushed. Here was a child who had twice been found a long way from home and apparently intent on travelling further if she had not drawn attention to herself and been questioned (in the first instance by a traffic warden, seeing her standing hesitantly at a crossing but never crossing, and in the second by a shopkeeper from whom she'd tried to buy a bar of chocolate with a 10p piece). In both cases, Camilla had been quite calm when challenged about what she was doing in an area such a long way from where she said she lived. She said she was just exploring. Taken to the nearest police station each time she gave her address and telephone number, perfectly self-possessed, and waited to be collected without seeming to have any worries about her parents being angry or distressed by her behaviour.

They hadn't been angry but they were bewildered. On one occasion, the parents thought Camilla safely at school, to which they'd delivered her themselves. She had slipped out at break time without anyone spotting her, though quite how she'd managed to do this when the playground gate was locked from 9a.m. to 3p.m. nobody had established satisfactorily. The teachers didn't yet know Camilla and none of them appeared to have noticed her disappearance until at least an hour later when for some reason there had been a name- or head-check, and one girl was missing.

Julia had listened patiently while all this was described by the parents, who blamed the teachers for being "slack". They ought, in the father's opinion, to have been keeping a watch on a new pupil. He didn't know how this school had been rated "outstanding" by Ofsted, if a nine-year-old girl could just leave it without anyone noticing for more than an hour.

"And the second time Camilla wandered off?" Julia asked, knowing this time the school could not be blamed. Camilla had been at home. It was an hour before her parents realised she was not watching the DVD they'd left her (they thought) engrossed in.

"We were decorating," the mother said, "we were painting the bedroom."

Julia nodded. She looked at Camilla, who returned her gaze with a slight smile.

"Why does she do this?" her father asked. "Why doesn't she tell us why she does it? I mean, think what could have happened? It's dangerous, we've told her that, we've tried to tell her without, you know, scaring her. We can't trust her any more, she won't promise never to go off again just when she feels like it."

There was a lot more in this vein. Julia listened, and watched Camilla, who appeared entirely unworried.

Visits to see little Reggie became regular. Julia and her mother now lived only ten minutes' walk away from where Iris still lived with her parents. Often, Julia and her mother babysat while Maureen and Iris went out. It was, Julia discovered, a deeply boring pastime. Hours, she seemed to spend, standing dutifully in the garden watching over a sleeping little Reggie. There was a canopy over his Silver Cross pram but this might not protect him from the attentions of stray cats even if it guarded him adequately from the sun. It was Julia's job to chase away any interested cats, and look out for wasps and bees. A bee sting, she was told, could be "fatal" for such a young baby. If a bee started to hover round the pram, she was to move its position at once. It occurred to Julia that, since bees flew, they could fly after the pram and it would be no good moving it, but she didn't mention this obvious fact. To do so would have meant being called "argumentative" by her mother.

Little Reggie was still very little. Julia listened to the conversations about his weight. They were interminable. Iris fretted about her baby's lack of substantial weight gain whereas Maureen saw nothing worrying about little Reggie only having put on a couple of ounces since regaining his birth weight. Julia's mother, however, supported Iris. Little Reggie was taken weekly to the baby clinic where all three women watched the scales intently while he was weighed. The nurse who did the weighing was reassuring, saying little Reggie was perfectly healthy, but Iris was sometimes tearful on the way home. Maureen and Julia's mother nudged each other when this happened, and cleared their throats, and began talking over-brightly to each other, until Iris recovered.

It was the last week of the school holidays. The weather went on being hot and sunny, but Julia didn't enjoy it much. She wished she could be at the seaside, any seaside, or at least near a lake or river. Their new home had a small garden but this consisted merely of a parched plot of grass and a ragged border full of weeds and not much else. Julia's mother clicked her tongue at the sight of these weeds but said she had no time to do anything about them and certainly couldn't afford a gardener. Julia wished they had a garden like Maureen's but as they didn't she stayed mostly inside, out of the sun. Go out and play, her mother urged, but there was no one to play with and outside it was too hot. Go and explore, her mother suggested, get to know the way to your new school. But Julia knew the way. There was no need to explore. The use of that word irritated her. "Explore" sounded exciting, and walking the roads round where they now lived was not in the least exciting. She would have liked to explore the canal at the back of the houses, but the gate onto the towpath was locked.

She was worried about starting her new school. On the one hand, she wanted the holidays to be over because she was so bored, but on the other she was nervous because she would know no one. She would be the new girl, and she had seen what it could be like to be a new girl. She'd be an object of great curiosity at first and then this interest would fade away and she'd be left struggling to break into groups and partnerships formed by the others long ago. She was resolved not to care about this isolation, but she was not looking forward to experiencing it. She didn't bother voicing her anxieties to her mother, knowing she would only get a bracing lecture on facing up to things. What her mother didn't appreciate was that in her imagination Julia had done just that and hadn't liked it. She had envisaged the faces peering at her, seen the crowd surrounding her in the playground on her first day, and her heart had started to beat loudly. She felt taut with apprehension. She could feel herself inside the heads of the other girls. Knew what they would be thinking about her and what they would say. She practised over and over again how to react.

The day before term started Julia and her mother spent the afternoon at Maureen's. They had lunch there after Julia had watched Iris bathe little Reggie. Iris was very tired because little Reggie had woken up every hour all night. He seemed to be hungry but had only half emptied the bottle he was given. Theories as to the cause of the baby's reluctance to accept all the milk were debated by Iris, Maureen and Julia's mother. Julia's mind wandered. She heard the voices of the three talkers but she didn't take in the words. Asking if she could be excused (her mother had brought her up always to ask if she could be excused from the table), she stood up and took her empty plate to the sink and rinsed it clean, and then she wandered into the garden, kicking the gravel on the path, but carefully, quietly, so that nobody would hear her.

Little Reggie was in his pram, finally asleep. Iris had said he would probably sleep for hours now, and his regular feeding pattern would be disrupted, but she didn't care, she wasn't going to waken him, he needed the rest and so did she. Julia peered into the pram, which as usual during this hot weather was under the pear tree, nicely shaded. She could only see the baby's head, a still bald head, unless the new darker fuzz on it was counted as hair. He was lying on his back, his eyes, of course, shut but his eyelids occasionally seeming to flicker. Julia thought he must be dreaming, and wondered what a baby would dream about. She thought she'd gently rock the pram, as she had been taught, though there was no need to because little Reggie was asleep and perfectly quiet. The pram wouldn't rock with the brake on so she released the brake. It now rocked satisfactorily. Julia looked back at the house. Her mother and aunt and cousin weren't in the dining room any longer. They had either all gone to wash up or they'd retreated to the cooler sitting room at the back of the house. They weren't watching Julia or the pram anyway.

Slowly, experimentally, Julia began to push the pram towards the gate. It was a broad wooden gate, painted green. When she reached it, she put the brake back on while she opened the gate. She would take little Reggie for a short walk, just up the road and back. It would only take ten minutes. She liked the idea of being in charge of the pram, of being capable enough to manage to push it without her mother's supervision. She could be back in the garden before her mother or aunt or cousin came to check on the baby. Walking very erect, head held high, she negotiated the way through the open gateway skilfully, turning the pram neatly to face down the road. She didn't close the gate. No need to, when she was going to be back in a few minutes.

She was at the end of the first stretch of the road in what seemed like seconds. Once there, she hesitated. There was a kerb, and then another kerb, with a minor road leading to the canal joining the main road. Could she safely manage the kerbs? Yes, of course she could, and she did. On she went until she came to the very end of the road, where she was resolved to turn and go back. Faint pricklings of guilt and anxiety were beginning to trouble her. Any moment she expected to hear her mother or aunt or cousin, or all three of them, shouting down the road at her, wanting to know what on earth she thought she was doing, pushing the big pram on her own, yelling at her to come back at once. But there was no shouting. The road, at two in the afternoon, was eerily silent. Most houses had blinds or curtains drawn against the fierce sun. Nobody was in the gardens, nobody mowing the lawn or clipping a hedge. It was much too hot. Julia turned the pram round, again taking great care. Then she set off back to the house, the sun now in her eyes.

Quite what happened she wouldn't have been able to say. It was something to do with going down the first kerb. She'd already gone over two kerbs, one upwards, one downwards, each time gently tipping the pram at the right angle. But now something happened. She turned the pram round, with no difficulty, and then, pleased that this manoeuvre was so easy, she put her hands under instead of on top of the handle, and pushed, so that the big front wheels would slide over the kerb. Immediately, much too quickly for her to correct the angle, the whole pram seemed to stand on end, the hood hitting the ground, the handle in the air, her hands trying to clutch it. She could see that little Reggie had slid down into the interior of the hood, his head separated from the tarmac road only by the fabric of this hood. But he was still asleep there wasn't a sound from him. Julia raised herself on tiptoes and pushed down on the handle with all her might. Thankfully the pram righted itself and she pushed it across the short width of the side road and got it up the other kerb without mishap.

"Phew!" she said out loud, just as her mother was in the habit of doing when a minor catastrophe was averted, and again, "phew." She put the brake on the pram and peered at little Reggie. He had come free of the white cotton cover (a lacy affair, very lightweight because of the heat) so she put it over him again, very neatly, and then carried on pushing the pram back to the garden. She went at a quicker pace than before, anxious now to get the pram back in the position it had been in when she had decided to go for a walk. Nobody was about. She looked to right and left and all was still in the afternoon heat. Turning into the gate, she stopped as soon as she was through and closed it and placed the pram under the pear tree, just as it had been. But then she realised there were wheel marks slightly to the left of where she'd parked the pram. They were only visible here because the grass was a little longer than on the rest of the lawn which had become parched in the weeks of sun. It took some struggling to get the wheels exactly set in the existing tracks but finally she succeeded. She scuffed the grass with her feet all around, went into the house and straight into the kitchen where she ran the cold tap and filled a glass with water. She looked at the kitchen clock but couldn't work out how long she had been. Not long, she decided.

When Julia and her mother left to go home, little Reggie was still asleep. "The lamb!" Iris said. "He's making up for last night." There was a bit of discussion about whether the pram should now be moved inside, and Iris decided perhaps it should be because the sun was moving around and there wasn't as much shade under the tree as there had been. She was pushing it inside the front door as Julia and her mother waved goodbye. They dawdled along the road. It was much too hot even for Julia's mother to rush. "What did you do with yourself in the garden?" she asked Julia. Julia could tell her mother wasn't asking this because she really wanted to know. It was what her mother once described to her as "a pleasantry", a polite bit of chat, just another way of saying hello or how are you? "Nothing" would be a perfectly satisfactory answer, so Julia gave it. "Nothing," she said.

Next day was meant to be Julia's first day at her new school, but she didn't go to school. The phone rang during the night. Julia didn't hear it, but her mother did, and answered it. She shook Julia awake at dawn, a startlingly lurid red dawn. "Get up, Julia," she said, "get dressed. We're going to Maureen's house. I'm needed there, and you'll have to come with me." Still half asleep, Julia said, "But what about school?" Her mother said, "School can wait."

★　★　★

"Were you lost, Camilla, when you left your new school?" Julia asked. Camilla said a little bit, but not much. "What did you find, when you were exploring?" Camilla described the running track she'd found and the shops she'd passed, and the railway bridge she'd stood on watching the overground train go by. "Were you going to go back to the school? Did you intend to?" No, Camilla had intended to find her way home when she got tired. She said she knew the right bus to get. "And when you went exploring from home, what were you planning to do then?"

"Don't know," Camilla said, "just wanted to be out. I like being out."

"But it worries your parents," Julia pointed out. "Think of being them, how would you feel if your daughter just disappeared? Wouldn't you worry?" Camilla nodded, but smiled at the same time.

The parents had made a mistake, moving Camilla from one school to another, which they believed to be a much better school and when she only had a year and a bit to go before changing to secondary school anyway. Julia thought they realised that, but wouldn't reverse the process. Camilla was quite likely to continue her "exploring" if she could, but probably she wouldn't be able to. She would be watched. Seizing an opportunity would be hard. She had no idea of how vulnerable she was, wandering the streets and parks.

"Well, Camilla," Julia said, "I think you're going to have to accept the new school and try to make the best of it. But you could still go exploring if you called your

76

parents on your mobile. You can't leave school to do it, but you could do it from home sometimes. Could you give that a try? Otherwise nobody will let you out of their sight and you wouldn't like that, would you?"

She watched from the window as Camilla and her parents walked to their car. Her mother was holding her hand. Her father patted her back tentatively. It was a reassuring scene. The parents were clearly sorry.

"Don't say anything," Julia's mother told her as they hurried to Aunt Maureen's. "Don't ask any of your questions, whatever you do." Julia, half asleep, absorbed these instructions. They were familiar, after all. Her mother was always forbidding her to ask questions, even obvious, simple ones. She was expected to be able to understand what was going on through some process of osmosis, and often she did.

It was only a ten-minute walk, but Julia's mother was almost running, dragging Julia with her. She gave a gasp as they turned the corner into Maureen's road, a sort of long drawn-out "Oh!" Julia saw the ambulance standing at her aunt's front door, its doors open. "My God," Julia's mother said, but quietly, whispering the words. The front door was open too. As she and her mother walked past the ambulance, almost tiptoeing their way across the gravel, they both looked in. It was empty. The house seemed at first to be empty too. Julia's mother didn't call out. She took Julia's hand, and together they walked into the sitting room. It was full of people. Julia took in the man and woman in uniform first. One of them, the woman, was holding

Aunt Maureen's hand and saying something to her. Uncle Tom was standing looking out of the French windows into the garden where a cat was slowly picking its way across the lawn. The woman stopped saying whatever she was saying to Maureen and in the silence that followed Julia heard a strange sound. It wasn't exactly the sound of crying, more a howl which rose and fell quite rhythmically. "Stay here," Julia's mother said to her, and left the room. Nobody stopped her. Julia heard her mother go up the stairs, heard a door being knocked on, and then Iris's name being spoken. The weird noise intensified for a moment, and then a door closed and there was silence.

A long time seemed to pass. There was some sort of discussion between the ambulance people and then the man went outside the room and Julia heard the crackle of what she supposed was a walkie-talkie thing. She couldn't hear what the man was saying, but he soon came back and spoke to his colleague, and they both shook hands first with Maureen and then with Tom. Then they left, and Julia heard the ambulance driving off. This puzzled her. Why was the ambulance going off empty? What did it mean? But mindful of her mother's warning, she didn't ask. Another vehicle had just pulled up outside the still open front door. Julia waited. This time it was another policewoman, and a man with her who was not in any uniform. Tom turned away from watching the cat, and the policewoman went up to him and said something. "Is that necessary?" she heard her uncle say, and the policewoman said, "I'm afraid so, sir."

Nobody said anything to Julia. Nobody seemed to notice her. She wondered if it would be wrong to say she was hungry, and thought that so long as she didn't *ask* for something to eat it would be all right. But when she tried to say the three words, she got no further than "I'm . . ." which came out as more like a throat clearing than a word. It called attention to her presence.

"Julia!" her aunt said, as though amazed to see her, and then, to her husband, "Where's Lydia?"

"With Iris," Tom said.

"She let her in?" Maureen asked.

Tom nodded.

"Well," Maureen said, "I'd better give Julia some breakfast. We have to eat. What time is it?"

Tom said it was seven o'clock, about.

"What do you mean 'about'?" Maureen said. "You've got a watch, we've got clocks, what time is it?"

Tom said it was 6.54a.m.

Maureen boiled an egg for Julia, talking rapidly all the time about eggs. She said she would have fried some bacon, but the smell might upset Iris. Smells, she told Julia, drifted upwards even if the extractor fan was put on, and it didn't work very well. Julia ate the egg and two slices of toast. She ate them so enthusiastically that Maureen offered her another slice and she accepted. "You've a good appetite," Maureen said, and then her face crumpled and she started to weep. Julia was embarrassed. She had no idea what to do, beyond daintily nibble at the remaining morsel of toast. Her uncle had left the room and there was only herself and her aunt there, facing each other across the table. The weeping didn't show any sign of stopping, so Julia got up, scraping her chair on the floor, and tore off a piece of kitchen paper. It was quite rough paper, but she couldn't see a box of tissues anywhere. She offered the paper to her aunt who balled it up and dabbed at her streaming eyes, to little effect. At that moment, Julia's mother was heard coming down the stairs. Relieved, Julia turned towards her as she came into the kitchen.

"Stop this, Maureen," Julia's mother said, "there's things will need to be done, and Iris is in no fit state." She put the kettle on, and banged about quite noisily, selecting a tea bag from a canister and a mug from a hook and a teaspoon from the cutlery drawer. There was more noise as the fridge was opened and the milk taken out and the fridge shut again. Julia, watching her mother, knew all this noise, such as it was, was deliberate. Normally, her mother did everything quietly, and objected if Julia so much as dropped a teaspoon on the draining board. Maureen took the tea offered and Julia's mother sat down with her.

"Julia," she said, "go and play in the garden a minute."

Julia stared at her. "Play?" she echoed.

"You heard. Just go in the garden, pick some flowers or something, some roses."

"For Iris?" Julia asked. "Is she ill?"

She'd broken the order not to ask questions, but, surprisingly, her mother didn't seem annoyed. She said that yes, Iris was feeling ill but wasn't actually ill. It was the baby. It was little Reggie, who had been taken from her and it was very sad. Julia immediately began to

80

want to ask dozens of questions but her mother said, quite sharply, "Go in the garden, I'll call you in a minute."

Feeling excited, Julia went into the garden and wandered aimlessly around, trying to work out who could have stolen little Reggie. Had he been kidnapped? Would there be a ransom note? And how had it been done? She looked up at Iris's bedroom window. There was a drainpipe to the right of it. Had the kidnapper climbed up the pipe and got in through the window? But how could he have climbed down holding the baby? Wouldn't little Reggie have cried? Wouldn't Iris have heard him?

She seemed to be in the garden much longer than the minute her mother promised. She did no playing and picked no flowers. Instead she lurked beside the kitchen window, which was open a little bit, enough for her to hear some of the talking going on inside. She stood to the left of the window, her back flat against the brick wall, and she strained to make sense of what she could hear. This consisted of words broken up as her mother moved between sink and table, doing whatever she was doing. Sometimes a tap would run and Julia could hear nothing, then there would be a minute of clarity and she'd hear a whole sentence. She couldn't hear her aunt at all, only the burr of her voice in the background.

It took a long time for Julia to come to the conclusion from which she finally could not escape. Little Reggie was dead. Her mouth went dry when this realisation came to her and her knees began to tremble.

She clutched the drainpipe next to the window frame to steady herself. No one had told her little Reggie was dead. Maybe she had pieced together wrongly the fragments she'd heard. But then her mother called her name, sharply, and as she stepped forward and walked towards the kitchen door where her mother stood, Julia remembered the phrase "taken from her" and knew she was right.

"Mum," she said, "is little Reggie —" But she got no further.

"Shh," her mother said, "come back inside, sit quietly; find a book or something. I'll tell you later."

"Later" turned out to be much later. They stayed all that day and the night at Aunt Maureen's. There was a constant procession of people coming and going, all of whom ignored Julia. She sat in an armchair in a corner of the sitting room with one of Uncle Tom's books about birds open on her lap. She turned a page occasionally, to look like an authentic reader, though nobody was watching her. She watched them instead. She had a good view of the hall and the first flight of stairs and saw how solemn everyone looked as they arrived. They spoke in hushed voices and if they were wearing a hat they took it off and clutched it awkwardly. Julia heard odd words which she didn't understand. One was something "mortem". They'd done a poem during her last term at her old school about King Arthur and his knights and the title was *Morte d'Arthur* which the teacher explained meant the death of Arthur. *Morte* meant death. *Mortem* must mean something to do with death.

At lunchtime, Julia was called into the kitchen and given a sandwich. Maureen said she couldn't eat, she'd be sick, the mere thought of eating made her feel sick. Julia's mother told her that not eating wouldn't help anyone and that Maureen needed to be strong and to be strong she needed to eat. Maureen said she was going up to see Iris. Julia's mother said that if she was going to do that she should be sure not to start crying again because Iris had had quite enough of crying already. She'd wept buckets herself and now she was exhausted and silent and needed comforting. One day, she could have another baby, Julia's mother said. She was young and healthy and little Reggie passing away was nothing to do with her, it was just one of those things. "They don't know that yet, Lydia," Maureen suddenly said in a surprisingly firm tone, "they have to wait for the result of the post-mortem." Julia's mother was scandalised. She said that whatever a post-mortem showed it still wouldn't have anything to do with Iris. "It might," Maureen said. Julia's mother said it was beyond her comprehension how her sister could say such a thing about her own daughter.

The argument carried on, becoming more and more confusing to Julia. She could tell this *was* an argument but what she couldn't understand was what lay underneath her aunt's words. What did it mean, that something to do with little Reggie being dead might be Iris's fault? Or had she picked that up wrongly? Her mother was angry with her aunt, and it was that sort of dangerous anger Julia recognised and feared, not the run-of-the-mill crossness. But this troubling discord between the sisters stopped when the doorbell rang and Uncle Tom answered and then came into the kitchen and said, "They've come for . . ." and didn't finish his sentence. Its meaning seemed to be understood, though. Julia's mother said, "Stay here, Maureen, stay here, Julia. I'll see to it," and she left the kitchen, closing the door firmly behind her. Uncle Tom sighed, and sat down. "This is . . ." he said, and again didn't finish his sentence. Julia couldn't guess how it might have gone on.

At six o'clock, Iris came downstairs. The curtains were drawn in the sitting room, where they were all sitting, their tea just finished. It hadn't been a proper tea, to Julia's disappointment. Nothing freshly baked; just some shortbread and the tea itself. Nobody was expecting Iris to come down, so when they heard her door upstairs opening and then the sound of her slowly descending, they all seemed to freeze, even Julia's mother. Julia was watching her closely, and saw how alarmed she looked, a frown creasing her forehead. But she didn't get up, and neither did anyone else. The door opened, creaking a bit, and Iris stood there, staring at them. "Oh, Julia," she said, "you're here!" Julia got up, blushing. Iris sounded so surprised, as though Julia should have been somewhere else. In her head, Julia was instructing herself to say something, say something, but nothing came. She felt strangled with embarrassment.

It was a feeling that didn't lift. Julia soon sensed that neither her aunt nor her uncle, nor inexplicably, her mother, knew what to say to Iris. It was much worse

84

than when Reginald was killed. Then, people spoke freely, even if they all said the same things, or so it seemed to Julia. But now there wasn't even a "I'm sorry, so sorry". There were no hugs either, and the tears were all dried up. Uncle Tom said he would have to go out. He didn't say why or where he was going but nobody questioned him. Once he'd gone, there was a slight easing of the tension. Julia's mother and her aunt began talking, in a stilted fashion, but still, it was talk. Iris didn't join in, but she picked up the newspaper her father had left there and turned its pages.

Julia thought that day would never end. For once, she was longing to be sent to bed but it was nine o'clock before her mother told her to brush her teeth and go to bed in the little box room. Julia said she hadn't got a toothbrush or her pyjamas. "For heaven's sake, Julia," her mother said, "have some sense." Julia couldn't imagine what sense had to do with pointing out that she had no pyjamas and no toothbrush, but she said sorry and left the room and went upstairs to the bedroom. On the bed lay a toothbrush and her pyjamas. Her mother must have packed them, in her bag before they left the house that morning. "Sense" meant that Julia should have known that her efficient mother would do so, whatever the emergency. It was oddly comforting, seeing her own pyjamas and toothbrush, and Julia, after brushing her teeth extra vigorously, went to bed more content and settled than she had been all day. But when she closed her eyes, she saw little Reggie, and quickly opened them again. It suddenly occurred to her that the dead baby might be in the next room, Iris's room, and after that she couldn't get to sleep. What did a dead baby look like?

It wasn't until the following day that the questioning began.

"It's a simple procedure," the nurse said, "only takes ten minutes." Julia asked what exactly was going to be done. "We cut it out," the nurse said, "and then put a few stitches in. You only need a local anaesthetic." She seemed dismissive, bored with Julia's anxiety. "Ready?" she asked. "Then sign here." Julia signed. Two other people appeared. A young woman and an older man, both wearing blue tops and with their hair covered. Julia didn't watch medical soaps but she'd caught the end of enough of them, turning the television on for other programmes, to recognise that their clothes identified them as doctors. They barely greeted her before the man indicated to the woman the black spot on her cheek. "It's a BCC," he said, "you need to cut right round." He said something else Julia couldn't quite catch. She felt stupid, as though she had no will or power, and cleared her throat to show she was there, a real person. Images of revenge rose up in her mind and she suppressed them hastily.

The anaesthetic took effect very quickly. She was on her back, staring into a harsh light which hurt her eyes. "Sorry about the light," the woman said, "but we can't give you protective glasses or a shade because they'd cast a shadow on your cheek." Julia felt small tugs on her face. "OK?" the woman said. She nodded. The man was watching the woman closely. It occurred to Julia

86

that she had never done this operation before. He was instructing her, telling her to do this, to do that. The woman's face was above her, a little flushed, and she was frowning. It was all over in ten minutes or so, just as they'd promised. "Well done," the man said, but he said it to the woman, not to Julia. "Neat stitches," he said, "very nice. You've followed the line running down her nose at the side. Good work. There won't be any scar." Then he left the room, and the woman smiled and patted Julia's hand and said the nurse would put a dressing on, then she could go. She only needed to keep this dressing on for the rest of the day and then she could remove it and let the air get at it.

When she got home, Julia removed the dressing and looked in the mirror. She didn't know how many stitches had been put in but the red line was livid. If this was good work she didn't want to see what bad work looked like. Her cheek would scare the children, but if she covered the stitches the plaster would have to be so large and prominent that would scare them too. She would have to spend precious time explaining, and going into details about basal cell carcinomas would not be a good idea. All she could say was that a bad bit had been cut out, like a bad bit from an apple, and that it hadn't hurt and in a few days her cheek would mend and look the same as it always had. But she decided to take some time off, two or three days. She would write up reports which she could do perfectly well at home. There were no referrals which would have to be cancelled. Her next appointment was on Tuesday, plenty of time for the stitches to stop looking so raw, and she might get away with a neat little plaster by then. Any questions could be dealt with in a matter-of-fact way, but few children did ask those sorts of questions, fascinated though they might be at the sight of any kind of sore or wound. Once, Julia had broken her arm and had to have it in a sling for weeks, but not one child had asked her what she had done to her arm.

She was the one who had always, as a child, wanted to ask questions but had been trained not to. She liked being asked them, too, or thought she did until the questions became tricky and she began to worry about what her answers were revealing, to herself as much as to the questioner.

All Julia was told was that a lady would ask her some questions. Nobody told her who this lady was, but she wasn't in uniform so Julia thought she couldn't be a policewoman. She thought what a funny job it must be, just asking questions, but one she might like herself.

The lady was gentle and kind. She smiled at Julia, and told her not to worry, she just wanted to go over exactly what had happened the day before the poor baby fell asleep. Julia wondered why she didn't say "died". She decided she would say it herself. "You mean," she said, "the day before little Reggie died?" The lady looked a little shocked, but nodded. Julia nodded back, and waited.

"Now," the lady said, "you and your mother were here that day, is that right, Julia?"

Julia knew that she knew it was right. It was such a wasted question.

"So," the lady went on, "tell me about that day, from when you arrived at the house. Tell me every little thing you can remember."

Julia told her. She rather enjoyed giving every little detail, right down to what kind of bread Maureen provided with the salad, stressing that it was granary, not straight brown, and not sliced, and the slices cut were thick and the butter spread thickly too and . . . The lady stopped her. She explained that by "every little thing" she meant actions, what was done, that sort of thing. Julia said that before this lunch when they arrived at her aunt's house she had gone with Iris to watch little Reggie be bathed. Iris thought he seemed hot, and a bath would cool him down.

The lady sat up very straight and looked expectant, her mouth opening slightly in encouragement. "Yes?" she said. "You watched the baby being bathed?" Julia agreed that was what she had done. "Tell me about how baby seemed," said the lady. "Did he like his bath? Did he cry?" Julia said yes, he'd liked it and he hadn't cried at all. Iris had lowered him very carefully into the water and splashed him a little bit and he'd kicked his legs, and then Iris had wrapped him in a white towel and cuddled him . . . This time, the lady didn't stop her.

It took a long time for Julia to get to later in the afternoon of that day. When she reached that point in her narrative, a strange feeling began to come over her. It was a feeling of dread, though dread of what she couldn't have articulated. "They said to go in the garden and look at little Reggie in his pram and so I did." Then she stopped.

The lady, whose attention throughout was unmistakably close, said, "Go on, Julia. Little Reggie, in his pram? Did you look at him, in his pram?" Julia nodded. "Was he asleep?" She nodded again. "Did you touch him, Julia?" She shook her head. "Did you touch the pram?"

Julia hesitated — she knew the lady saw her hesitate — and said, "I touched the handle, the way Iris showed me. Just a little. Just once."

There was a silence, and the lady stared at her. "And then," she said, "what did you do?"

"I walked round and round the garden," said Julia, "and then I went back inside."

She had lied. The moment she had missed out the next bit, about taking little Reggie for a walk, she started to feel sick. Lies led to more lies, her mother always said, and ended up making a terrible mess. Lies, her mother taught her, always got found out in the end. This lie could easily be found out if someone in the road had after all seen her without her realising. Then what would she do? Julia started to tremble, and then to cry. The lady comforted her. She said yes, it was very upsetting, the baby dying, and that she, Julia, had been brave, not crying up to now. Julia cried harder, and the lady went to get Julia's mother who, when she came into the room, said quite sharply, "Really, Julia," but then she did put her arms round Julia, briefly, and said, "It's enough to make anyone cry, all this." Julia was taken into the kitchen and given a glass of water, and soon after that she and her mother at last went home.

The next day, she started her new school, after her mother had rung the headmistress and explained why Julia had missed the first two days.

The stitches came out of Julia's face, and all that was left was a thin red line which hardly stood out. It could have been nothing more than a scratch. She was glad not to attract attention when she returned to work, though really there had been few questions about the plaster and what it was covering. People probably thought, she reckoned, that it would be a trifle indelicate to ask a middle-aged woman what was wrong with her face.

But she saw that Eva was scrutinising her face and wondering about the scar. Eva had a scar of sorts herself, a birthmark in the centre of her left cheek. Because she was fair-skinned, the red blotch, which was quite large, stood out more than it would have otherwise done. Presumably, Julia thought, nothing could be done about it. When Eva was older, she could cover it with make-up, if it bothered her. She was a pretty girl, in spite of the birthmark, with thick, auburn hair, a mass of curls, framing her face. Julia noticed in particular the child's mouth. Her lips were full, the upper lip a perfect bow, and when she smiled a dimple appeared in her right cheek. She was, Julia estimated, aware of her own good looks, sitting with an air of absolute confidence on her chair. She was used, no doubt, to being looked at and admired, the birthmark notwithstanding.

The mother was a single parent. Julia thought at first she was a divorcee, but she had been misinformed. Eva was the result of a sperm donor insemination. She knew, the mother told Julia, all about her origins and always had done. That was not a problem. The mother said this emphatically and Julia didn't contest the assertion, though she was tempted to say that remained to be seen. The problem was alleged to be disorder, extreme disorder of every sort. Eva trashed things. She deliberately tore her clothes, deliberately knocked things over, deliberately created mess wherever she went. Her own room was, said her mother, like a tip, heap upon heap of rubbish, most of it taken from skips in the street. It was shocking, the mother said, that such a young child should collect such disgusting junk. There must be something wrong with her, and she wanted it put right before Eva became a teenager and got totally out of control. Julia prayed silently for patience, and asked the mother to wait outside. There was such antagonism between mother and daughter that it would be hopeless trying to talk to Eva while her mother was present.

Studying Eva, once she had her on her own, Julia was struck by her neat appearance. No sign of disorder there. The mother, of course, would have made sure Eva was tidily dressed, but there were plenty of ways the girl could have sabotaged her efforts if she had wanted to. Buttons could have been buttoned in the wrong order, socks shoved down, sleeves shoved up —

there were all kinds of small rebellions possible if Eva wanted to be disorderly. But she had made none of them. Julia thought about commenting on this, but didn't.

"Tell me about your room, Eva," Julia said.

"What?" Eva said.

"Your room at home — describe it to me," Julia said.

Eva thought for a minute. The hesitation seemed prolonged. "I don't know what to say," Eva said, and then, "It's not a very big room. It has my bed, and a chest thing, with drawers, you know the sort." Julia nodded. "The carpet is blue. The curtains are blue. That's all."

"It sounds quite empty?" Julia said.

Eva shook her head vigorously. "It isn't empty."

"What do you have in it, then?"

Eva began to itemise everything that she'd filled her room with, from things she'd found in the park, just left lying abandoned on benches or dropped on paths, to items she'd picked up from outside people's doors. "They just leave stuff there," she told Julia, "anyone can take it." She'd found a little cabinet with six drawers, only one of them broken, and a lamp which didn't work but had a pretty frilly pink shade, and an umbrella which was like one she'd seen in a picture, a white-and-black umbrella, intact except for two bent spokes. It looked lovely opened out on the floor of her room, Eva said, but her mother said it got in the way and was always closing it up. Her mother didn't like clutter. Her mother liked everything neat and tidy.

"Like the *Mr Men* books," Eva said helpfully, "Miss Neat & Tidy."

"And who are you?" Julia asked. "Miss Messy?"

Eva smiled then seemed to change her mind. "I'm not messy," she said, "I'm just not like my mother."

How true. How common, how familiar the situation, about which there was very little Julia could do. She talked a little more to Eva, discovering that the child was well on the way to being a real collector. She collected buttons, she said, but only green ones, and purses, she loved purses, especially very small ones that hardly held more than a few pence. Her enthusiasm grew, as she told Julia about the stones she had, picked up every year from any beach she was taken to, and Julia began to think this was an extraordinary girl who might one day become an expert on something unusual. There was nothing at all wrong with her. The mother was simply being unreasonable, dictating standards of tidiness way beyond the norm. Julia didn't believe anything remotely approaching "trashing" was being done.

Eva didn't like her mother. Her mother didn't like Eva. She'd wanted a clone and instead got a rebel. It had been so difficult for her to have a child at all and now, ten years later, she was realising nothing about Eva was how she had thought it would be. None of this could be spelled out. All Julia could do was try to affect a compromise, persuade Eva to be neat and tidy everywhere at home except in her own room, and her mother to let her have that room as she wished to have it. Julia told Eva's mother that she had a very special daughter, and that she shouldn't worry about her resistance to tidiness. Eva was going to try hard to meet her mother's standards.

Difficult, of course, but both Eva and her mother left without the hostility between them bristling so fiercely.

CHAPTER
FOUR

Julia was almost daunted when the application form arrived, both by its length (eight pages) and by the detailed nature of the many questions. For a week, she didn't touch it. Every day, coming in from work, she'd see it lying on the kitchen table and think no, I'm too tired, it was a mistake to think I could be a magistrate. She had got carried away, reading about a certain case in the newspapers where it seemed to her the magistrates (according to the report) were completely out of touch with the lives young people led. *She* was not, she was sure she was not. And so she sent off for the application form in a fit of what she now saw was self-importance.

But when finally, on Sunday afternoon, she picked up the form, she was struck by how suitable she seemed for the post. "Do you have the ability to sit and concentrate for long periods of time?" — Well, of course she did, she was expert at concentration. Only one question made her hesitate: "Is there anything in your private or your working life, or in your past, or, to your knowledge, in that of your family or close friends which, if it became generally known, might bring you or the magistracy into disrepute, or call into question your integrity, authority or standing as a magistrate?" What a complicated question. How could anyone be certain that they were answering it truthfully? Leaving aside her own qualms about some of her behaviour when she was young, how could she be sure that her family was blameless? She didn't know enough about all of them. None had been murderers but what about all the lesser crimes and misdemeanours that existed and were frowned upon by the law? She knew nothing at all for example, about her dead father.

She was taking the question too literally, as she tended to take so many questions. "Not so far as I know," she wrote. Would that do? She filled in the remaining questions, returned the form to its envelope and went out to post it before she changed her mind. The three people she had given as referees would, she knew, give her a glowing report. She'd already discussed her application with them and they were all standing by. "You are good, Julia," her boss had said. There was an edge, she was sure, of sarcasm there but she ignored it.

Julia thought how her mother would have said that Janice, the girl now in front of her, had a shifty look. Her eyes darted constantly about, from door to window, restlessly checking her surroundings. When Julia spoke to her, she momentarily made eye contact, then looked over her left shoulder, as though someone there might require her attention. She sat with her knees tightly together, one hand gripping each of them. Her voice was light, and a little breathy. Julia, studying her while asking some routine questions, wondered if Janice's mother had combed her hair for her. It was so very neatly parted in the centre and pulled into two bunches, each secured with a thick elastic band.

The alleged problem with Janice, who was aged ten, was that it seemed she would take no part in any communal activities. Her mother was worried because she had no real friends, and she wouldn't join any group. She was, the mother said, a real Billy-no-mates. Her mother thought this was going to be a dreadful handicap in life, and wondered aloud if possibly Janice might be autistic. Patiently, Julia defined what autistic meant then reassured the mother that Janice didn't come into this category. This seemed to disappoint her. Something must nevertheless be wrong, she persisted, with a girl who chose to have no friends. Julia said this was not necessarily so — unusual, yes, but "wrong", no. If Janice liked being on her own it was her nature. She would make friends eventually, slowly, if she came to want them. The mother was not convinced. Janice, she feared, was becoming what she called "a serious loner", and everyone apparently knew where this might lead.

So here Janice was, answering questions politely, controlling her nervousness well.

"Do you play games, Janice?" Julia asked her. She said she didn't like games. "Do your classmates play games together?" Janice nodded. "Doesn't this make you feel left out?" Janice shook her head. "What do other girls say to you when you won't join in?"

Janice smiled slightly. "They think I'm weird," she said, "or a snob."

"Do you care about this?" Julia asked.

Janice said no, she supposed she was a bit weird, preferring to be on her own. She didn't know why her mother fussed about this, there was nothing wrong with it.

Julia agreed. "No," she said, "there's nothing wrong so long as you can truthfully say you're comfortable with this state of affairs, that you're not just pretending." She looked Janice in the eye and asked, "Is it true?"

New home, new school, new bus route. Julia didn't know where she was. Not in a dream, she didn't feel as though she were in a dream, or even a nightmare, so much as in a fog. Her mother became increasingly impatient with her. "Stop wandering around like that, for heaven's sake," she said to Julia. "What on earth are you looking for?" Julia had no idea. She found herself going up and down the stairs, in and out of rooms, for no reason at all, just to be on the move. At her new school, she had more scope for this eternal movement. There were many corridors, many flights of stairs, and so many people using them that she wasn't noticed. Staying in a classroom for a lesson was agony, but if her attention was caught by whatever she was asked to do, it helped. Concentrating on work helped, especially if the lesson was maths of any sort.

In the playground she had masses of space to patrol. There were areas where younger girls were not supposed to go but she flitted through them, keeping to the brick walls, and was never stopped. There was a big field at this school, where games were played, and walking round it could take 20 minutes. Lots of girls did walk round it, in twos and threes, arms linked or round each other's shoulders. Julia knew she was conspicuous, walking on her own, but if she positioned herself between two groups she hoped nobody would challenge her. One girl did, in the second week. She was a tall girl, who also wandered around on her own. "Are you new?" she asked Julia, as she plodded beside her the length of the field. "You are, aren't you?" Julia nodded. "Do you want to sit beside me at lunch?" Julia said no, thank you, she wasn't going to have school lunch. She was going home.

This was only partly a lie. It was true that she wasn't going to have the school lunch. She had a lunch her mother had packed for her. But it wasn't true that she was going home. Now that she'd told this girl she was going home, though, she couldn't go and eat her lunch in the room where the packed-lunch pupils ate theirs, so she slipped out of the school gate when it was opened to let in the van that delivered food. The gates were never locked, but pupils were not supposed to leave the grounds, and Julia was careful to use the van as a screen for any eyes that might be watching from the staff room windows.

Once in the street, she didn't know where to go to eat her lunch, but it was a relief to be out of the school. She found her way, accidentally, to a park, but that proved not a good idea. Sitting on a bench, eating her sandwiches, on a dull, cloudy day, she felt conspicuous. Someone might see her and report her to the school, whose uniform she was wearing. Hurriedly, she finished eating, and started walking through the park to the other gate. A woman was coming towards her pushing a pram. It was a Silver Cross pram. Julia recognised it at once, and her heart began to thud. The woman was smiling into the pram, making little clucking noises to the baby. Julia started to run. She ran out of the far gate and down the road and then stopped at a crossing because she was lost and didn't know how to get back to the school. She had no idea where she was. The only thing to do was turn round and run back into the park and go out of it the way she had come in. But this meant passing the Silver Cross pram again, if the woman and the pram were still there, and she was afraid. What she was afraid of she couldn't have said, as usual, but it was there, the dry mouth, the jumping heart.

She got back to the school safely, just in time for the bell. Her teacher, the next lesson, commented that she was very flushed, was she all right, and Julia said yes, she was. She kept repeating it to herself: I am all right, I am all right. But the feeling of dread wouldn't go away. Her hand was shaky. When she had to write down what was on the blackboard she could hardly manage to form the letters. And there seemed to be something wrong with her eyes. She kept blinking, to clear away the blurred vision, but this didn't work. She kept them shut, and when the teacher noticed, she was asked if she had a headache. Yes, she said, yes, my head aches, I can't see, and she was taken to a little room next to the headmistress's room, where there was a camp bed, and told to lie down for a little while. She was so grateful to obey. In the background, she could hear the teachers talking, two of them, their voices concerned. She couldn't make out their words, just their tones, gentle, soothing.

Her mother was sent for. Julia never realised this would happen. She thought she could go on lying so comfortably on the bed until it was time to go home. When she heard a teacher say, "Your mother is on her way, don't worry . . ." she struggled to sit up and said her headache had gone and she could see again and please could they call her mother and tell her not to come. But she was already on her way, the teacher said; she'd be here in five minutes. And she was. She came click-clacking down the corridor at a great pace. Julia lay down once more and closed her eyes. "Whatever is the matter?" she heard her mother say, in her usual sharp way. "Julia? Sit up, for goodness' sake." Julia sat up. She looked straight into her mother's stomach, not lifting her eyes to her face. "Stand up," her mother said, "let me look at you properly." Julia's chin was held in her mother's hand — the hand was quite hot and sweaty, Julia noticed — and her face tilted up so that she could no longer avoid looking her mother in the eye. Whatever her mother saw there made her hesitate. "I'll take her home," she said to the teacher. "Could someone get her coat and her bag? Thank you."

They walked home in silence. Julia had been asked if she thought she could manage to walk and she'd said yes. Good, her mother said, the fresh air will help. What it would help she didn't say. Surprisingly, she held

Julia's hand though Julia would much rather she didn't because this hand felt sticky. But she let her hand be taken and the two of them walked along, still nothing being said. When they got home (though it still didn't feel like home yet to Julia) her mother told her to lie down on the sofa and she'd get her a drink. "Probably," she said, "you're just dehydrated." Julia didn't know what that meant, but she felt quite pleased that her mother had given a name to her condition. Lemonade was brought and she drank it thirstily. "There you are," her mother said, "dehydrated." But she was watching Julia closely, and in a way that was unusual, as though she were on the verge of saying something but didn't know whether to or not. "Julia," she began, and then stopped. Julia didn't encourage her. She didn't say "What, Mum, what were you going to say?" She kept quiet, and after a minute or so her mother sighed, and said, "We're all upset, no wonder."

Later, Julia heard her talking to someone. Aunt Maureen she guessed, telling them about Julia's "funny turn" at school. Dehydration wasn't mentioned. Her mother's voice was low, and she was not speaking in her normal rapid, clipped way. There were long silences when presumably Aunt Maureen, or whoever was at the other end, was talking. It was unlike Julia's mother to allow another person such a long run without her interrupting them and bringing a conversation to a swift close. But this time, she was listening. She listened a long time without saying anything then said, "What does that mean?" Whatever the reply was to her question, it produced a "No!" said very definitely, and then repeated. This was followed by "Oh dear, oh dear me" and then, soon after, Julia heard the click as the telephone receiver was replaced. Her mother came back into the room and stood looking down on Julia, still lying on the sofa.

Julia wondered if she should risk asking what was the matter, but decided not to. Instead she said, "Who were you talking to, Mum?"

Her mother sat down, quite abruptly, almost squashing Julia's feet, and said, "Aunt Maureen." Julia waited. Surprisingly, her mother continued. "You'll have to know," she said, "they are going to ask us all more questions, just a formality, I expect."

Questions. Julia pondered this. She was always, of course, wanting to ask questions herself, and enjoyed being asked them, on the whole. Sometimes she enjoyed it because it was a game trying to avoid giving truthful answers, if the truth would cause trouble. So she usually had no fear of questions. But when her mother said *they* were going to ask questions, without identifying who "they" were, Julia felt all the feelings of earlier in the day return. Her mouth felt unbearably dry, her heart gave little leaps and thuds, and her skin prickled. She was glad she was lying down and could keep still and close her eyes.

"You're tired," her mother said, "try and have a nap. Then we have to go to Maureen's. It's better than them coming here."

Them? Was that Maureen and Uncle Tom and Iris? Somehow Julia didn't think so. She tried, as instructed, to sleep, but failed. Quietly, she got up. On tiptoe, she left the room. Her mother had gone upstairs and was moving about in her bedroom. Julia recognised the sound of drawers being opened and closed. Her mother would be looking for clothes to wear, clean blouses and cardigans. Carrying her shoes in her hand, Julia crept to the door and very, very carefully turned the knob that opened it. It had a rubber strip all the way round it, to keep out draughts, her mother said, and the rubber squeaked a little as the door gave way. Julia froze, waiting, but her mother was now shutting the door of her wardrobe and there was no shout of what are you doing, where are you going. Once outside, Julia put her shoes on, and then hesitated. Her mother's bedroom was at the front, over the front door. She might, if there were any sound of footsteps on the gravel path, look out and see Julia leaving, so Julia took her shoes off again and walked painfully along the gravel path in her stockinged feet. Only when she was through the gate and hidden by the privet hedge, did she slip her shoes back on. Then she began running without knowing where she was running to.

It felt so good to be running. She was a speedy runner, with a lolloping stride which she could keep up over long distances without pausing for breath. One of the few things she knew about her father was that as a young man he had been a champion runner, winning races, and Julia was said to run like him. She'd always liked this comparison, though she had no way of knowing if her running merited it, and she had not as yet won any except school races. Her father, she knew, had excelled at cross-country but she had never run cross-country. Now, racing along these strange streets, she wished she were in the country and could run up hills and jump over streams and not have to watch out for traffic. She reached the park, where she had been at lunchtime, and ran through the gates and followed the fence which enclosed it. Round and round she ran, lap after lap, glad the place was empty and there was no one to wonder why a girl was running as though someone was chasing her.

But she couldn't run forever. The running had to stop when her legs began to hurt and her breathing became ragged. There was a kind of shelter in the far corner of the park, near the children's playground, and she sank down on the bench inside, leaning back against the wooden wall. Her body and face were clammy with perspiration, and her hands trembled slightly, so she folded her arms tightly. Then she began to shiver, though she was so hot, and she staggered up again and braced herself against the corner post of the shelter. It felt better to be standing up, even though she was so tired. Slowly, she set off across the park again, knowing she would have to go home. She had no choice. If she didn't go home, her mother would start a search for her. She might even phone the police. At the thought of this, at the thought of the very word "police", Julia began to cry. Why she was so frightened, she didn't know, but she was. There was something lurking in her mind, some half-formed idea, that scared her but she couldn't say what it was even to herself.

Her mother was at the gate, looking up and down the road distractedly. The moment she saw Julia, who was still a long way off, she began shouting her name, and then she hurtled down the road calling, "Wherever have you been?" When she caught up with Julia, she seized her by the shoulders and looked at her and said, "What's wrong? What is the matter with you? You've been running, haven't you?" and she shook her slightly. All Julia could think of to say was that she felt sick. In reply, her mother said she wasn't surprised at all this ridiculous behaviour, but the explanation, though it made no sense, seemed to satisfy her. She stopped talking and marched Julia back home. She said they must go to Aunt Maureen's at once. Julia tried to say that she wanted to wash and to change her clothes but her mother said there was no time for that, they were late already. She would just have to suffer the consequences of all that silly running.

Aunt Maureen's sitting room was again full of people. To Julia's relief none of them, so far as she could tell, appeared to be police. There were two women and one man, and they all looked serious, but smiled when Aunt Maureen said this was Julia, her niece.

"Hello, Julia," one of the women said. "I'm Linda, and this is Mary, and this is Mr Robertson. We just want to go over again what happened that sad day when baby Reggie fell asleep."

Julia once more registered "fell asleep", and for a moment wondered if Linda knew that baby Reggie hadn't just fallen asleep but that he'd died, really died. But at the mention of little Reggie's name, Aunt Maureen began quietly weeping, and Linda, who was sitting next to her, patted her hand, so Julia knew there was no doubt in anyone's mind that the baby was dead.

Then Linda said, "Maureen, why don't you go and make that tea you offered?"

Maureen got up, looking quite grateful to be given something to do, and left the room.

"Would you like to help your sister?" Linda said, looking at Julia's mother, but Julia's mother said Maureen was perfectly capable of making a pot of tea by herself and she would stay with her daughter if, as she'd gathered from Maureen's call earlier, there was to be any more questioning.

Hearing her mother's tone of voice, strong and faintly challenging, Julia felt comforted, and found herself slipping her hand into her mother's hand. Her mother squeezed it.

They sat down, facing Linda and Mary, and with Mr Robertson on a chair to their right. He took a pen out, and sat with it poised over a pad of paper, the sort, Julia noticed, with a spiral top. Linda started asking her questions, and Julia's mother began answering them, only to be stopped. "I'd like Julia to tell us about that day, in her own words, if you don't mind. Julia? Do you remember coming to this house on the day of 4th September?" Julia nodded. "Could you actually say 'yes' or 'no'?" Linda urged. Julia said yes. The man, Mr Robertson, was writing something down. Julia thought it looked as if he was writing down more than her "yes", and she wondered what it might be. But Linda was pressing her to continue. "So you arrived at this house," Linda said, "and what did you do?" Julia told

108

her yet again. She described the lunch they had had, in minute detail. Out of the corner of her eye, she could see that Mr Robertson, far from writing down her every word, had stopped writing anything at all. "And after lunch?" Linda repeated.

"I went into the garden."

"Did you look at the baby in his pram?"

"Yes."

"Was he asleep?"

"Yes."

"Did you touch the pram?"

"Yes, I shuggled the handle a bit."

"Shuggled?"

"I just moved it a bit. That's what Iris said to do, to keep little Reggie asleep."

"Did he wake up when you stopped?"

"No."

"So what did you do then?"

Julia took a deep breath, and frowned. They were all waiting, including her mother. This was the hard bit, this was where the lying had to begin again if she were going to carry on lying. But she had already lied, by omission. She knew that. She'd pointed that out to herself already. Don't be stupid, Julia, she'd said to herself, you didn't tell anyone about tipping up the pram. She could tell them now. This was her second chance. She could burst into tears and tell them and say she was sorry. Tipping the pram up, and little Reggie's head getting knocked (but not much, there was no blood or cut) might have nothing to do with anything. They would tell her that. They would say they were glad she had told them the truth at last and that she was not to worry about it. Julia opened her mouth to tell them about her walk with the pram, but instead of telling the truth she said, "I pushed the pram round the garden a bit, then I put it back where it had been, in the shade." She was astonished at her own words. Where had they come from? Why had she said that?

But Linda seemed satisfied. Mr Robertson wrote some more, and then looked at Linda, and nodded. Mary, who hadn't said anything, just smiled and watched Julia, then got up. "I think that will be all for now," she said. "Thank you, Julia, you've been very helpful." That was when Julia started to cry. Everyone fussed over her, providing handkerchiefs to mop her eyes and wipe her nose, and a glass of water appeared, sent for by Linda. Maureen arrived with the tea at the same time as Mary came with the water, and there was a lot of bustle as the tea things were set down: proper cups and saucers, and a sugar bowl (lump sugar) and tongs, and a small milk jug, and the pot itself. Julia recognised it. It was Aunt Maureen's best teapot, a flowery thing, not the plain brown one. Everyone took tea. There was no talking, except remarks about how delicious, and welcome, the tea was.

After Linda, Mary and Mr Robertson had left, Aunt Maureen didn't immediately clear the tea things away, as she usually did. Instead, she leaned back in her chair and closed her eyes and said, "I'm so tired, but I can't sleep, not a wink." Julia's mother said it wasn't surprising, and that she'd hardly slept herself. Julia's head whirled with questions but she asked none of them, much too alarmed at what the answers might be. She wished she had someone to talk to, someone she could tell everything to. Her mother? No.

"Sometimes," Janice admitted, "it would be good to be with someone, just for a bit, but I don't care, really, it doesn't matter."

Julia asked on what sort of occasions Janice might like to have a companion. She said, walking in a crocodile to the swimming baths she always got stuck with girls she didn't like, who nobody liked, or wanted to walk with, but the class had to walk in twos. If that day there was an uneven number, she had to walk with the games teacher and she hated that. It would be good to have a walking partner, that was all.

"To talk to?" Julia asked, knowing perfectly well that would not be the reason.

Janice shook her head vigorously. "I wouldn't talk," she said, "I'd just have someone regular to walk with."

"Who would you prefer, of all the girls in your class?" Julia asked.

Janice shrugged. She waited. Janice then began a list of elimination. She named eight girls very rapidly and then, more hesitantly, another six. "Does that leave ten, or twelve, who wouldn't be so bad to walk with once a week?"

"Ten," Janice said.

"And who, of the ten, would be the most bearable?"

Long pause. A lot of looking at the ceiling, and then, "I know what you're trying to get me to say," Janice said.

"Do you?" Julia said. "You tell me what you think I'm trying to get you to say and I'll tell you if you're right."

She told her.

"Very good," Julia said, "spot on. And now you've said it, how reasonable does my theory sound? Do you think I'm right, and in fact there *are* at least two girls you would quite like to get to know and walk with and maybe become friends with?"

"Possibly," Janice said, "but I don't care, I won't try to get them to walk with me anyway, I wouldn't ever ask them."

"Of course you wouldn't," Julia said, "you wouldn't *ask,* that would be against your own rules. It's called pride, Janice. You're too proud to show you would quite like occasional companionship."

"No," Janice said, "I'm not too proud."

"So," Julia said, "if one of those girls actually asked you to walk with her to swimming, what would you say?"

"Nobody would ask," Janice said, "nobody does any asking, it just happens."

"Well then," Julia persisted, "suppose it just happened, suppose one of these girls gravitated towards you and assumed you'd be happy to walk with her, what then, what would you do?"

"Walk with her, of course," Janice said.

Julia had no worries at all about this child. She wasn't as peculiar as her mother suspected, just content with her own company. She might never develop any liking for being in any kind of social group but in time she would make one or two friends of like mind, people who shared her outlook on life and were as discerning as herself. Her mother was fretting about nothing.

But Julia was doubtful if she could convince Janice's mother of this.

There was a call from the police station that afternoon. An appropriate adult was needed to attend with a young girl who had thrown a bottle of Coca-Cola at an elderly woman and was going to be charged with assault. It was not Julia's job to be an appropriate adult but her name had been suggested by the social worker who knew Julia had worked with this girl before. The social worker couldn't be there herself, and there was no parent available — the girl was in a home after her foster-mother refused to keep her following a fight — so the need was urgent. All Julia was required to do was be present at the questioning. It wouldn't take long. A car would collect her and take her back.

Julia remembered the girl. She'd been about nine at the time, so must be around fifteen by now. Julia couldn't remember exactly why this girl had come to her but it had been for some kind of unexceptionable bad behaviour, stealing of some sort, nothing too unusual. Walking into the police station, something she hated doing and hadn't found got any easier, she wondered if she would recognise the girl, who was surely bound to have changed dramatically in the intervening years. But she did recognise her, from the hair alone, black and unruly, dropping heavily all round her face, quite distinctive hair. The girl, Gill, didn't recognise Julia, though, or if she did she was determined not to admit it.

"Who's this?" she said to the policewoman sitting with her.

The policewoman told her who Julia was and why she was there.

"I don't care," the girl said, "doesn't matter to me."

"Shall we get started, then?" the policewoman said.

Julia settled in at the new school quite quickly, to her mother's relief. She even made a friend, Caroline, in the third week. There were no more "funny" episodes. But at home, she was "not right", as her mother described it to Maureen. But then nobody in the family was quite right. Iris barely stirred from her bed. Her mind, Julia heard her whisper, was full of images in which her baby was being cut to pieces, hacked at with saws and knives. Julia immediately had these same images herself. When the autopsy was over, and Iris was taken to see little Reggie, Julia scandalised her mother by asking if she could go too. But whatever the dead baby had looked like, Iris came back calmer. "He looked perfect," she told Julia, which disappointed Julia. There was a lot of talk that day about the cause of little Reggie's death but Julia understood hardly any of it. She caught odd words, but not clearly enough to retain them in her mind so that she could look them up afterwards.

Eventually, there was a funeral. Julia, to her fury, was not allowed to go to it. Her mother said she had been through enough and it would do her no good to see the tiny coffin and Iris in a state of collapse. So Julia stayed at home, sulking, in the company of a cousin of her mother and Aunt Maureen, who had turned up at the house saying she couldn't after all face the funeral but she wanted to pay her respects. She was an odd woman. Julia was embarrassed to be left with her and tried to retreat to her room to read. The cousin wouldn't allow this. "You need company," she told Julia, "it isn't good to be alone on a day like this. Come on now, we'll bake a cake." Julia said she didn't want to bake a cake. There was plenty of mother's gingerbread in the cake tin already, thank you. The cousin said in that case they could play I spy — that was harmless enough. I'll start, she said, something beginning with F. Julia wanted to say "fool" and "it's you" but instead went into the kitchen and banged about, running the tap and boiling the kettle, pointlessly, just as her mother did when she was cross.

The hour the funeral took passed so slowly Julia began to think the clock had stopped. It sat on the mantelpiece, fair and square in the middle, a toby jug to the right, a toby jug to the left, both exactly the same distance from the clock. Julia hated the clock and hated the jugs. She wanted to be at the funeral, she wanted to see the little white coffin. Then, it would be real. Real, and over. Nothing could be done, once she'd seen the coffin buried. She didn't know what might have happened if she'd been allowed to go to the funeral. She would have cried, of course, but she might not just have cried. She might, at last, have said something, and then what would have happened? Julia looked away

115

from the clock, and stared at the cousin: small, stupid, horrible skirt, horrible jacket, ugly shoes. She thought about shocking her. She thought about telling this cousin, whose name she hadn't even listened to, that she, Julia, might have killed little Reggie. She thought about describing the walk she'd taken with the Silver Cross pram, and what had happened on the way back. She opened her mouth to begin talking just as the cousin said, "My baby died, Julia, same thing, six weeks old, no reason." There were tears running down the cousin's powder-encrusted cheeks. "Well," the cousin said, "it was a long time ago. I never have got over it, though."

So Julia said nothing. She couldn't do the shocking she'd thought about. Instead, she made the cousin a cup of tea, and was thanked for it. The remaining time was spent listening to the cousin reminisce about when she and Aunt Maureen had been children. Julia noticed that her mother wasn't mentioned in any of these rambling anecdotes, just Aunt Maureen. She vaguely wondered why. Then her mother came home. "Thank you, Doris," she said, "you'll be wanting to get to the tea. Tom's waiting to take you. I hope Julia has been no trouble." There was no pausing for the answer. "Julia, get Doris's coat. Have you got your bag there, Doris? Good. And thank you again." Cousin Doris was out of the door before she had time to say a word.

"Thank God," Julia's mother said, "she never stops talking."

"Her baby died," Julia said, "just like little Reggie."

116

Julia's mother said, "She told you that, did she? Just like Doris, just like her, typical."

"Of what?" Julia asked, and was told not to be irritating. As usual, this didn't make sense, but Julia didn't point this out. She wanted to hear about the funeral.

Later, she went with Aunt Maureen to the cemetery. Julia's mother never knew about this. Julia had tried asking her mother if she could go and look at little Reggie's grave, and her mother was appalled. "What an idea!" she said, and that was that. But Aunt Maureen, when Julia got her on her own, responded quite differently. "Of course, my pet," she said, "of course you can, we'll go together, no need to mention it to you-know-who." Julia knew who. She was spending the day with Aunt Maureen anyway, while her mother went to see a solicitor about something to do with money. Julia didn't know what it was all about, all questions being ignored, but the visit to the solicitor was important enough, Julia noticed, for her mother to dress in her best outfit and put lipstick on. Julia was told to go straight to Aunt Maureen's after school, which she did. Aunt Maureen gave her a glass of orange juice and a biscuit and then they went down to the cemetery, closing the door very quietly behind them because Iris was resting.

Julia had only ever been in one cemetery, the one where her father was buried. Her mother didn't believe in what she called "making an exhibition" of herself by frequent graveside visits, but on the anniversary of her husband's death she and Julia always put flowers in the

117

metal holder before the gravestone. Julia rather liked the ceremony of it. She felt important, and enjoyed filling the holder with water and arranging the flowers. Tulips, the flowers were always tulips, white ones. Julia sometimes suggested yellow or red tulips but her mother just gave her a withering look and bought white ones. They would stand in front of the grave for a moment or two, Julia's mother with her eyes closed, and then she would say, "Come on, that's enough," and they'd leave. Julia was never sure what her mother's closed eyes signified. She'd scrutinised her mother's face, when the eyes were closed to see if any tears were leaking out, but they never were. Once, she'd asked her mother if closing her eyes meant she was praying, to which her mother replied, "Certainly not." So Julia concluded that when her eyes were closed her mother must just be remembering her father. She liked that thought, but never put it to the test, in case her mother disillusioned her.

But the cemetery in which little Reggie was buried was nothing like the place where Julia's father lay. Julia's father's grave was in a small cemetery, a churchyard, in fact, a pretty place on a hillside. Little Reggie was buried in a vast cemetery lying between two thunderingly noisy main roads. Aunt Maureen led Julia under an archway and then up a long, broad path that was almost another road. There were flower beds at intervals, full of rigid rows of violently coloured blooms, and beyond them masses of gravestones, crosses and angels and peculiar stone columns. They seemed to walk forever along this gruesome highway,

118

the thought of so many people under the earth horrifying Julia, but then Aunt Maureen turned off along a narrower path, and then almost immediately turned again, down a grassy path this time, until they came to some trees planted in a circle. "Here," Aunt Maureen whispered, "it's where they lay the babies to rest." Inside the circle of trees the wind that had been stinging their faces all the way up the main path was lessened. They were sheltered, standing there, and the sound of traffic could no longer be heard. "There," Aunt Maureen was saying, still in a whisper, "that's little Reggie's place. There'll be a stone later. An angel, white marble, we think, with his name and dates on."

Julia never told her mother she had been to the cemetery and Aunt Maureen kept quiet about it. Weeks later she took Julia aside and asked her if she'd like to "slip off" again, to visit little Reggie and see the stone angel. But Julia shook her head. She'd seen the grave once. She could visualise the stone angel well enough. Little Reggie was dead and buried, and the police asked no more questions. "We just have to get on with life," Julia's mother said. She said this repeatedly. If Iris was in the room and heard her, she left it. But Julia agreed with her mother. She had to get on with her life, and part of getting on was not to think about her mishap with the Silver Cross pram. Ever.

CHAPTER
FIVE

The conference was in Manchester. Julia went by train, dreading the arrival at the station, fearing she would be troubled, even after the thirty-year gap, by upsetting memories, but none surfaced, which seemed like a victory of some sort. Manchester, as she passed through the streets in a taxi, looked much the same. It was raining, hard, and the grimness she recalled hadn't changed. Colleagues of hers were fond of Manchester and could never understand her aversion to the city. They'd told her she should go again, she would be surprised at how vibrant the place now was, how cleaned up and splendid. She could see no sign of splendour out of the rain-battered taxi windows.

She was staying one night only, sufficient time to fit in two sessions at the conference, both of them to do with trauma experienced by children. The speakers were known to her and were highly regarded in their field. She'd read the book one of them had recently published (and which she privately considered she could have written better herself) and the paper the other had contributed to an American journal. She reread the paper that evening, in her hotel, after a room-service meal, marking it with pencilled queries.

She wasn't intending to ask any questions of the speaker, but just in case she might be tempted she wanted to be prepared. She'd sit at the back, as near to the door as possible. These sessions could go on far too long, in spite of the best efforts of the organisers. She intended to slip out if it all got too much.

Although tired, she didn't sleep well. The hotel was not exactly noisy, but there was a constant padding about along its corridors and the frequent opening and closing of doors. At six she got up and had a long, hot shower, and then made herself tea. There was a selection of individual tea bags, all neatly stacked in a box. She remembered the contempt Aunt Maureen and all her generation had for tea bags of any kind. Loose tea and a proper teapot had to be used at all times. Watching her Darjeeling bag float in the hot water, pressing it down with a spoon until the water was the right colour, Julia saw in her mind's eye the look of disgust on Aunt Maureen's face and heard her say that's not proper tea, Julia.

For months, all that grief had floated on tea, until one day Iris said she preferred coffee. Just like that; Julia had been there. "I prefer coffee, Mum," Iris had said. Aunt Maureen looked aghast and said she didn't have any coffee, as Iris knew perfectly well. They were a tea-drinking household, and that was that. Iris said she'd bought some coffee from a new coffee bar, which was also a shop, near where Iris now worked as a secretary in a solicitor's office. Julia and her mother had passed it, and the aroma drifting out as the coffee beans were being ground was overpowering. Julia loved it but, predictably, her mother did not. She said it made her feel faint, it knocked her out as if it were a poisonous fume. "Iris is going to buy some ground coffee," Julia had volunteered, "and a machine to make it in." "Her mother won't like *that*," Julia's mother had said, with grim satisfaction.

The machine was a percolator, and Iris kept it in her bedroom, only bringing it down to the kitchen when her mother wasn't in it because the mere sight of it resting beside the teapots could upset her. Julia loved to watch this strange machine bubbling away, though she found the actual coffee it produced a bit strong. So did Iris, but she persevered bravely and came to like it. Julia went with her sometimes to buy the coffee. She'd imagined the man who managed it would be foreign, Italian or French maybe, and old, but he was young and English, and though not conventionally handsome (in Julia's opinion) he was tall and strong-looking and had black curly hair, worn quite long. He gave Iris a great welcome, and Julia saw how she blushed and smiled and, on the way out, hummed.

"Do you like him?" Julia ventured.

"Who?" Iris said.

"The coffee man," Julia said.

"Oh, him? Well, I don't know him, do I? I just buy coffee there sometimes."

"He likes you," Julia said, and Iris laughed and said she was being silly.

It was good to hear Iris laugh, of course. Julia's mother and Aunt Maureen agreed; they commented to each other that "things" were "looking up" and "turning round", and it was about time. "I think," Julia heard Aunt Maureen say, "it's that Michael Osborne in the office, you know, the boss's son. He seems, from what she's said, to pay a lot of attention to her." Julia kept quiet. Maybe Iris wouldn't like the coffee man mentioned, but she was sure he, and not this Osborne man, was the one making Iris happier. Maybe Iris would prefer this to remain a secret, and Julia was still good at keeping secrets. It had only just recently struck her that other girls were not. At school, secrets were traded ruthlessly. Girls told by other girls not to tell a soul almost immediately told someone else, adding "Keep it quiet" to cover themselves. The secrets involved were not, in Julia's opinion, interesting, or even worthy of the name "secret". *She* knew what a secret was. She had one, and had never told anyone, and never would.

She wondered often whether Iris perhaps felt the same about secrets. She had never, Julia knew, revealed what it was that Reginald had given Julia to give to her. After a long time she had unwrapped it, but afterwards had carefully rewrapped it so that no one could see that it had been unwrapped. No one except Julia, who had seen it in Iris's bedside cabinet drawer one day and spotted straight away that the little white ribbon had been snipped off and not replaced exactly in the centre. She shouldn't have been looking in drawers, of course. This, as her mother had told her long ago, was snooping, and a very unpleasant activity, something to be ashamed of. But Julia was not particularly ashamed.

A little bit, yes, but not much, so long as no one found out. All she did was gently slide drawers open, and just look. She didn't touch. She simply liked to see what others had in the drawers of their different bits of furniture. What was wrong with that?

She had been in and out of Iris's bedroom quite a lot while little Reggie was alive. Iris was always sending her to get something to do with the care of the baby, so Julia had plenty of opportunity to have a quick look in Iris's familiar drawers. Reginald's secret after-the-wedding present was always there, never touched again after its one unwrapping, or so Julia reckoned, but kept tucked in the back left-hand corner of the small, shallow drawer, behind a packet of tissues (opened) and a pair of spectacles in a soft leather case. After little Reggie died, Julia was not as often in Iris's bedroom because Iris herself practically lived there, with the curtains drawn, but as things improved, and Iris began getting up, she would send Julia up to her room to get some item she hadn't the energy to go and get herself. Julia would go to collect the nail scissors, or whatever it was Iris wanted, and she sometimes allowed herself a quick peep in the drawer which held Reginald's present, just to check it hadn't been thrown out. She was always pleased to see it was there, and would touch it lightly with one finger, nothing more. She had no wish to ask Iris about this object. It appealed to her, in an odd way, to have it remain mysterious.

Then one day, eight months after little Reggie died, Julia and her mother were summoned by Aunt Maureen who said she had some news. Julia heard her mother on the telephone saying, "News? What sort of news? Good, or bad?" Whatever the answer, Julia's mother responded by telling Julia to get her coat on, quickly. The news, which was described by Aunt Maureen as "a shock", was that Iris had become engaged. No, not to Michael Osborne, which Aunt Maureen could have understood, and welcomed, but to a man who sold coffee, who was half Italian and had an unpronounceable surname. Julia smiled.

"What are you grinning at?" her mother said.

"He's nice," Julia said, "he has curly black hair."

Aunt Maureen and Julia's mother stared at her, their expressions similar, a mixture of barely suppressed curiosity, and distaste.

"*Curly* black hair?" Aunt Maureen queried, as though curls in themselves were deeply suspect in a man.

Julia nodded. "Sometimes," she said, "he ties it back in a pony tail."

Stunned silence.

"Not with a ribbon," Julia added hastily, "just with an elastic band, I think. Iris likes it tied back."

"How do you know?" Aunt Maureen asked, her tone incredulous.

"I asked her," Julia said. "I asked her, 'Do you like Carlo's hair loose or tied back?' and she said —"

"Carlo?" her mother queried.

Julia nodded. "Carlo Annovazzi," she said, lingering on the surname, breaking it up into three syllables and emphasising the "Anno", making it long drawn-out, the way Carlo himself did.

"What a name," Aunt Maureen said, and then, "Why she couldn't fall for someone English I don't know, someone like —"

"Maureen!" Julia's mother said warningly.

"Well," Maureen said, "someone like him, where's the harm in saying that, what's wrong in a mother wanting her daughter to get engaged to an Englishman and not a foreigner?"

But Carlo Annovazzi was not really a foreigner. He'd been born in Manchester, of an Italian father and an English mother. His father was born in Naples but came to Manchester with his parents and two sisters when he was two. All that was foreign about Carlo was his name. Otherwise, he was Manchester born-and-bred. He talked like a Mancunian, and couldn't speak more than a few phrases of Italian. All this emerged the very first time Iris brought him home, and helped a great deal to make Aunt Maureen reconciled. She didn't like Carlo's job though. Selling coffee, no matter how fashionable the place it was sold in, or how good the coffee, was not a profession. Carlo was a shopkeeper. A shopkeeper and a salesman and that was that. "Maureen," Julia's mother told her, "you are a snob, you always have been." Maureen said she didn't care. If wanting the best for your daughter meant you were a snob, then she was happy to be one.

Gradually, though, Aunt Maureen came round to liking Carlo, who worked hard to charm her. He was naturally charming (Julia's mother recognised this, and was consequently suspicious from the start) but he made extra efforts with his future mother-in-law,

126

quickly realising no flattery was too excessive but that all the same she was not a fool. He was open about his business prospects, letting Iris's parents know that he was the co-owner of the coffee shop and cafe, and his income considerable. Iris's father liked him because he was a Manchester City, and not a United, fan and they could talk football. Carlo was sporty, playing both golf and tennis, which went some way to offsetting the long hair and ponytail.

Iris wanted a quiet wedding. A registry office, not a church. "Not a church?" her mother said. "But, Iris —"

"Mum," Iris said, and gave her mother what Julia's mother said was a significant look.

"What was significant about it?" Julia asked later, and was told "think". Thinking in the end did for once explain what her mother meant: Iris didn't want to marry in a church because she'd married Reginald in a church and the memories would be overwhelming. This led to more thinking: did it mean that Iris didn't love Carlo as much as she'd loved Reginald? But she seemed happy with him. All the times Julia saw them together over the following months she noticed how light-hearted her cousin seemed, how much she laughed, how readily she showed her affection for Carlo, and he for her. She'd only seen Reginald once with Iris but it was enough to know there was a difference in how she regarded him. Julia couldn't exactly remember what that difference had been but it had existed, she was sure.

It set her doing yet more thinking: what about Reginald's secret present? Would Iris now throw it away? It made Julia's heart flutter to think that she might, and she could hardly wait for an opportunity to check Iris's drawer. It was an opportunity that took a long time coming. Iris, when Julia was in Aunt Maureen's house, no longer seemed to send Julia to get anything at all from her room. She was suddenly full of energy herself, running up and down the stairs, singing as she went. "Someone's happy," Julia's mother would comment, but in an ominous tone, followed by a further remark, "Let's hope it lasts." Julia asked why it would not and her mother shook her head and said, "Julia, Julia."

Finally, Julia accepted that she was never going to be sent to fetch anything from Iris's room, which left her with no option. She and her mother were at Aunt Maureen's house for tea, as they often were these days, with so much about the approaching wedding to discuss, and Julia was left to amuse herself, which she usually did by reading in the sitting room, away from the kitchen where her mother and aunt were talking. She put her book down on the sofa, and said out loud, "I am just going to the bathroom." Indeed, she *would* go to the bathroom, she needed to. Up the stairs she went, making sure she could be heard if either her mother or her aunt cared to listen, plodding heavily on each stair, and when she got to the bathroom she opened, then closed, the door noisily. No reason why she shouldn't be in there quite some time. Then she slipped into Iris's bedroom, went straight to the bedside cabinet, and opened the drawer.

Reginald's secret gift was no longer there.

The wedding was as quiet and simple as Iris had wanted it to be. Julia wore a blue-and-white flowery dress she already owned, but being a bridesmaid turned out this time to be meaningless. All she did was stand beside Iris for the photographs which, this time, were taken at home in the garden. There were only thirty guests for the lunch at an Italian restaurant, owned by Carlo's uncle. No speeches. Carlo kissed Iris lovingly, and everyone cheered and clapped.

Julia sulked throughout.

The conference room was not even half full, which would upset the speakers, Julia thought, and most people were sitting well to the back, leaving the first four rows entirely empty. She sat in the fifth, an aisle seat, as she had intended, though it was obvious that it would be impossible to slip out undetected. She would have to last the course, however boring it turned out to be.

The first speaker, the man who had written the book on childhood trauma and its effect on later life, was clearly nervous, though it couldn't have been the first time he'd spoken at such an event. He had not just notes for a talk but the entire talk itself written out. Never once did he lift his eyes from the paper in front of him on the lectern. His audience might as well not have been there. Julia felt that in the circumstances it was excusable to close her eyes, and once she had done, aided by the monotone he delivered his talk in, she began to drift. Only certain words the speaker was using penetrated the haze which descended on her —

"retrograde", "cognitive", "simulation" — all quite unconnected. There was no applause at the end, but the speaker didn't seem to expect any, moving straight on from his last sentence to ask "Any questions?" Julia would like to have asked why he had not troubled to explain his definition of "trauma", which these days had become an overused word constantly applied to situations which no psychologist would describe as traumatic. But she kept silent, as did everyone else. She saw the speaker smile as he gathered up his sheets of paper. Clearly, he thought that no questions had been forthcoming because he had cleverly answered them all in advance.

The next speaker was a woman whose name was unfamiliar to Julia. Glancing at the programme she saw that this was a clinical psychologist who had previously and most unusually been a police officer. The jump from one profession to another obviously couldn't have been easy. It hadn't been easy for Julia herself, switching from teaching, and having to take the accredited psychology conversion course, and what this woman had done had entailed far more studying, so Julia was instantly impressed. The woman was self-possessed rather than confident, rather stiff in manner but her expression was pleasant. She introduced herself with a smile, looking along the rows of people steadily as she spoke. She stood, not in front of the lectern, but to its left, resting her right hand upon it, where she had placed some notes. But these notes were not consulted. She had either memorised what she wanted to say, or else was speaking off the cuff. She told her audience, first of all, about her

130

experience of being a police officer and how it had brought her into touch with the more violent crimes committed by children. It was always difficult, she said, for an adult to believe that a child could intend to kill somebody, "intend" being the crucial word. She had, she went on, begun to think that she didn't understand how a child's mind worked, and this had led to her change of profession. She had wanted to know how a child thought, how this was different from how an adult thought, and what she wanted to talk about was her realisation that some children do not think in a childlike way. Some children, so far as cognitive development goes, are mature far beyond their years. They can think like an adult and they can carry those thoughts through to behaving like an adult. "And that," said the woman, "is both alarming and challenging." Exactly, thought Julia. She recalled the day she'd realised this herself, faced with a ten-year-old girl in a class she was teaching who had shown a cunning Julia had been astounded by. It had been the start of her own determination to try to understand how a child's mind does work.

"Could you kill someone?" Julia once asked her friend Caroline. They were walking through a cemetery at the time, a short cut on their way home from school.

"Kill someone?" Caroline said, "I wouldn't know how."

"I wasn't thinking of the method," Julia said, "I was thinking of wanting to do it. Do you think you could hate someone enough to want to kill them and think of doing it?"

"No," said Caroline.

"I could," Julia said.

"But you wouldn't really," Caroline said, "not when it came to the bit."

"I might," Julia said, "I nearly killed a cat once — with a spade. It was attacking a little puppy in the garden next door. I saw it over the wall, a big, black tomcat with its claws digging into the puppy's back, and I took a spade and jumped over the wall and bashed the cat. I could have killed it."

"But you didn't," said Caroline.

"No. But only because the puppy's owner heard the screeching and came out."

"Lucky, then," said Caroline.

"Lucky, why?"

"Well, killing anything is wrong, isn't it?" Caroline said.

"Oh, Caroline, you're such a goody-goody."

"Fine," said Caroline.

They walked on through the cemetery in silence. When they were almost at the top of the main path, near the grave of a woman about whom it was said on the stone "She was ever quiet" (which always amused them), Julia spoke again.

"What I meant was could you hate someone enough to think about killing them?"

"I've never hated anyone," Caroline said.

"You haven't?" Julia was incredulous. "But if you did, if someone came into your life and made it a misery, and was cruel, wouldn't you hate them then?"

"Probably," Caroline said, "but hating them wouldn't make me try to kill them."

"It would make me want to," said Julia.

"Well, that's where we differ," Caroline said, "and anyway, I don't believe you would kill anyone. Don't be silly."

Julia said nothing. Her mind, she knew, worked in a different way from Caroline's. She was beginning to think it worked in a different way from everyone's. She wished someone would explain how minds did work.

Iris had another baby, nine months ("to the day" Aunt Maureen kept saying, with emphasis, which puzzled Julia) after she and Carlo married. It was a girl. "Just as well," Aunt Maureen said, and this time Julia understood. Julia and her mother saw the baby, named Elsa, often. Just as with little Reggie, they helped look after Elsa, taking her for walks in her pram. This was not a Silver Cross pram. It was another pram called a buggy, what Aunt Maureen said was "a new fangled sort". The body could be lifted off the wheels and served as a carrycot, and the rest of the pram could be folded up and put in the boot of a car. It was dark green in colour and not at all impressive, in Julia's opinion, but Iris and Carlo were pleased with it. By now, Julia was taller and, since the pram was smaller, she could push it easily. The days of having difficulty going up and down kerbs were over.

Julia was entrusted, from almost the beginning, with taking Elsa for walks. Just up and down the road, not to the park. The first time she pushed the pram, her mother stood at the gate and watched her. Julia counted her steps to the first kerb. Sixty. When she reached it, her mother called out "Now turn, *carefully!*" and she turned the pram with exaggerated care. Her mother made her walk up and down twice more, then said, "You've got the hang of it." After that, she was often ordered to take Elsa for a walk up and down the road. It was a very dull walk. At the time of these walks, nobody ever seemed to come out of the houses. The whole road appeared in a deep sleep. Julia looked at the gardens and, as ever, saw no activity, not even a lawn being mowed, even though all the lawns were trim and obviously must be regularly mowed. She was so bored.

Julia, on these promenades, wished something would happen. Anything, it didn't matter what. And yet, even though she was longing for some drama, there was often the old uncomfortable feeling in her stomach. It always began, this churned-up sensation, as she approached the first kerb and the moment to turn the pram. She knew she could do it without any trouble so it wasn't nervousness that made her feel churned up. On the way back along the road, the feeling disappeared, but then it would return the next time she approached the same spot. Julia tried experimenting. She stopped a good couple of yards from the kerb and turned the pram early. This worked quite well; she still felt a bit funny towards the moment of turning but nothing like she had felt before.

Iris had another baby, ten months after Elsa was born. "Far too soon," Aunt Maureen said, sounding quite cross. Julia asked why it was too soon, and was told that it was better for children to be spaced out. Her following "why" was treated to an exasperated "because". This too-soon baby was also a girl. This time Aunt Maureen didn't say it was just as well. What she said was "a pity, but never mind". Julia correctly supposed that this meant Aunt Maureen wanted the baby to be a boy. The new baby was named Francesca, after Carlo's Italian grandmother, which Aunt Maureen thought "unnecessary". Fran, as she quickly became known, had Carlo's black curly hair whereas Elsa's was fair, like Iris's. "You wouldn't know they were sisters," Aunt Maureen commented. Julia couldn't interpret her tone. But Julia's mother reprimanded Aunt Maureen, saying something Julia found interesting. "Really, Maureen," she said, "just because they have different hair. We have different hair. People never thought we were sisters."

Julia looked at her mother's hair and at Aunt Maureen's hair. She couldn't see much difference. They both had brown hair. Aunt Maureen's was maybe a little more stylish, but then she went to the hairdresser every month to have it cut whereas Julia's mother only went about twice a year, and in the meantime trimmed it herself. Julia knew, though, that there was a deeper meaning to her mother's comment. It often seemed to her that her mother and her aunt were engaged in some sort of complicated battle but what this battle was about baffled her. Sometimes she sensed that her aunt was winning, even though she didn't know exactly what was being won, and sometimes it was her mother who gave off a victorious air. Once, Julia had asked her mother if she liked Aunt Maureen. "Like?" her mother replied, and then again, with emphasis, "Like? We're sisters, Julia." This was obviously supposed to satisfy Julia but it didn't. She pondered the information deeply and came to the conclusion that if you had a sister there was no choice about liking her.

She would have liked a sister herself, of course. Or a brother. But a sister preferably. Someone she could talk to and who would be an ally against their mother when she was at her most infuriating. They, her sister and herself, could then gang up together, and complain to each other about whatever it was that their mother had said which they objected to. And she would have been able to tell a sister anything. When she considered this, Julia felt there was something just out of reach in her mind which was bothering her and which a sister would have known about in a telepathic way. It was something that Julia wanted rid of, but first she had to identify what this something was. A sister would have guessed. Julia had seen this happen between her mother and Aunt Maureen. Her mother would tell Maureen what she was worrying about. "Your trouble, Maureen," she would say, "is that you can't see what is happening under your nose." And then Julia's mother would tell Aunt Maureen what indeed was happening, and over Aunt Maureen's face would spread a look of relief mixed with astonishment. That was what having a sister meant: knowing things about them that they didn't even know themselves.

136

Julia didn't need to ask the question she had been ready to ask because it was asked by someone who was quicker at attracting the speaker's attention than she was. The answer was fairly satisfactory, so Julia didn't feel any need to make the point she'd been going to make about how it was tempting to confuse a child's evasion of the truth with a calculated piece of lying.

As she left the hall, successfully dodging several people who she could see were going to come and greet her, her mobile, which she had just switched back on, rang in her bag. She waited until she was outside the building before she answered it. It was from the social worker attached to the case of Gill Boothroyd, apologising for calling her when she knew she was in Manchester but there'd been a new development and she wanted Julia to see Gill again. This was not how things were done, as the social worker knew, and Julia didn't have to agree, but she did. She said she'd see Gill Boothroyd the next day and asked where she now was. "In hospital," the social worker said. Julia didn't ask why. This social worker sounded almost apologetic, though nothing that had happened, whatever had happened, was likely to be her fault. Instead, Julia said she would be at the hospital at ten the next morning.

There was a mother and a three-year-old girl sitting opposite her on the train, making Julia recall Elsa at three years old. She was the sweetest child, so pretty and lively, an absolute delight. That's what Julia's mother called her, "an absolute delight". Julia played all sort of games with her, quite willingly. Hide-and-seek was Elsa's favourite, but it wasn't the usual game, in which one person hides and the other seeks. They both hid together, and waited to be missed, waited for the shout of "Julia, Julia" or "Elsa, Elsa" to sound through the house when Julia's mother registered that she hadn't seen either of them for a long time. Even when Julia heard her mother, she didn't let Elsa leave their hiding place. She liked her mother to begin to sound frantic before she let Elsa out of the cupboard or from under the bed. Elsa would yell, "Here, here!" and run off excitedly, while Julia followed on, nonchalantly, and Julia's mother would eye her suspiciously yet never say what these suspicions might be.

Whether she did indeed have anything to be suspicious about, Julia herself would have been unable to say. There was something about hiding with Elsa that troubled her. The little girl was so small, so eager to cling on tightly to Julia when they were hiding, shivering with the thrill of it, squealing softly when she heard her name being called. Shh, Julia would whisper, shh, and Elsa's grip would tighten. To be so powerful was a feeling Julia relished, but she was also afraid of it. But these games of hide-and-seek stopped as Elsa grew bigger. Julia found she didn't want to be squashed any more into confined spaces with the increasingly sturdy Elsa. She suggested treasure hunts instead. The treasure hunts had a purpose Elsa knew nothing about. Julia wanted to find Reginald's secret present which she believed Iris must have hidden among her things, her personal things.

138

What she wanted to do was to go through the wardrobe and the drawers in Iris's bedroom, but she couldn't do it herself. She didn't feel she could go into the bedroom unless Iris sent her there for something, but the occasion, these days, never arose. Elsa could go there, though. There would be nothing unusual about her going into her parents' bedroom. But however hard she tried, Julia couldn't make up a clue in her treasure hunt that would lead to a search of Iris's bedroom, so she had to change the game. The new game was the dressing-up-as-ladies game, with Iris's permission to play with her clothes, so long as they were all put back afterwards.

Elsa loved dressing up. Julia chose the clothes for her, carefully picking brightly coloured garments. Luckily, Iris was not only a woman who had lots of clothes but was also someone who never threw anything out. Stacks and stacks of dresses were jammed into her wardrobe and the shelf inside held dozens of hats. The dresses, even the short sixties ones, were too long for Elsa but Julia used scarves to hoist them up and tie round what passed for a waist on Elsa. The scarves came from the dressing-table drawers. Lots of scarves crammed there, chiffon and silk, spotted and striped and patterned, some long and thin, some square, and all in beautiful colours. Julia's heart beat a little faster when she got Elsa to pull out these drawers. She felt instinctively that they made the perfect nest for a secret present. But she was careful to touch nothing in the drawers herself. "You choose a scarf to use as a belt," she'd said to Elsa, and Elsa had promptly pulled out all of them so that they fell into a heap on the carpet. But when the drawers were quite empty, Julia saw there was nothing else in them. She folded all the scarves and replaced them. "No more dressing up," she said to Elsa crossly.

Gradually, it dawned on Julia that Iris and Carlo were well off. According to Julia's mother, "Those two spend money like water." Julia didn't see how water could be spent, but she took her mother's point. She went shopping with Iris quite often, because she was useful holding the pushchair (a double one) with the girls in it while Iris looked at clothes. Iris bought a lot of clothes, paying in cash from a purse which seemed to bulge with it. Sometimes she would ask Julia to get a twenty-pound note out for her while she attended to one of the girls. "Here, Julia," she'd say, handing over the purse, "Get a twenty out and give it to the girl at the till for this, will you?" and Julia would carry out the transaction and bring the skirt, or top, back to Iris, in a bag, together with the change, if there was any. "Oh, keep it," Iris would sometimes say, and Julia did.

She wondered if she ought perhaps to tell her mother how generous her cousin was, but decided not to, in case, as was quite likely, she was told not to accept the money. She saved it, week by week. Although there was no such thing as a place where her mother would never look, Julia thought that keeping the money she got from Iris inside an old toy bear she had once been fond of might be safe. Her mother had bought that bear for her and had been pleased by Julia's affection for it when she was small, and would never throw it away, as she had a habit of suddenly doing with Julia's discarded things, nor would she whip it away to wash it, another habit she had. So Julia carefully unpicked the stitches round the back of the fat bear's tummy, took out a lot of the stuffing, and kept Iris's money inside it. The bear, on a top shelf, would only be touched when the shelf needed to be dusted and Julia's mother had started making Julia clean her own room so the bear should be safe.

Eventually, the hiding place inside the bear began to be hardly big enough. Julia was adding to it every week, and not just the money Iris had told her to keep. The first time she took a pound coin from Iris's purse she hated herself so much that the next time she was given the purse she put it back. The knowledge of the coin in her pocket during the intervening half-hour, going from shop to shop, had filled her with shame, so much so that she found herself trembling and Iris said, "Oh, Julia, you look hot, this shop *is* hot, let's go out for a bit, would you like some lemonade, we could go to the cafe and have a drink . . ." Iris's words all ran together and Julia's head thudded. The relief when she returned the pound coin was immense. Never, never would she do such a despicable thing again.

A week later, she took a five-pound note, one of a thick wad of notes inside Iris's wallet. Iris didn't miss it. The note didn't seem to burn in Julia's pocket the way the coin had. For three weeks after this, she took nothing from Iris's money, though she had plenty of opportunity. Her own virtue began to please her. She would look at all the money in Iris's purse or wallet whenever she was told to go and pay for some item and congratulate herself on resisting the temptation to take some more. She thought it a pity that no one knew how honest she was being. But occasionally she succumbed again, filching a note or a few coins to test that Iris was unaware that she was stealing from her. When she did, she immediately missed the glow of virtue that had filled her when she had stopped herself from taking money. But still, she couldn't give up the habit entirely.

I am a sometimes thief, Julia decided. That was not so bad.

Gill Boothroyd had her right arm in plaster and a bandage round her head. She opened her eyes when Julia, accompanied by the social worker, walked in, and then closed them again. The social worker, Maggie, looked at Julia and raised her eyebrows. Julia nodded, and Maggie left the room. Julia sat down beside the bed, and waited. She didn't attempt to say anything to Gill.

A nurse came in, announcing that she'd come to do obs. "How are you feeling now, Gill?" she asked. Gill, clearly reckoning that it was not a good policy to ignore the nurse as she was ignoring Julia, said that she had a splitting headache. The nurse, wrapping a blood pressure cuff round Gill's arm and sticking a thermometer in her mouth, said she would see if Gill could be given some more paracetamol but that meanwhile she should keep as still as possible, head wounds were nasty things. When the nurse had left the room, Julia quietly unhooked the clipboard hanging at the end of the bed and looked through the notes. The patient was reported to be "very quiet" and "unresponsive", but her temperature and blood pressure readings were steady. Julia put the notes back. The clipboard made a slight rattle as she put it back, and Gill opened her eyes.

"Just looking at your notes," Julia said.

"None of your business," Gill said.

Julia, who had been briefed before she came into the room, knew how Gill had received a head wound and how she had broken her arm. She'd been pushed out of a window when caught breaking into a warehouse to steal an iPad. The security guard thought she was a boy, and when she tried to make a run for it, and to exit through a window, he had lunged at her and pushed her when she was already half out of the window. His torch had hit her head, and then she'd been cut by the glass, and he wouldn't have been so rough if he had known the intruder was only a girl.

All for an iPad. There had previously been a fight with the foster-mother over a bag she'd stolen, and now these injuries, all to try to get an iPad she couldn't possibly afford and wanted so much.

"Gill," began Julia . . .

CHAPTER
SIX

The first, crucial, interview came at an awkward time, just as plans were being made to do with the centre being moved to different premises, but Julia's boss said of course she should attend, in view of its importance. She went for it eagerly, considering herself good at interviews, and intrigued to discover what form it would take.

When she arrived, she was given a hypothetical case to study, the sort of case which apparently came before magistrates quite regularly, and then she was asked questions about it by a panel of six people. Most of these questions were straightforward, to do with her political affiliation, but when they moved on to her reaction to the case she'd been given to study they became harder to answer. What, she was asked, was her response to the mythical defendant having sworn at, and spat in the face of, a policewoman? She said that of course though this was offensive the police were probably used to it and knew how to deal with it. She felt this hadn't been a wise answer. Two of the panel frowned. Then she was asked if she had any prejudices. Yes, she said. She was prejudiced against anyone showing a lack of respect for others in public places, and gave as her example a man she'd seen, on her way to this interview, urinating against a wall in full view of children going to school. She was also prejudiced against those who played music at a deafening level, and against people who were bad-mannered and rude. But these kinds of prejudices were, it seemed, commonplace and wouldn't obstruct her in her duties if she became a magistrate. The panel was more interested in prejudices to do with race, religion and class. She was able to state she believed she had none.

The check-up was, Julia was sure, unnecessary, but she kept her clinic appointment too, the same busy week, and was duly discharged after she'd been looked at by a very young and nervous junior registrar who issued warnings against sunbathing and tanning salons which Julia didn't need.

"Probably the damage to your skin was done years and years ago," this doctor said. "Did you live abroad in the sun when you were growing up, or go on holiday somewhere hot?"

"No," said Julia, "I grew up in Manchester, and we had no holidays abroad."

"Oh well then," the doctor said, "it's a mystery."

One of many, thought Julia as she left the dermatology clinic. Her childhood seemed full of mysteries, most of them trivial, some important, none now able to be solved. A child's memory, she had long ago discovered, was no more reliable than an adult's. A child of eight, so near to their past, could not always recall it vividly. They would have to wait until they were eighty to remember suddenly in absolute detail events that happened when they were four or five.

"I'm not going back to Karen's," Gill Boothroyd said, "I'd rather be put back in the home. I'm not going back to her. I'm telling you, I'll just run away. I'm telling you."

"I heard," Julia said, "I was listening."

"Well, then."

"You've been in the home already, Gill. I'm sure you remember what it was like."

"Nothing wrong with it."

"Is that why you ran away at every opportunity?"

"I didn't mean it. I just wanted out. But there was nothing wrong with the place. I want to go back, I don't want to go to Karen's."

"There's a problem," Julia said. "Karen wouldn't have you back anyway —"

"Good."

"— and you're too old now for Hilltop House. Where would you like to be placed, ideally?"

"What's that mean?"

"If you could choose, where would you choose to live?"

"With my mum."

Julia looked at the girl steadily. Gill's mother was in prison. Gill knew that. Julia knew Gill was waiting for her to say, does that mean you want to be in prison? Gill held her gaze for a while, and then said, "But she's in Holloway, so why did you ask that when you knew what I'd say and why I couldn't be with her?"

"I wasn't sure you *would* say you'd like to live with your mum."

"Anyone would."

"No, they wouldn't, not if things had been tough when they lived with their mum before."

"They weren't tough. What's tough anyway? They were all right."

Again, Julia kept quiet and met Gill's look. The bandage was off her head now, with only a neat line of stitches showing where the wound had been. Some of her hair had had to be shaved off but this small patch hardly showed. Someone had washed Gill's hair and now it settled gracefully around her sullen face.

"You've got beautiful hair," Julia suddenly decided to say.

"You softening me up, or what?" said Gill.

"I was just admiring it and thought I'd pay you the compliment."

"Then don't," Gill said. "I don't like it. I don't like it. It isn't your business, it isn't your job, going on about my hair," and she imitated Julia saying she had beautiful hair, sneering.

"I think," Julia said, ignoring Gill's tone, "you're going to be reckoned too young for any sort of hostel, though that might suit you best, give you some independence."

"Are you talking to yourself?"

"I'm just thinking out loud about possibilities."

"Then don't bother. I won't have any say in it anyway. They'll just put me where they want."

"You're still at school," Julia said. "What would you like to do when you leave next year?"

"*Like?*" Gill said. "What's like got to do with anything?"

"No harm in thinking about it," Julia said, knowing she was irritating the girl with her deliberately charming smile. "What kind of work do you see yourself doing?"

"I don't. I don't care. There aren't any jobs anyway. Everyone knows that."

"You're a bright girl," Julia said, "or so some teachers have said. You've got some brains, apparently."

"Apparently," Gill repeated, sneering again.

"But you don't use them."

"That's my business."

"And mine."

"How the fuck is it yours?"

It was the first time Gill had sworn in her presence though there was plenty in the notes about her filthy language and constant use of the F-word. Karen, the foster-mother, said Gill hardly opened her mouth without attaching this word to everything she said. But Julia let it pass. It had been said without heat, in an incredulous voice, not an angry one. "Your brains," she told Gill, "and your refusal to use them are my business. It's my job to work out why."

"For fuck's sake," Gill said, almost laughing now, "this ain't real."

"It is," said Julia, "very real. When you hit Karen, you knew the consequences. It was deliberate. You'd thought it all out."

148

"I was mad at her, that's all. I couldn't stand her a minute longer. I hate her. You don't know what it's like hating someone you're made to live with."

"Karen knew you'd stolen that bag."

"So?"

"She had to make you take it back."

"I wasn't going to do that, no way. The shop hadn't even fucking well missed it."

"Karen was in charge of you. It was her job to —"

"Oh, shut the fuck up!"

Julia turned, without speaking, to leave the room. "Where are you going?" Gill said.

"I'm shutting up," Julia said, "and going home."

"Just because I swore? Oh, for . . . oh, I don't believe it, taking offence, just because, it's your job, you said it was, you can't just eff off, is 'eff' all right, is it?"

"Yes, it's all right," Julia said, "but I'm finished anyway. I know enough to give my opinion."

"But I haven't said nothing yet, you don't know nothing."

"You're shouting."

"Yeah, I'm effing shouting, you'd shout if you was me, someone walking out on you just like that. Job done, I don't fucking think . . ."

The shouting went on as Julia walked down the corridor. She'd go back in half an hour.

Julia, as she grew older, still saw a lot of Iris's girls, especially Elsa, the older one. Elsa loved Julia, She'd shriek with delight when Julia arrived, and leap into her arms and hug her fiercely. "You're the favourite," Iris

149

said, "you're her idol, Julia." At first, Julia liked being an idol. She found being adored pleasing. But as Elsa grew, and became an incredibly energetic child, demanding so much more of her idol, wanting to play games that were becoming tiresome, Julia found the experience not quite so agreeable. Elsa was never still. At four years old, she literally was only still when she was asleep. "Come on, Julia!" she would yell, and try to drag Julia into the garden just as Julia felt like slumping on the sofa. "Let me read you a story," she'd suggest, but Elsa was not interested in being read to. The demands on Julia's time became heavier and coincided with a total lack of energy on her part. She was a teenager now, and didn't care for bouncing about all the time, or chasing Elsa round the garden. She started saying to her mother that she didn't feel like going to Iris's house, it was too tiring, being at Elsa's beck and call.

Her mother was quite shocked. "Tired? At your age? Really, Julia, that's ridiculous. You can say you can't be bothered with Elsa any more but don't claim to be *tired*. That's just an excuse." Julia shrugged. Of course it was an excuse, but her mother needn't have pointed this out. "Anyway," her mother said briskly, "you'll have to get over this so-called exhaustion because I've said we'll have Elsa to stay next week."

"To *stay?*" Julia said. "You mean, sleep and everything?"

"Yes. It's the least we can do. Maureen can't manage the two of them and Fran is the easier, so I said we'd have Elsa, and Iris was not to worry. Elsa's not been told yet, it would make her too excited. She'll be thrilled to bits."

Iris was going into hospital, for an operation. Julia had only the vaguest idea of what an operation might mean, but once she had wondered aloud — her newly contrived subtle way of asking questions — whether Iris was having a leg cut off, or something cut off, and her mother had said no, she relaxed. The mysterious operation went on being mysterious, and Julia asked no more. She was told that when Elsa came, she was not to mention anything about hospitals or operations, but just to say, if Elsa wanted her mummy, that she would be home soon.

Elsa didn't once ask. She was entirely happy to be with Julia, whom she followed everywhere, even to the toilet, which embarrassed Julia greatly, much to the scorn of her mother, who informed her that urinating and defecating were natural functions and not something to hide from children. This enraged Julia, who knew perfectly well about natural functions but saw no reason to perform them in front of others, even Elsa. It was one of the contradictory things about her mother: you'd expect her to be prim and proper in this respect, as in all others, but she wasn't. She never closed the bathroom door, which horrified Julia now. She liked the door not just to be closed but locked when she was using the bathroom. But Elsa howled and roared and hurled herself at the closed door whenever Julia tried to get some privacy, and then Julia's mother came alongside Elsa and demanded that Julia stop being so silly. Later, her mother took the bolt off the

151

door. It was only a slim metal bolt, which would never have held the door if a determined onslaught upon it had been made, but it had been a great comfort to Julia.

Elsa slept with her. Not in the same bed, officially, but on a camp bed next to Julia's bed. She stayed in it perhaps five minutes after Julia's mother had wished her goodnight, sleep tight, and then she was straight into Julia's bed. She snuggled up to her, and played with Julia's hair, and her little body was warm and soft. It was not at all like cuddling a toy, nor even the big bear she'd been so fond of. When Elsa finally fell asleep, after Julia had sung all the nursery rhymes she requested, Julia tried to detach her from her own arm, which she had insisted should be around her, and to move her body away from her side, to which it clung. But this was impossible to do without waking her, as Julia soon discovered, so she had to let the little girl stay as she was until, in her sleep, she naturally moved and Julia was free.

Julia didn't complain about this to her mother because if she did she would have to explain her feelings about Elsa sleeping with her, and she couldn't have done this because she didn't understand them herself. It made her uncomfortable to think about the possible reasons why she didn't want Elsa there. It was about bodies. She said that to herself: it is about bodies. She didn't like having Elsa's body curled up against her own. But why not? What was wrong with it? That was the bit she couldn't explain. It was dangerous, somehow. But who, or what, was in danger? Julia had bad nights trying to work this out and was cross with Elsa in the mornings.

It was the first week of the Easter holidays, and they were "blessed" with fine weather, as Julia's mother put it. "Good," she said, seeing blue sky and sun when she opened the curtains, "you can be out in the garden with Elsa." Julia wanted to say that she was too old just to be sent into the garden to play with a four-year-old, but she didn't. It would be no use. And she preferred being outside with Elsa rather than inside, it was true. Outside, Elsa running manically about, wasn't as exhausting. Julia became quite skilled at thinking up games which involved Elsa running up and down while Julia stood still. "I'm timing you, Elsa," she shouted. "See how many times you can run from the kitchen door to the fence at the bottom of the garden. Ready, steady, go!" Elsa loved ready, steady, go. She never managed to wait for the "go" but charged off at "steady", and then was made to do it again.

Julia, timing her, but cheating, couldn't help but reflect on the power she had over Elsa. Elsa, she realised, would do anything she suggested. It crossed her mind that if she said go and jump in the fish pond Elsa would unhesitatingly do it. Julia knew her mother would be furious if she did any such thing, but then she could pretend it had been Elsa's own idea. Quite easy, really, to plant the idea that, contrary to appearances, she had no control over Elsa, then she'd have some fun. The minute she'd thought like this, Julia had another thought, a mischievous thought, definitely only a bit of fun. There was some gravel on the garden path. Julia

153

picked up a handful and offered some to Elsa. "Let's see who can throw the furthest," she said, and threw some of the tiny stones ahead, up the path towards the house. Elsa was delighted with the new game and, just as Julia had known she would, was not content with picking up just a few stones to throw but began scooping up whole handfuls and hurling them wildly, with no sense of where they were going. She was running along the path as she did this and, inevitably, was near the glass doors of the French windows when she chucked her last handful. The clatter against the glass brought Julia's mother rushing out. Elsa was screaming and laughing, then rushing back to gather more stones. "Stop it, Elsa!" Julia said, and then, to her mother, who was examining the panes for damage, "Sorry, I couldn't stop her."

For the rest of that day, Julia was particularly kind to Elsa, but the following day the same impulse to make the little girl do something she should not do overcame her. At the end of the garden there was a gate, usually locked (but Julia had recently discovered where the key was kept), which led onto a lane leading to a pathway along the canal. "Shall we have an adventure, Elsa?" Julia whispered, and of course Elsa jumped with excitement, then mimicked Julia's "shh", and put her finger to her lips, just as Julia was doing. Julia got the key and, with difficulty, opened the gate, with Elsa squealing and shhing beside her. Once out in the lane, Julia did exaggerated tiptoeing along, holding Elsa's hand, and then once on the towpath they both ran until, out of breath, Julia stopped.

"Where's the adventure?" Elsa asked, stumbling over the word.

"This is it," Julia said, "unless you want to go on a boat. Do you want to go on a boat, Elsa? Do you?" Elsa nodded vigorously. "Come on, then."

There was only one canal boat tied up on this stretch, quite a smart boat, newly painted by the look of it, and with red-and-white gingham curtains at the windows. Julia, holding Elsa's hand and telling her to be very quiet, studied the boat. It was hard to tell if the owner was in residence or not, and, if he was not, whether he would come back soon, but she thought, from the lack of any sound, and the very tidy appearance, that it was empty. Experimentally, she picked up a tennis ball she'd noticed lying in the undergrowth and tossed it onto the boat. It made a satisfying bang on the deck before bouncing off into the water. Nobody appeared to investigate the noise. "Right, Elsa," Julia said, "let's go on the boat." This wasn't easily managed. The boat was lower than the path and though Julia, by sitting down, could get her feet on the deck and then stand up on it, Elsa couldn't. So Julia first had to manage this before holding her arms out and telling Elsa to jump. The jump was a bit too enthusiastic and Julia was almost knocked over, so she was cross with Elsa. Suddenly, this "adventure" seemed stupid. Julia couldn't remember what the point of it had been meant to be.

Because there had been a point to it. She knew that. In the back of her mind there had been a plan, or if not a plan then an urge to make Elsa suffer for being such a pain. It wasn't pleasant to think about it, so Julia tried to shake it off, but this thin smear of nastiness lingered. Elsa meanwhile was wandering around the boat looking in at the windows and shouting she could see a cake, a chocolate cake and two plates. Smartly, Julia dragged her away. "Time to get off," she said, "they'll be coming back soon," and she led the way back to the point where they'd climbed onto the boat. She went first, finding it much harder to clamber onto the bank than it had been to get onto the boat, and then she turned to help Elsa. But jumping was no good here. She needed to lift Elsa, but she couldn't do it. Elsa pulled and Julia was going to fall back on the deck, so she let Elsa go. Then she stood up. Elsa's now tearful face stared up at her imploringly. "Sorry, Elsa," Julia said, "you'll just have to stay there till the owner comes back," and she began to walk away, the rising note of Elsa's screams quite alarming to hear.

She only walked a couple of yards. She never had any intention of abandoning Elsa, of course she didn't. But in that short fragment of time she felt an intense excitement which immediately made her feel shaky and sick. Quickly, she turned back, and shouted to Elsa to stop it, stop it, and then she lay down full-length on the bank and told Elsa to stretch her arms as high as she could and slowly, slowly, she was able to haul the child up, but only just. If Elsa had not been so light, she would not have been able to do it. "There," Julia said, panting, "now stop crying, there's nothing wrong with you." But clearly there was. Elsa did stop crying, but she went on trembling. Julia held her tight and soothed her and told her what a brave girl she'd been and what a great adventure they had had. "Don't tell anyone about it, though," she added, "it's our secret, OK?" Elsa didn't nod in agreement. She was silent all the way back to the gate, though Julia chatted away to her and sang her favourite songs. When they were safely in the garden, Elsa broke away from Julia and ran into the house. Following her, Julia found her mother looking astonished and Elsa with her arms wrapped round her mother's legs.

"Good heavens," her mother said, "what's brought this on? What's the matter with Elsa?"

"Oh, she's tired," Julia said carelessly. "I walked her too far." Her heart beat rather hard as she said this, but Elsa, for the moment, stayed silent. That night she stayed in her camp bed. Julia was excessively kind to her, but it made no difference, she wouldn't be coaxed into Julia's bed. Next day was the last day, then she went home.

Julia's mother had a phone call from Iris. Iris thanked her for having Elsa, said she was so grateful, and grateful to Julia too. Elsa, it seemed, had had such an exciting time with Julia that she'd been having nightmares. Iris said this quite nicely, Julia's mother reported, but there had been "an edge" to it. The nightmares were about boats and chocolate cake. "What on earth could have caused that?" Julia's mother asked her, watching her closely. "You didn't take her onto a boat, did you?" Julia said of course not, but they'd seen a boat and seen a cake through one of the windows. She excused herself the lie because strictly

157

speaking she hadn't "taken" Elsa onto the boat. Elsa had jumped.

After that, Elsa was not so keen on Julia. "It's to be expected," Julia's mother said, "she's growing up."

Afterwards, Julia regretted telling her friend Caroline about the boat thing. She couldn't remember why she'd broken her own rules by confiding in Caroline. Needing to confide anything to anyone was a weakness. But she had done it, while walking to school the next morning. Caroline was odd. It was this oddness that had drawn them together, though they were each thought odd in a different way, Julia because of how she kept herself to herself, and Caroline because of her accent and her appearance. She was from Motherwell, near Glasgow, and had a strong Scottish accent, and she had a brutal haircut, clipped round her ears and in at the neck, which looked strange when her figure was so full-breasted and womanly. Girls were not comfortable with Caroline but Julia was interested in her because she was different and clever.

They were both clever, particularly at maths and science. Julia's cleverness was of the quiet, unobtrusive variety. She didn't speak much in class and it was not until marks were given out that her ability was revealed. But Caroline was a show-off. She had her hand almost permanently raised aloft in lessons, answers to everything at the ready and always correct. Neither girl made any approach to the other, but they had been put together to work by their chemistry teacher. Outside the laboratory they went their separate ways but then they began meeting each other accidentally on the way to school and soon this developed into a habit and from this they discovered they shared a liking for a sharp comment about a whole list of things. Neither of them yet knew much about the other, so the name Elsa meant nothing to Caroline when Julia suddenly began this tale, told in a laconic tone, of dumping her cousin on a boat and almost leaving her. Caroline said nothing at first. She realised that Julia was pitching for some reaction but she wasn't sure if she was supposed to be shocked or amused, or something else. It seemed to her that Julia was trying to tell her something, that this story about the cousin indicated some undercurrent worrying her. So Caroline said nothing, except that maybe Julia should keep away from this Elsa.

"Why?" asked Julia.

"Well," said Caroline "you seem to like hurting the kid, no?"

"No!" said Julia. "Of course I don't, that's stupid."

She didn't speak to Caroline for the rest of the day.

When Julia got home and saw a letter lying on the mat behind her front door, she thought it might be to say she'd been appointed as a magistrate, but one glance, as she picked it up, showed her it could not be. It was a personal letter, the address written in a round, almost childish hand. Julia held it, playing her mother's annoying game of spending ages wondering who this unexpected letter could be from when all she had to do to find out was open it. But she rather liked the suspense. A letter was, after all, now a rare event. Who

159

wrote to her? Caroline, occasionally, very occasionally, and Iris, on her birthday and at Christmas, but everyone else emailed or phoned.

The letter was from Sandra who Julia had neither seen nor heard from for something like forty years, ever since she and her mother had left Cumbria. It was written on two small sheets of blue paper with another thicker page folded up and stuck between these two sheets. Julia read the letter first, without unfolding the other sheet. It reminisced about their primary schooldays together, with Sandra apparently having crystal-clear memories of incidents Julia could not recollect at all, and then moved on to (as Sandra put it) bringing Julia "up to speed" on how her own life had developed. She was married and had two children, both boys, of twenty and nineteen, who still lived at home. Sandra was a full-time wife and mother, which she didn't regret at all (the "at all" underlined) but nevertheless she was full of admiration for what she'd heard from others about Julia's career, and often thought about her, and how well she'd done.

By the time Julia was onto the second sheet of paper, she was wondering what the point of this letter was going to turn out to be. Could it really just be a "for old times' sake" letter? Or was Sandra writing with a purpose and if so what would it be? She noticed that right at the beginning Sandra had revealed how she had got Julia's address, a complicated sequence of encounters with someone who knew someone who knew someone else who knew Julia's cousin, Iris, who had provided the address. Once she had it, Sandra had felt she really must write, especially as — and here the point of the letter began to emerge — she had recently seen, in the extract from the magazine she enclosed, a photograph she was sure was of Julia.

At last, Julia unfolded the page from the magazine enclosed in Sandra's letter. It seemed to have been taken from a feature about wedding-dress styles over the last fifty years. There were three photographs on this page. The bottom one was of Iris's first wedding. There she was, in 1973, Reginald at her side, in his uniform. Iris, Reginald and bridesmaids Sylvie and Pat all had their names listed underneath. Then Julia realised that though Sandra was correct, she was in this photograph, her name was not in the caption, which simply said "unknown bridesmaid". Unknown? She felt strangely shocked seeing that word: Unknown? What would it signify to people? Who had sent this photograph to the magazine? Who had not known her?

But then, still staring at the photograph, Julia thought that *she* did not know that child either. The description was correct. She was unknown to herself. It was a stage she was beginning to suspect, that all adults reached. She knew that she had been that child but nevertheless the child was a stranger to her and it was distressing.

She would not reply to Sandra.

One day, when she was fifteen, Julia came home from school to find the house, as she thought, empty. She banged the door shut as she entered, and waited for her mother to shout "Don't bang the door", part of the

161

ritual of coming home, but no shout came. Assuming her mother was out, Julia went into the kitchen to look for something to eat, and only after she'd cut herself a piece of cake did she notice there was a pan on the cooker, its contents bubbling away. So her mother wasn't out. She trailed into the living room and put the television on and half watched *Blue Peter*. There was homework to do, but she hadn't the energy yet. When *Blue Peter* finished, she went back into the kitchen to make some tea and saw that the pan was still bubbling but now there was a slight smell of burning. She lifted the lid and peered in. There was a chicken carcass inside, with only a tiny bit of water at the bottom of the pan. Stock. Her mother had left the chicken bones simmering to make stock, and she'd forgotten it and gone out.

But her mother never forgot such a thing. She was incapable of leaving the house while a pan was bubbling away. Julia went to the bottom of the stairs and called out, "Mum? You've left the stock pan on and it's nearly boiled dry." She realised she sounded scornful, and added, "I've turned it off." Then she waited. Even before she mounted the stairs she knew something was wrong. Outside her mother's bedroom, she hesitated. The door was half open, but she didn't go in straight away. Maybe her mother was having a nap. But Julia knew this was another impossibility. Her mother had nothing but contempt for those feeble enough (like Aunt Maureen) to need naps in the afternoon. So Julia pushed the door further open and went in. At first, she was relieved to see that her mother

162

did indeed appear to be having a nap. She was lying on her back, her eyes closed, her arms by her side, neatly arranged, slightly tucked into the folds of her skirt. But Julia knew.

She behaved in an exemplary fashion. Calmly, though she did not feel calm, she went towards the bed and touched her mother's shoulder, shaking it slightly. No response. "Mum!" she said loudly. There wasn't a flicker. Julia went back downstairs and rang Aunt Maureen. She got Uncle Tom. He seemed a little irritated by Julia's call, asking twice if she was sure her mother wasn't just having a well-earned rest. Julia said she was sure. He came round ten minutes later, in his car, looking grumpy (he'd been watching the cricket), but then when he'd gone upstairs, he changed his attitude.

If Julia's mother had suffered from headaches or blurred vision, she hadn't mentioned them to anyone. No doctors had been consulted. The aneurysm, when it happened, must, everyone said, have taken her by surprise. Much was made of this to Julia. "Painless" was a word used frequently. "There would have been no time," Aunt Maureen assured her, "to worry about you." Julia resented this, but said nothing. She said nothing for days. There was plenty of talking around her, but she didn't take part in it. Everyone was kind, but she hated them all. She longed for them all to go away, but that was the one thing they would not do. She must, they said to each other, never be left alone. There was no doubt about it: she needed her family and must be looked after by them. So she was taken to Aunt Maureen and Uncle Tom's.

Nobody consulted her about her future. She was told, gently enough, that though Aunt Maureen and Uncle Tom were her legally appointed guardians she would be going to live with Iris and Carlo and their girls. "You'll be happier there," Aunt Maureen said, "part of a young family instead of stuck with middle-aged folk like your Uncle Tom and me." Aunt Maureen seemed to want Julia to be pleased, or so Julia thought, but she was not pleased. She couldn't take anything in, or find words to express the strangeness she felt. Her mother had ruled her life. Everything she did, or did not do, in some way referred back to her mother. Recently, she had begun to rebel against her mother's absolute authority but she needed her mother to be there to be rebelled against. Without her presence, there was only a void, and that was frightening.

For weeks afterwards, going home from school to the Annovazzi house, Julia would find her footsteps coming to a halt at the point where the road to her old home and the road to theirs met at a corner. Sometimes, she took the old route, not because she'd forgotten where she now lived but deliberately, to see how it would feel. How it felt was good. She had no wish to be back in that house. She didn't feel distressed looking at it. It didn't make her yearn for her mother (though she did want her to be alive again). She stood on the pavement outside the garden of her old home and looked at it not with longing but something near to contempt. What a miserable house, what a miserable place this was. She had never liked it, she had never liked Manchester. Home, in her head, was in Cumbria, where she was sure she and her mother had been happy. Why her mother chose to come here had never been explained to her, and she wanted to know the reasons now more than ever.

When she began being able to talk properly once more, Julia asked her Aunt Maureen why her mother had moved to Manchester.

"Oh, you don't want to fret about that," Aunt Maureen said, "don't you worry your pretty little head about it."

"But I want to know," Julia insisted, "it's important."

"Good heavens," Aunt Maureen said, "important? It's all water under the bridge. What's important about it?"

Julia just managed to stop short of saying it was important because from that move onwards everything in her life had gone wrong so she needed to know why her mother had chosen to come to this place she hated. There had to be a reason, and perhaps if she knew the reason she might not feel so angry and resentful. But she didn't say any of this. Confessing a hatred of Manchester might be taken as also hating her aunt and cousin, and she was smart enough to realise this would do her no good. Instead, she said stubbornly, "I just want to know, that's all."

"I'll tell you one day," Aunt Maureen said, "not that there's much to tell." And that was that.

Julia believed in the theory that dreams were a sort of dustbin for the mind and had no significance. But when she had a particularly clear, vivid dream, in which the sense of reality was so strong that, on waking, she was still within it, she had difficulty accepting that there was no hidden meaning there.

As a child, after little Reggie died, she didn't have nightmares. She slept soundlessly, dreamlessly. It was during the day, while she was wide awake and moving through her life, that she had what seemed like waking dreams. She'd be sitting in class, doing something as practical as long-division sums, when there would rise before her a vision of the Silver Cross pram, tilted on its hood, and she'd hear the thump it made on the kerbstone. But it was the next bit that confused her. She would hear voices in her head, as she sat, petrified, pencil clutched in her hand. One of them, she was sure, was her own, pleading, crying, saying over and over that she was sorry, sorry.

Gradually, these episodes faded and she began to forget they had ever occurred. But then, when her mother died, she had the nightmares she had never had before. In them, her mother was dragging her along the pavement where she had wheeled the pram but it was no longer a solid pavement. Instead, it had become a river of blood and the level rose and rose until it engulfed her, and her mother, and filled the pram, and the baby floated out of it, and she woke up sweating and terrified. But she was certain the baby was alive.

Naturally, she told no one about these nightmares and, in time, they, too, became infrequent and finally ceased. But she felt there had been some message there, if only she could interpret it. Whether it was

166

about the baby, or her mother, or merely her own hidden guilt, she could never work out.

The letter finally arrived: she was appointed a magistrate. The first training session was on a Monday morning. The district judge was dealing with people charged over the weekend, and all Julia and the others had to do was observe. She observed intensely, noting the judge's decisiveness, which impressed her, but also his politeness towards those charged. There was no harshness in his manner, and she saw how kind he was to anyone obviously terrified that they would immediately be sent to prison. She observed, too, the widely varying demeanours of those accused. Not all of them were nervous. One young woman, accused of stealing a pair of shoes from a chain store, objected violently when the shoes were described as leather, claiming only the uppers were leather and the shoes "rubbish" on examination. She thought she saw the merest suggestion of a suppressed smile on the judge's face as he gave her a conditional discharge for six months. The woman shrugged when she heard this, as though she didn't care either way, and Julia felt surprised, expecting her to realise how lucky she'd been.

Some people did. There was another woman, middle-aged, very soberly and neatly dressed in a grey suit, charged with a driving offence. Her car had neither insurance nor an MOT certificate, and she had been driving it after drinking enough to be just over the limit. She hung her head in what looked like genuine shame, and appeared grateful for the fine she received, obviously having expected worse. Julia was not at all sure that a fine was enough, thinking maybe the woman should automatically be disqualified from driving, but there were apparently extenuating circumstances disclosed to the judge but which they did not hear.

But the case that worried her most was concerning bailiffs. If the bailiffs managed to gain entry into a household where debts had not been paid they could cart off belongings in payment, though only non-essential goods. The case that morning involved a distress warrant applied for by a managing director of a firm of bailiffs. He wanted permission to seize the belongings of a man who had a wife and four young children and who had defaulted on many and various debts, for the 32-inch plasma TV, a three-piece suite, a stair carpet and a kitchen table among other things. All non-essential items, but Julia immediately visualised the denuded home and the effect on the wife and children. The warrant was granted, and rightly so, but she found herself heartily disliking the bailiff who looked extremely pleased and smug.

She warned herself sternly against this kind of reaction. It was her job to be impersonal, dispassionate. The law insisted upon it.

Julia lived with Iris and Carlo and their girls for only three years, but they were years which when they came to an end seemed to have gone on much longer. Those three years seemed, later on, to have almost obscured the years that had gone before. It used to make Julia panic when she found that she could not successfully reconstruct the earlier years. She could not place herself in the house she and her mother had lived in, could not *be* in it though she could answer any questions about it. When the memory of her mother also began to be less sharp, as painfully sharp as it had once been, she was filled with despair, and also a kind of shame. How could her mother, whose opinions and habits and rules of conduct had filled every moment of her life, how could she fade, becoming instead a vague picture in her head, fuzzy at the edges and entirely silent?

Yet she was judged to be happy during those years. She heard Aunt Maureen and Iris tell other people how quickly she had "settled", as though she were a bird who had found a nest, and how easily she had fitted into the Annovazzi family, adored by Elsa and Francesca. This, of all the false assumptions made, was, to Julia, the most absurd. There had been no "fitting in". She resented from the very first day being cast in the role of elder sister to her two cousins (she was described to outsiders as the girls' cousin, though they were her first cousins once removed, a pedantic fact which mattered to her). Once she might have wanted a sister, indeed she could recall clearly wanting one, but now that she had, in effect, two sisters she longed to be an only child again. There was never any privacy, never any real stretch of time to herself. She had her own room, at least, and was grateful for it, but it was either regularly invaded by Elsa in particular, or else she was called out of it to do something for Iris. The Annovazzis in general liked togetherness. They were all highly social animals for whom silence and being on one's own were afflictions. "Are you sulking, Julia?" Carlo would ask her when she said she was going to her room. "What's the matter, what have we done?" Told that she was not sulking and that nobody had done anything, that she just wanted to go to her room for a bit and read, Carlo would say "Funny girl", and shake his head. Neither he nor Iris ever stopped Elsa and Fran from following her to her room. Instead, they encouraged them. Julia heard Carlo urging his daughters to "Go and cheer Julia up", a suggestion they followed at once, running up the stairs and pounding their little fists on her door. She always had to open it. If she didn't, Carlo or Iris would come up and make anxious enquiries about what was wrong with her.

Homework was the only thing that did give her the right to be shut in her room for an hour or two. Neither Carlo nor Iris knew much about examinations but they were prepared to take them seriously, aware that Julia was clever and might do well. Hard work Carlo certainly understood, and agreed with, whatever kind of hard work was involved. "I have a lot of homework tonight" became the magic password to being allowed seclusion in her room. Julia did the homework, but did it far quicker than Carlo and Iris could possibly have guessed since both of them had laboured over their own homework at school and shuddered at the memory of it. Julia's bag, bursting with books and files, filled them almost with awe — "The weight!" Iris would exclaim. But most of the stuff crammed into Julia's bag was not needed for her homework. She kept half of the books there all the time, for the look of the thing. In the hour after she had done her homework, she would often just lie on her bed, thinking, daydreaming, not daring to play music or make any noise in case she gave the game away.

Her room, which overlooked the garden, was small, but then all the rooms Julia had ever had as her bedroom had been small. She would have liked space, though she was used to her quarters being cramped. There was no room for a bookshelf, but Carlo had put up three planks across an alcove and these were crammed with her books. In front of each line of books she had propped up photographs, some in frames, some not. They were mostly of herself, though the most prominent was of her mother and father, taken on their wedding day. Her mother had always had it on their mantelpiece. It had been dusted daily, and the silver frame polished once a month. But commanding attention though it did, with its posh frame and its size, compared to the other photographs, Julia rarely concentrated her attention on it. It was photographs of her younger self that fascinated, and even troubled, her.

She would have liked to ask someone about these photographs, someone who had been there when they were taken and had watched her smiling, or trying to smile, for the camera. She wanted reassurance that she really had looked sweet (at three years old), happy (at five), mischievous (at seven) and so on. Most of all, she wanted to ask someone about the photograph of herself at Iris's wedding, as a bridesmaid — the first wedding.

There was a photograph of her on her own, holding the posy of flowers in front of her in an attitude that looked defensive. Julia couldn't believe that the girl there was herself. She didn't recognise it at all, though of course she could remember the dress and flowers. What she wanted was to be that girl again, and for everything that had happened since the photograph was taken to happen differently. She didn't want to have lost that girl.

Once, she had tried to talk to Iris about that photograph and how she felt. Iris was always kind and friendly, but there was rarely any chance to talk to her on her own. Elsa and Fran were always there when Julia got home from school, and when they had been put to bed, Carlo was there, and often other members of his gregarious family. Time alone with Iris was incredibly rare and only happened when Julia was ill with flu or something similar. Then, Iris would make time to bring her hot drinks and literally soothe her forehead with a cold flannel. Iris was always bright and cheerful, assuring Julia that she would be better soon, and asking her if there was anything she wanted, an approach to illness which Julia could distinctly remember had not been her mother's.

"Iris," she murmured, on one such occasion keeping her eyes shut, "do you remember that photo of me being taken?"

"Which one, pet?"

"The one of me as a bridesmaid, there," and Julia opened her eyes and pointed.

172

Iris looked at it for a moment, and then went over to the shelf and picked it up. "Yes, of course I do," she said, her voice soft, "my dad took it," and she put it back.

"It doesn't look like me," Julia said, "I can't believe it was me."

"Well," said Iris, "we all change, we all grow up."

She looked so sad suddenly that Julia felt guilty. She'd reminded Iris of Reginald, that was it, Reginald who had given her the secret present, Reginald whose baby son had died — all those things, things Iris, so far as Julia knew, never talked about. Julia's mother had approved of how Iris had dealt with two tragedies. She had admired Iris for not allowing them to "get her down", except, naturally, at first, and most of all she had admired how Iris never, ever referred to either Reginald or little Reggie once she had met and was happy with Carlo. "An example to us all," Julia's mother had said, and when Julia had asked, "An example of what?" had replied, "What do you think, Julia?" and that had been that.

But Julia wondered if how Iris reacted was a good example or not, even though she followed it for years.

The girl was described in the referral notes as possibly seriously depressed. This comment had a red asterisk next to it, which irritated Julia — as if she would have missed the significance of this! Depression in any teenager was taken very seriously but these days she felt the term was used to cover many lesser states of mind, all of them perfectly normal. To be fed up, miserable, lethargic was not necessarily to be depressed. But schools panicked, and so did parents. They were afraid that "something" might happen.

However, there did seem grounds for Sarah Baxter, aged fourteen, to be a cause of genuine concern. She had begun refusing to get up in the morning. She lay in a darkened room unless her mother hauled her out of it and forced her to go to school. Once there, she would not speak. This had been going on for some time. Julia could see this Sarah Baxter already in her mind's eye, right down to the sullen expression and aggressive frown. The session she would have with her was likely to be very wearing.

When Julia returned to school after her mother's death, Caroline was at her side instantly, shielding her from the curiosity of other girls, and from the pity she dreaded.

Caroline had never met Julia's mother. She'd never been to Julia's home. But she knew about death, sudden death. She had had a brother who was an epileptic and had died, aged sixteen, when Caroline was twelve. She had never told Julia this, though they had got to the stage of telling each other about their families, and she didn't make the mistake of saying to Julia that she knew how she felt. Mature for her age, Caroline found other, subtle, ways of expressing concern and showing sympathy, and Julia recognised what she was doing and appreciated it. From that point on, they were truly friends, soon thought of by the teachers as inseparable. Everyone was pleased that these two clever girls, excellent students both, had become so devoted.

It took even longer, though, for them to see each other out of school hours. Julia didn't want to invite Caroline to the Annovazzi household, where Elsa and Fran would run riot and give her and Caroline no peace or privacy, and Iris would be far too interested, plaguing Caroline with questions. And Julia knew, too, that Iris wouldn't think much of Caroline, though she would say nothing. Caroline would not be deemed a fun person, with her rather solemn habitual expression, and the frown she had when anything puzzled her could make her look cross. The Annovazzis liked pretty girls and were wary of plain girls who might turn out to be clever. They knew Julia was clever, and forgave her for it, since she was family, but they didn't want her friend to be of the same mould. They wanted a friend who would lighten her up and they would know, Iris and Carlo, at first glance, that Caroline was never going to do that.

But Julia knew that she couldn't put off much longer inviting Caroline to what was now her home. Caroline never said anything, never hinted that she was hurt, or thought it odd, that she hadn't been taken home by Julia, but all the same the omission was becoming glaring because Caroline had taken Julia to *her* home often. Julia liked going there. Caroline's mother was a rather vague, scatty woman, completely disorganised but welcoming and, best of all in Julia's opinion, not given to asking searching questions or referring in any way to the death of Julia's mother. She usually drifted off, once she'd invited Caroline and Julia to help themselves to what they could find in the way of biscuits, and she could be heard playing the piano, a sound Julia was unused to and liked. There was a younger brother sometimes around but he gave no trouble, occupied as he seemed to be with a variety of pets, and constantly going next door to play with his friend there who also had a cat and rabbits and a guinea pig.

It was a relief to be at Caroline's house, lolling in Caroline's room and listening to records, of which she had a surprising number, or else discussing books and films. They wouldn't be able to enjoy such seclusion in the Annovazzi household. Julia said this to Caroline, who shrugged, and said it didn't matter, she didn't mind about not going to Julia's home. Julia said that Iris — Caroline knew who Iris was — minded. "She's always on at me to bring you home. She says things like am I ashamed of them all, which is stupid." "You can see what she means, though," Caroline said. "It probably worries her, even though it needn't." That was what Julia liked about her friend. She was always able to put herself in the other person's head and imagine how they would think.

So Julia finally braced herself and took Caroline home. She didn't warn Iris in advance. To do so would provoke ridiculous preparations, endless fussing about what should be provided for tea, and Elsa and Fran probably dressed in their best to greet the visitor. What Julia was counting on was that nobody would be at home on the day she chose, a Wednesday. On

Wednesdays, Iris and the girls always went to spend the afternoon with Maureen, usually not returning until around six o'clock. Carlo never came home before seven, so the coast would be clear. If everyone arrived back when Caroline was still there, it wouldn't matter, she would be about to leave and would only say hello on her way out. Julia knew that this was a sort of cheating, inviting her friend to her house but not to meet its inhabitants, but she didn't care. Iris would be a little hurt, but that couldn't be helped.

But the plan went wrong. As Julia and Caroline approached the Annovazzi house, Julia saw Iris's car in the driveway and, worse still, Carlo's. She almost told Caroline that she couldn't invite her in after all (and Caroline would not have been the least bit offended, she was sure), but Elsa was at the window and had already spotted them. "Oh God," Julia said to Caroline, "I thought they'd all be out. It's Wednesday, they should be at Maureen's." It didn't really occur to Julia, at that moment, that something unusual must have happened to alter normal routines, especially Carlo's, but it was obvious when the two girls walked in that there was some sort of excitement disturbing the family. Elsa and Fran were jumping up and down in the hall, both talking at once, both unintelligible, and through the kitchen door Julia could see Iris with her head in her hands and Carlo shouting down the telephone. Then there was the mess. Julia could see drawers pulled out and overturned, cupboards open and the contents spilled out, and along the hall floor and going up the stairs a trail of assorted clothes. It was

Caroline, who didn't know the house at all, who murmured, "Julia, I think maybe there has been a burglary."

Which was correct. The house had been ransacked while Iris was taking her daughters to their grandmother's, a daring daytime burglary. A neighbour had seen two men carrying two bags each, hurrying through the Annovazzi's garden and she had phoned the police, reporting "suspicious behaviour". There had been no breaking-and-entering because it hadn't been needed: a window had been left conveniently open, which led to Carlo berating Iris, and Iris attempting to excuse the open window on the grounds that there was a loose catch which he had failed to mend and *maybe* it had just blown open. At any rate, all her jewellery had gone, plus £200 in cash, and, as well as various electronic items, and far more disastrously, all Carlo's cups, the silverware he had won for his sporting prowess in tennis and golf.

There was a policeman still in the house, who came down the stairs, on his walkie-talkie, as Julia and Caroline stood uncertainly in the hall. At the sight of him, Julia started to shake.

Julia was sworn in as a JP together with nine others and taken by the legal advisers to the court through all the rules to do with verdicts and sentencing. There was a rota made out so that she and the other new JPs would never sit together but always be with two other experienced magistrates. Then they were all taken on a visit to the cells. She had been pretty sure she knew what a cell would look like but even so the reality felt dramatic. They were each invited to put themselves in a cell and be locked in for a few minutes so that they could experience what it would feel like to the people they would be sending down here. Only Julia accepted the invitation.

She sat on the hard bed for five minutes. When the door was unlocked again, she had to control her trembling, but before she'd succeeded it was noticed by one of the other new magistrates, who smiled at her. "More than you bargained for," he said, "or were you imagining yourself there for possible crimes?" She managed to smile back, and nod, and agree that she had an overactive imagination — that was all.

Except the trembling hadn't been because of that.

Sarah Baxter was composed. She was not sullen or miserable-looking, nor was there anything neglected about her appearance, which was neat and tidy. Her short hair was brushed, her fingernails were clean, and carefully attended to. She held her head up rather high, as though straining to see something above Julia's head. Her complexion was pale, with traces of acne over the forehead, but there were no dark shadows under her eyes. Only her shoulders, slightly slumped, showed faint signs of possible dejection, but maybe she had poor posture.

Julia smiled at the girl. She smiled in return, but with her lips tightly closed.

"Sarah," Julia began, "I see you have two sisters."

"Half-sisters," Sarah said quickly.

"Half-sisters," Julia repeated. "Six and five, is that correct?"

Sarah nodded. "And you help look after them, is that right?"

Sarah hesitated. "I don't help," she said, "I do it all. I look after them. My mum doesn't."

"What do you do for them?" Julia asked gently.

"I get them up, and dress them, and give them breakfast, and take them to school, and I pick them up from after-school club and take them home and give them tea and watch telly with them and put them to bed. That's what I do." The anger was barely controlled.

"I see," Julia said, "and how do you feel about this?"

"I hate it," Sarah said, "I've got no life. I might as well not live. I'm just a slave."

Julia cleared her throat. "I don't expect this will go on too long," she said, "your sisters —

"Half-sisters."

"— half-sisters will soon be able to get themselves up and dressed and so on."

"Years," Sarah said, biting her lip, "not *soon* at all."

Sarah's father had died when she was five. She had been looked after by an aunt, for almost a year, because her mother had had a breakdown and been hospitalised for some of it. Julia had read all this. She'd read that when Sarah had rejoined her mother she at first hadn't settled well. She'd wanted to stay with her aunt (who had no children). But eventually, her relationship with her mother had slowly improved until Jack, who was to become her stepfather, had come to live with them. He

180

seemed, from what Julia read in the notes, to have tried hard with Sarah, and not only in the obvious ways. She'd never had a pet, and longed for a puppy, so Jack took her with him to choose one from the litter his friend's cocker spaniel had produced. He taught her how to look after it, and they went for walks together. So far so exemplary. But then he married Sarah's mother, with Sarah as bridesmaid. Two babies quickly arrived, within a year, and Sarah's mother began struggling to cope just as Jack's firm required him to travel more, meaning he had at least two overnight stays a week away from home.

Julia looked up again. "What happens, Sarah, when you stay in bed and refuse to get up?"

"They cry," Sarah said.

"And then?"

"Mum rings Jack, and shouts at me."

"Does Jack come home?"

"If he can."

"What does Jack say to you?"

"He begs me to get up and take over. For Christ's sake, he says. He says he'll pay me."

"And what do you say then?"

"No. I say I'm not moving. It's awful, everyone shouting, crying."

"Who is crying?"

"The girls, my mum."

"But not you?"

"Me?"

"Yes. Do you cry when all this is going on?"

"No."

"How do these situations end? Usually."

Sarah thought for a minute. "Jack gets the girls ready and takes them to school and gets his sister to take them to her home until he can collect them."

"And what do you and your mum do?"

"We stay in bed."

"Together?"

"No!" said Sarah indignantly. "I'm in my bed, in my room, and she's in hers."

"And when Jack and the girls come home?"

"He puts them to bed."

"It's hard for Jack, isn't it?" Julia asked.

Sarah frowned, and said, "Suppose."

"And hard for the little girls, upsetting for them."

No response.

"Do you remember being five, six, Sarah? What was it like when there was a lot of crying, and you didn't know what was going on?"

"It isn't my fault," Sarah said.

"No, it isn't," Julia said, "but it isn't sensible, is it, to take the line you're taking, and you're a sensible girl, I think."

Sarah suddenly looked down, her head bowed where before it had been held up so proudly. It was impossible to tell if she was upset or merely adopting what she might think of as a thoughtful air. Julia gave her a minute or two, and then said, "I wonder, did you like being a bridesmaid, when your mum and Jack married?"

Sarah looked up, surprised. "What?" she said.

Julia repeated her question.

182

Sarah frowned. "Why do you want to know? What's it got to do with anything?"

"It hasn't," Julia said. "I was just curious, thinking it may have been a great day in your life, a happy time, not like now"

"It was," Sarah said. "My mum was happy again."

"And she isn't now, is she?"

"No."

"Why do you think that is?"

"It's obvious, she can't cope."

"She can if you help her."

"But I'm tired of helping, I told you, it isn't just helping, it's doing everything."

"Yes," Julia said, "yes, I realise. You're on a kind of strike, aren't you? A withdrawal of your labour. So, what would your terms be?"

"What?"

"To end this strike. What would be reasonable, in your opinion?"

Sarah told her. Julia passed the news on. The only puzzle was why Sarah had needed to take such drastic action? Why, instead of staying in bed and letting chaos reign, she hadn't said to Jack that her mum would have to have help. And why this stepfather, Jack, hadn't realised this himself, when surely he'd realised Sarah was standing in for her mother and this was making her not depressed but rebellious. There was no need to imagine Sarah might "do something". She'd already done it.

CHAPTER
SEVEN

The hardest part of sitting on the bench was, Julia found, the coffee that preceded it. The routine was that she and whoever else was sitting that session met in a small room before going into the court. The idea was that they got to know each other just enough to feel comfortable in each other's company, but Julia would have preferred to have gone straight into court, keeping her fellow magistrates at a distance. She felt that during the deliberations that would arise, it would be better not to know what the others did, what their lives were like, what state of health and spirits they were in, all subjects that came up during the preliminary chatting. She didn't like revealing anything about herself either.

But some of those with whom she sat on the bench made determined efforts to be friendly, going so far as to express concern about her pallor. "You're looking pale," this woman, a university lecturer, said, staring straight at Julia. "I'm fine," Julia said, ignoring the implicit request for information. There was then, because of her clipped tone, what her mother would have called "an atmosphere", and afterwards, when they had a particularly tricky case to consider, Julia felt this atmosphere influenced the other woman's decision to go with the opinion of the third member of their panel and not with hers. It was a nasty business: a woman found with twelve wraps of crack cocaine. She looked weak and ill, gripping the ledge of the witness box tightly to hold herself up. Her clothing was minimal. The shortest possible skirt without it not being a skirt at all, tights with holes and tears all the way up her legs, a scoop-necked T-shirt, showing bruises across her throat. There were bruises on her face too, making her look what she obviously was, a victim as much as a dealer.

The woman was so clearly ill that Julia thought it automatic that she would be treated in some sort of hospital. But she had previous convictions for shoplifting and soliciting and the decision to send her for trial was made by the other two with only Julia wanting her instead to be released from custody into a rehabilitation unit. The chairman said it would not be appropriate, and that if she was committed to serve a sentence she would be treated in prison.

"She's had more than a second chance," the chairman said. "She really has to face up to the penalties of disregarding the law."

"But," Julia said, "she's never had a chance. Look at her history. Fostered from the age of two, then a children's home when the fostering failed, then the abuse from the staff member, then —"

The other woman interrupted her. "All this is true, and dreadful," she said, quite gently, "but she could have turned herself round. She made choices, bad ones, which is why she is here, and has been here before."

They were right, the other two, but losing the argument made Julia despair.

"Hiya, Julia," Caroline said, "it's me, how are you?"

How long since they'd met? Julia couldn't remember, but quite a long time.

"I'm in London for two days," Caroline went on, "how about a catch-up? I've lots to tell you. Where shall we meet? Your place?"

"No," Julia said quickly, "I'm having the flat decorated and it's a terrible mess. Why don't we meet in the caff at Tate Modern? I've got to be on the South Bank tomorrow morning, to see someone at ten, so how about having lunch there, one o'clock?"

She wasn't having her flat decorated but she didn't want Caroline there. She hadn't wanted her in her home last time they'd met either. They'd met in the rose garden in Regent's Park, on a lovely sunny day. Julia almost hadn't recognised her old school friend. She'd always been big but now she was enormous, disconcertingly so. Her hair, however, was an improvement, no longer viciously short but grown into a shapely bob. And the sharp intelligent eyes were the same. Caroline gave her an enthusiastic greeting, enfolding her in a bear hug, which Julia slightly recoiled from. They had not been, as girls, used to this kind of embrace, and she found it embarrassing. It was a strange hour they spent, sitting on a bench in the rose garden, with Caroline doing most of the talking in her still strong Scottish accent, unaffected apparently by living in Manchester more than thirty years. They spent

186

a good deal of their time reminiscing about their school-days, seeing who could recall the most names of teachers and classmates. They laughed a lot. People passing by smiled at their apparent happiness, two women, side by side, thoroughly enjoying each other's company. But Julia wasn't sure she was enjoying Caroline's company as much as she must seem to be doing. She felt false, as though she were acting a part. Yet, unlike Sandra, during her primary schooldays, Caroline had been a real friend, with whom she had kept up some contact, however vague. The trouble was that Caroline seemed to be assuming a past intimacy that Julia felt had never really been there, or only briefly.

But now here was Caroline again, and she'd agreed to meet her, as she had done the previous time. What would they talk about? More reminiscing? There were things Caroline knew that Julia felt uneasy about and did not want to have brought up. Last time, she'd managed to steer the conversation away from memories of Elsa, and Carlo, and only hoped she would be able to do this again. She must keep the chat light, and encourage Caroline to talk about herself.

Elsa was sporty, to her father's delight. By the time she was seven she could wield a tennis racket effectively, and she was a good swimmer. Often, Julia was given the job of taking Elsa to the junior clubs Carlo had enrolled her in, a task she resented. She didn't want to be Elsa's chaperone. She wasn't the least bit interested herself in tennis or swimming, and didn't want to have to watch

Elsa bashing balls over a net or ploughing up and down a swimming pool, though when she complained Caroline said she didn't know what she was making a fuss about.

Quite often, Julia slipped out of the tennis club grounds, or the swimming pool building, and wandered about till it was time to collect Elsa. Caroline, told this, didn't approve. Julia was in charge of Elsa and should stay with her. "Oh, don't be so pompous," Julia said, "I'm always back in time." But one evening, she wasn't. She'd left the swimming pool building the moment she'd delivered Elsa instead of waiting till she'd seen her actually in the water, in charge of the coach. But then she got lost. That was the simple truth. She turned left out of the swimming pool instead of right, the usual direction she took when escaping for a while. All the streets to the right were familiar. She could walk them without thinking, and knew how to retrace her steps by another route, arriving back well before time at the pool. But she turned left, walking quickly, defiantly, though no one was watching her. Left led her to a huge, ugly, blackened church. She crossed the street and went down a narrow lane opposite which in turn led to a series of streets where the traffic was heavy. She had to go all the way down the main thoroughfare, off which the smaller streets ran, to find a pedestrian crossing, and once she was across she hesitated over which route to take. In her mind, she was walking in a square and had now done three of the sides of it, so all she had to do was turn left down one of the streets and she'd be back where she started.

But she wasn't. She came out on another main road and didn't recognise it. For nearly a year she'd been taking Elsa to swimming club, always catching the same bus, always getting off at the same stop and walking the same way to the pool. The first time, Carlo had gone with them, pointing out landmarks so she would know the right stop to get off at. It had been easy. But the hinterland of the building the pool was in was unknown to her. It was only the area to the right that she'd become familiar with. And now she was lost. An edge of panic crept into her mind but she pushed it away. All she had to do was retrace her steps exactly. It would take longer than completing the square, but if she ran she would be back in time, just. So she ran, but running along crowded pavements was not a speedy process. She had to dodge round people, and sometimes she banged into them and had to stop and apologise, and then, at the pedestrian crossing she had used before, the green light wouldn't come on though she pressed the button over and over.

The big clock in the entrance to the pool building said ten past seven. She was ten minutes late. Elsa would be standing waiting, clutching her bag, her hair still wet. Surely they would never let her go without there being someone to collect her. Julia prepared her apologies, her excuses, and what she would persuade Elsa to tell her father, or rather what not to tell him. There were still three girls coming out of the area where the changing cubicles were. Julia stopped the last one and asked if Elsa was still getting ready. The girl said she didn't know, so Julia went in herself and went

189

up and down the cubicles. They had half doors, which didn't have locks and swung open easily. All empty. Now that edge of panic, which before she had suppressed, firmly took over. She rushed out of the cubicles to find the coach. He was standing talking to a parent, his back to the doorway into the entrance hall. "Excuse me," Julia said, "I've come to collect Elsa, where is she?"

But Elsa was by that time safely at home. She said she'd "waited and waited" (though really only for a very short time) and when Julia didn't come she just decided she could get home on her own. She knew which bus stop to wait at, which bus to catch, and she had money in her pocket to pay her fare. Bouncing with pride at her own daring and cleverness, she arrived home at the usual time, just as the coach rang to report that she seemed to have left the pool unaccompanied and that her cousin was now here to collect her. The moment he turned to Julia and said Elsa had found her own way home Julia started crying. She was taken to the cafe and given a cup of tea and told not to worry, all was well, nothing awful had happened. Eventually, snivelling, she went to catch the bus home herself, but then while she waited she changed her mind. She didn't want to go home. It wasn't her real home, it never had been. It was just a place where she had been put. People told her how lucky she was to have a cousin who was willing to give her a home, and she knew this was true but the truth didn't make her feel better about it. Iris was kind, but Julia resented this kindness more and more. She'd rather Iris was not kind at all, and her

190

resentment would have an excuse. She hated thinking how much she owed Iris, who didn't even know half the things she'd done, the small, mean things. Some of these, whenever she thought of them, made Julia feel hot and embarrassed, they were so petty. Nothing was worse than having to feel grateful to a cousin she'd consistently wronged.

She had enough money to get herself by bus to the centre of Manchester, where she wandered about staring into shop windows and trying to get up the courage to go into a cafe and have some tea. But by then it was long past the time to be having cups of tea. People were eating their evening meals, the tables were all set with knives and forks. There would be no room for someone just wanting a cup of tea. And she was intimidated anyway, at the thought of walking into any cafe and having to ask for something. She couldn't do it naturally, as though she was always doing it. It seemed a huge step, bold, defiant, and she hadn't the nerve. So she walked round and round the Piccadilly area, slower and slower, and when it began to rain she sheltered in the doorway of a department store, trying to look as if she were waiting for someone.

It got to ten o'clock. She'd never been out on her own so late at night. She'd moved doorways several times, and now she felt there was a man watching her. He was selling newspapers when she arrived but had put what he hadn't sold into a van where he was sitting smoking and staring at her. She left the doorway she'd been sheltering in and walked off rapidly, with purpose. She knew she'd have to go home. There was no alternative. She had no money, except for the bus fare and a little loose change, which she fingered nervously, in her coat pocket, and nowhere else to go. Iris and Carlo would be worried. She felt such prickling shame, thinking of how concerned they would be. What would they have done? Half running by then, along a street she didn't recognise, but hoped was leading her in the general direction she needed to go to catch a bus to get home, she suddenly became convinced that Carlo would ring the police. That was what you had to do when people went missing. But did she count as "missing" yet? She didn't know. Maybe at this moment a police car was cruising around looking for her. The thought terrified her — the police, looking for her.

She reached home a little before midnight, her hair plastered to her head with all the rain that had fallen on it, her clothes and shoes soaked through, not an inch of her dry. She had a key, but her fingers, cold and wet, slipped on the metal as she tried to get it into the lock. Every light in the house was blazing, making it look dramatically different from all the other houses in the road, like in an advert. She bent to pick up the key, and with great care, though she could hardly control her shaking hand, this time she managed to insert it in the lock, and successfully turned it. The next moment, before she had got through the doorway, she heard Iris shout, "Oh! The door! Carlo . . ." and then Carlo came charging down the hallway, followed by Iris, both of them rushing towards her with such force that she flinched and cowered and gibbered sorry, sorry,

192

covering her face with her wet hands, half convinced that they would attack her.

"I'm getting married," Caroline said, as soon as Julia sat down in the cafe. "Ridiculous, isn't it, at my age, but I am. Can you believe it?"

Julia asked all the obvious questions about the husband-to-be, and was rewarded with detailed answers.

"I'm in love," said Caroline, "can you tell? Forty-eight years old and in love — oh God, how silly that sounds, but I am. What I wanted to ask you, Julia," she went on, "was will you be my bridesmaid?"

Julia laughed, loudly. "A bridesmaid, me? Come on Caroline, think about it. I'm forty-eight too, I can't be a bridesmaid."

"A maid of honour, then?"

Julia, still smiling, shook her head.

What she wanted to say, she couldn't say without unnecessarily hurting Caroline's feelings. They had only seen each other perhaps a dozen times since they left school. Surely, in this long interval, Caroline had made other friends? Julia felt a stranger. It was embarrassing, this request. And she had no desire to return to Manchester, or meet Caroline's family again, or her bridegroom.

"Really, Caroline," she said, "I can't, it's not my kind of thing. I'd be useless as a maid of honour."

"Well, then," Caroline said, "come to my wedding anyway, as my oldest chum, for old times' sake, yes?"

193

It was impossible to refuse. The only way out would be to cancel at the last minute, to make something to do with work the excuse. But she'd send flowers, and a good present, and if Caroline was offended by her absence that would put a convenient end to this awkward, late-burning friendship.

I am ashamed, Julia thought. I live constantly with shame and guilt but neither makes me behave better.

Carlo adored Elsa. Julia despised the way he doted on her, the way he cuddled and kissed her and called her his golden girl, his little princess. Sick-making. Fran didn't merit the same attention but didn't seem to resent this because she was her mother's favourite. Julia thought both Carlo and Iris spoiled their girls something rotten. They were hardly ever reprimanded for bad behaviour and, when they were, a few tears from either of them, but especially from Elsa, had an immediate effect. Whatever the punishment threatened, it was withdrawn, and there would be pleas to stop their crying. It was no way, Julia thought, to bring up children. She would like to have seen Elsa in particular given a smack. Thinking this shocked her. She'd never been smacked herself, but on the other hand she had been firmly disciplined, at their age, by her mother. It was too late for Elsa to be disciplined. A stinging smack, just on the legs, would be best.

Julia never voiced this opinion but Elsa seemed to sense it. Ever since the swimming pool incident, she had been wary of Julia, whom she knew she'd got into a great deal of trouble. She was made to say sorry for leaving the swimming pool building on her own but Julia was the one punished. Going on a school trip to Paris was cancelled which made Julia hysterical with rage and disappointment. Elsa could hear her sobbing behind the closed door of her room and when she came out of it her eyes were all red and blotchy.

"Sorry," Elsa whispered, but unfortunately, without realising she was doing it, she smiled.

"You little bitch," Julia said.

"Dad!" Elsa shouted. "I said sorry to Julia and she called me a bitch."

But her father didn't storm up the stairs and make Julia apologise. He just called out to her that she should leave Julia alone and come downstairs, enough was enough.

Now that Julia wasn't trusted to take Elsa to her swimming club any more she found herself alone in the house on Friday evenings. Iris took Elsa, with Fran in tow, and Carlo picked her up. It gave Julia the rare freedom of the house and she relished it, wandering in and out of the different rooms, thinking how she'd change them if they belonged to her. She stayed longest in Carlo and Iris's bedroom, looking at the clutter on Iris's dressing table and trying on some of her jewellery, most of it either gold or glittery and not to Julia's taste at all. Looking at herself in the triple mirror, she saw how wrong the glitzy necklace looked. She didn't have the right complexion or face. Her own silver chain suited her better. Silver, she decided, was nicer than gold.

She'd given up, a long time ago, searching for Reginald's present, beginning to think that Iris had either lost it or discarded it. This didn't seem very likely, but Julia had come to realise that Iris often banished troublesome things from her life, if she could. Reginald's present might have come under that heading, loaded with a pathos Iris could not tolerate. It depended, a little, on what this present had been, which was what Julia had most wanted to know.

When, one Friday evening, she discovered the small, wrapped box, the old excitement gripped her. It hadn't been in the drawers of the dressing table at all. Julia found it only because she was poking about Iris's wardrobe, an old-fashioned thing which had a series of shelves inside to the right of the rail from which the dresses hung. Julia had been fingering a clutch bag covered in sequins. When she opened it there was the tiny package, just as she remembered it. Her hands trembled as she undid the faded ribbon and unwrapped the flimsy paper.

Her disappointment was huge. She'd invested Reginald's present with such significance, imagining it to be something glamorous, something unique, though she'd never been able to decide what that would be. And there it was, a silver bracelet, quite ordinary. It was hardly worth taking, but she took it, contemptuously. She didn't care if Iris discovered it was missing. Back in her own room, she hid the bracelet in the toe of one of her winter boots. She'd think about what to do with it later. There was a half-formed plan in her mind, involving Elsa, but it needed thinking about carefully, to achieve maximum effect.

Julia walked with her friend over the Millennium Bridge towards St Paul's, where she was going to catch a bus. By then, Julia had begun to feel less distanced from Caroline, with some of the old connection emerging after all. They walked slowly, pausing in the middle of the bridge to look down the river, ruffled today by a sharp wind from the east.

"Do you see much of the Annovazzis?" Caroline asked. "Elsa? Fran? You were so mean to Elsa, weren't you? I could never understand it. She was such a pathetic girl, all eager to please you. Until the car accident, well, the *almost* accident. Do you remember?"

"I don't think I want to," Julia said.

She'd just passed her test, the day of her seventeenth birthday. Elsa was in the back of the car, Caroline in front, beside Julia. Caroline had passed her own test two months before, and was there to offer support, though Julia was not admitting to nerves. They'd driven sedately along the quiet road where the Annovazzis lived, and onto the busier main road.

"Where shall we go?" Julia asked. "Elsa? Where do you want to go?"

She hadn't wanted Elsa to be in the car at all but it was a condition of being allowed to have Iris's car, a treat for Elsa who had just recovered from flu.

"The seaside!" Elsa shouted. Any seaside was miles and miles away.

"OK," Julia said.

Caroline laughed. "You must be joking," she said, but Julia turned onto the slip road for the motorway. "Steady on," Caroline said, "I don't think you're ready for the motorway yet."

They were soon doing seventy miles an hour. Caroline pointed this out to Julia, urging her to slow down, but Elsa, wildly excited, yelled, "Faster, faster," laughing and bouncing up and down in her seat. "Seaside, here we come!" Julia shouted. The accident, when it happened, wasn't her fault. She had slowed down after they left the motorway and were on an A-road heading for Southport, and then she'd mistakenly taken a B-road and was lost, and regretting the whole trip. The accident was caused by a tractor driven by a man who didn't seem to have gauged the width of the equipment he was pulling behind the tractor. It had spokes sticking out of it, metal prongs, and as he passed Julia, who had sensibly pulled into the side, one of these prongs pierced, the side-back window of the car and shattered the glass, showering Elsa with the fragments. Elsa wasn't hurt, only shocked, but returning home with Elsa still whimpering and the window smashed was likely, Julia knew, to send Carlo mad with worry about what could have happened. It would be no good saying it hadn't been her fault, and that the tractor driver had fully admitted it was his fault, and given her all his details for insurance purposes. Explanations, justifications, excuses — they'd all be no good. Elsa was bound to report that they'd been going really fast, even if they hadn't been at the time of the accident, and of course she'd say they'd been on their way to the seaside, which would make Carlo erupt. Julia had been trusted with the precious car and the even more precious Elsa and had risked both with her dangerous and absurd attempted drive to the sea.

The penalties were severe. Grounded for a month, and never allowed to have Iris's car on her own again. But the excitement, the thrill, stayed with Julia, compensating for the aftermath. Whenever she recalled the speed on the motorway, her heart raced, and she had to shut her eyes to relive the experience all over again. Even the car window exploding, and the sight in her mirror of Elsa shielding her head from the glass shards flying in her direction, excited at the same time as frightened her. It was Elsa who had nightmares, not Julia.

Caroline, to Julia's irritation, was still reminiscing. "What about their parents, how are they? They were such nice people. And the grandmother, how about her? I forget her name. She was quite a presence, wasn't she?" Julia said yes, Aunt Maureen had been a presence.

The last time Julia had visited her, Aunt Maureen was thought by Iris to be losing her memory. But Maureen told Julia that if she had Alzheimer's (which she said she did not) nothing really could be done about it. "Look at your grandfather," she said to Julia, "now *he* had Alzheimer's, though it wasn't called that then. Remember him?"

Julia said how could she remember him when he had died before she was born. Both her grandfathers had, and one of her grandmothers. The only grandparent she had a vague recollection of was her father's mother. She lived in a farmhouse near Alston, in the Pennines, and she had hens, which Julia remembered more clearly than her grandmother.

"Tell me about him," she said to Maureen, a request which led to the pulling out of photograph albums and a happy hour (from Aunt Maureen's point of view) of looking at people now dead and giving summaries of their faults.

"The male line in my family has died out," Aunt Maureen declared, as she neared the end of the last volume. "I had a daughter and your mother had a daughter, and that's it."

"But," said Julia, "even if Iris and I had brothers the male line wouldn't have carried on. It was your father, the grandfather with Alzheimer's, who ended the male line by not having sons."

"Oh, it's the same thing," Aunt Maureen said crossly.

One of the photographs of her mother, unusually smart and dressed up, reminded Julia, that day, of her mother's visit to the solicitor all those years ago. It wasn't that Julia had forgotten about it but that anything to do with her mother, any memory, was hard for her to deal with. She had trained herself for a very long time not to conjure up images of her mother. They only distressed her. More than that, they frightened her

200

because instead of seeming comfortably solid and reassuring, proof that her mother had existed and loved her, they were insubstantial, lacking all authenticity. And the memory of the day her mother dressed up to go and see a solicitor was particularly troubling. Julia could see her, as she could so often "see" some episode in her past, but she couldn't put herself in the frame even though she knew she had been in it. She remembered, though, her mother being unlike herself, being nervous and agitated and Aunt Maureen attempting to give her confidence, an unusual state of affairs. When her mother returned, she was abstracted. She couldn't, Julia suddenly recalled, eat the cakes.

She said this out loud. "Mum couldn't eat the cakes," she said. The final album was still open at a photograph of her mother taken at Iris's wedding to Reginald.

"What are you talking about?" Aunt Maureen asked. "Cakes? What cakes?"

"The ones you and I made that day, the day Mum had to go and see a solicitor."

"This is a photograph of your mum at Iris's wedding — there's no cake in it."

"I know that," Julia said, "I'm not talking about the photograph itself. It's just that I suddenly remembered about the promise you made, ages ago, to tell me about the visit to the lawyer, when Mum was all dressed up like she was in this photo."

"It was a wedding," Aunt Maureen said, "of course she was dressed up."

Julia knew what she was going to say next, and she did.

"I can't remember anything anyway," Aunt Maureen said, giving a melodramatic sigh, and passing a hand over her eyes, "my memory has gone entirely, so it's no use bothering me."

"That's a shame," Julia said, "I'll have to find out some other way."

"Find out what?" Aunt Maureen said. "There's nothing to find out. You're always suspecting things, Julia."

"Yes, I am," Julia said, "and I'm usually right. Mum went to see a solicitor that time because something was wrong. It was to do with money, and another woman, wasn't it?" She'd made the last bit up, a wild guess which, if it were wrong, would be laughed at by Aunt Maureen.

"Who told you?" Aunt Maureen said, suddenly no longer concentrating on being vague.

"I can't remember," Julia said, playing her aunt's own game.

"You can't trust anyone any more," Aunt Maureen said, "dragging things up, years later, smearing the dead. Your mother was innocent as a lamb."

This made Julia smile it was such an unlikely analogy. There'd been nothing lamb-like about her mother. But her smile annoyed Aunt Maureen, and annoyance made her talk. It was a simple enough tale, one Julia had come across often enough in her work. Her father had committed bigamy when he married her mother, nothing more heinous than that. He'd secretly married a girl Aunt Maureen quaintly described as "a buxom wench" when he was eighteen, and then he'd left her and moved away to Manchester where he met Julia's mother and "married" her. Only after his death did Julia's mother find out about his first marriage.

There had been a report in the newspapers about the accident that killed Julia's father, with a photograph of him taken with his wife and child. The first wife, the real wife, saw it, and was shocked. As far as she was concerned, her husband had simply vanished years ago. She didn't know what had happened to him, and thought he might be dead. But she rang up the newspaper, who sent a reporter to see her, and she told this man her story, producing her marriage certificate. It was, said Aunt Maureen, shown to Julia's mother, who was incredulous, but obliged to believe the evidence before her. There was then a battle over the insurance money. The first wife claimed it, and started legal proceedings to get it. She claimed the house Julia and her mother were living in, too. The whole business dragged on and on for years, and the day Julia remembered was the day her mother went to hear the final outcome from the solicitor.

There was another embrace from Caroline before they parted. This time Julia felt more comfortable about it. She thought she might even go to her old friend's wedding, though weddings in her life had never been entirely happy experiences. Standing, waiting for the number 4 bus, she looked up at St Paul's and tried to remember the churches where she had attended weddings. Not many. But she could recall the church where Iris had married Reginald. She could see that church clearly in her mind's eye, as she could see everything about that day. When she got on the bus, her head was full of it.

Elsa suddenly shot up in height when she was nearly nine, a growth spurt viewed with alarm by her father. "She's going to be a giantess," he exclaimed, and made poor jokes about limiting her food so that she wouldn't grow any taller. Her hair changed too. She could no longer be described as his golden girl because the gold had dulled to a light, undistinguished brown. The final disaster was that Elsa needed spectacles. Carlo didn't care for girls in glasses.

Julia observed all these changes in Elsa, and how they affected Carlo, but felt no sympathy for the girl who had to cope with them. Instead, she felt smug. She herself was not tall, and her hair was a rich dark brown, and she didn't need specs. She was aware that she now compared favourably with Elsa, though she realised that the age gap between them made any comparison false. All the same, she, in that last year she lived with the Annovazzis, constantly drew attention to what were regarded as Elsa's new defects, addressing her as beanpole, and wondering aloud if she needed a white stick. This sniping was cruel, and she knew it was cruel, but she couldn't restrain herself. There had always been in her this meanness which every now and again got out of control.

204

She did nothing about the silver bracelet she'd stolen from Iris's drawer. She'd thought of planting it somehow on Elsa, but realised this would never work. Elsa, discovering it, would simply be puzzled, and take it to her mother saying, look what I found in my sock drawer, where did it come from? Iris would know she was innocent of having taken it. It was no good either waiting for Iris to miss Reginald's present and start searching for it because she hadn't realised it had gone, and might never do so. Stealing it had been stupid, but Julia didn't replace it, hoping she would suddenly see a way of putting it to use.

It was easier and more effective to sabotage anything Elsa did. She did this very, very carefully, never going too far. She removed things from Elsa's school bag, things Elsa had packed neatly the night before, and put them in the living room under a cushion or beneath the television, in the shelf that held the video. Elsa would come home from school upset because she'd got a detention after failing to hand in the homework due. She was absolutely certain she'd put the exercise book in her bag, but it hadn't been there. Carlo would say she was getting careless, the book must be somewhere, and they would all start looking for it, and when it was found Elsa would be left without any defence. No one believed she had ever placed the book in her bag.

This kind of thing was trivial but, to Julia, immensely satisfying. It was wrong, and she knew it was wrong, but nobody was really harmed, not even Elsa. There were other petty pieces of mischief she carried out, damaging to Elsa, but it was not until she started lying to Carlo that she began to step over a line she had always assured herself was there.

Julia went to Aunt Maureen's funeral, a small affair, only Iris and her family, some elderly cousins, some neighbours, no more than twenty-odd people in the church. Aunt Maureen, Julia reflected, counting the heads, would have been offended by such a turnout. They were mostly dressed in black, though, which would've mollified her. And the older women wore hats, as Julia herself did. It was her magistrate's hat, never worn. She'd bought it recently, when first appointed to the bench, under the misapprehension that women JPs had to wear a hat. She had suffered such embarrassment discovering no hat was required and she was thought odd to be wearing one, as though a parody of a female magistrate.

There was quite a lot to clear out of Aunt Maureen's house, where she'd lived for almost fifty years, managing to avoid being moved into a home, though it had been a close-run thing the last eighteen months. Julia stayed to help. "Some of all this stuff might be your mother's," Iris said. "Mum took a lot of things to keep for you, remember?" Julia didn't remember. The time of her mother's death had become swallowed in a fog that had never really lifted, and she'd come to believe she never wanted it to. But she said she'd help, she'd share the job of clearing out her aunt's house. She stayed with Iris for three days after the funeral, going over each day to her aunt's old house. The furniture went first, collected by a charity Iris had contacted, and then the clothes and shoes and bags, all bundled into bin liners and taken to an Oxfam shop. Iris didn't want any of them, not even the excellent quality, fairly recently purchased cashmere cardigans. "It was ridiculous," Iris said, half laughing, "Mum going on buying these things when she hardly went out and had plenty anyway, but she loved shopping." As you do, Julia thought, but did not say. She'd never worked out what the relationship between Iris and her mother had been. Yes, they were "close" but was it a stifling closeness, or an easy, relaxed one, and had it changed during Aunt Maureen's last years? Iris didn't seem too upset by her mother's death. There were no tears, no betrayal of any emotion as she dealt with her mother's belongings.

The drawers were the problem. Not the drawers with clothes or linen in them, but the ones in the bureau in the sitting room, and in the dressing table in the bedroom. They were both crammed with papers of various sorts and each item would have to be looked at in case they included unpaid bills or bank details or investments. Julia settled down to the dressing-table drawers, three of them (but two full of jewellery). It was raining, and the wind was bashing the rain against the windows, just like it had done on the morning of Iris's first wedding. The memory depressed her. She wondered if Iris was remembering it. The house felt cold, though it was June, so she put down her shivers to the chilly atmosphere, but knew that had nothing to do with them. She didn't like this house, she never had done. Pressing in upon her was a threat. She was threatening herself. I dare you, confess, she said in her head. Go on, do it, now. This is your chance. How many years is it? So many. Get rid of it, don't let it linger there forever, niggling away every time the behaviour of some child touches it. But then she shook her head. There was nothing to confess. No, that was not it. There *was* something she ought to tell Iris but telling it would do no good. It would do harm. The only good it would do would be to herself. She might, through confessing, rid herself of this worry which had embedded itself all these years in her mind. When it surfaced, it was like a discordant note being struck. It made her wince, and then it was gone.

"Julia," Iris called up the stairs, "come and look at this."

CHAPTER
EIGHT

Photographs. Just two, both black and white, one of them torn across the top right-hand corner. They seemed, at first glance, to be the same, except for the tear in one of them. "That," said Iris, "is your father. But the woman he's got his arm round is not your mother. It must be 'her'." There was no mistaking how Iris said "her". Julia made no comment. She held the snapshots up to the light and scrutinised them, as though the very action of doing this might reveal something. She wasn't sure if she recognised the young man in the picture as her father. Could be, but she couldn't say for certain, though Iris seemed able to. The woman she definitely had never seen. The phrase "buxom wench" sprang ludicrously into her mind. Her father (allegedly) with his arm round Aunt Maureen's "buxom wench".

She hadn't known that Iris knew about the buxom wench, but she realised she should have guessed. Aunt Maureen wouldn't have been able to keep the information to herself forever, and who better to astound than her own daughter. "It was a long time ago," Iris said, in her most sympathetic tone. Julia thought this must mean that she was looking shocked at being presented with these photographs, so she smiled at Iris and said it was indeed a long time ago and not really all that exciting. But Iris was looking at her, still, with concern.

"I'm sure he loved your mum, Julia," she said. "I mean, he was only a teenager when he . . . when . . . I mean, that's what used to happen."

"I know," Julia said, "it doesn't bother me." She tried to be brisk. "What bothers me," she said, "is how did your mother come to have these snaps?"

"I expect they were among *your* mum's things," Iris said.

Julia raised her eyebrows. "I don't think so," she said, "I don't think my mum would've kept a picture of my father with his buxom wench. She'd have destroyed it, hated it."

"Well," Iris said, "I don't know how it came into my mother's possession, unless someone sent it to her, because she was your mum's sister."

"What would've been the point?" Julia said. "How would anyone have known her address? And why didn't *she* either give it to my mum, or tear it up herself?"

There were no answers. They spent the rest of that day finishing off the paper stuff, the letters and bills (all ticked, with "paid" scribbled across them) and statements and policies. It had looked overwhelming and untidy, but in fact there was some sort of order. There were no more discoveries to intrigue. Julia took the two little photographs, slipping them into her bag. "Might as well keep them," she said to Iris, "they've lasted this long." Iris nodded, pretended to be

210

uninterested, but Julia saw in her expression the same sort of "you-don't-fool-me" look that Aunt Maureen's face used to show in direct contradiction to something she was appearing to agree with. But Iris was not her mother. She was kinder, she would say no more, Julia knew.

It occurred to Julia, when she lay awake in her old room in the Annovazzis' house, that she might have a half-sibling somewhere. What she couldn't decide was whether she would like to find out and, if it were true, meet this half-sibling. And that's when the thought of her mother's pain became distressing, as such thoughts always did. Stupid, self-indulgent distress she had tried so hard, and for so long, to eradicate from her mind. Her mother had suffered the humiliation. She had borne it, and now she was dead, and this pain was long since over. To imagine it, to empathise to such a degree that it was being suffered all over again was not just stupid but masochistic. It had to be controlled, dealt with, this obsession with a tiny fragment of the past.

But Julia thought she would keep the photographs.

The word "blackmail" was not used, but it was clear it was implied. A ten-year-old girl had been found to be consistently exerting pressure on other children to give her money. She used threats and carried them out. Those who did not pay had books stolen, paint poured over clothes, shoes filled with mud. All relatively minor acts, but hurtful to the children involved. It was felt by the girls' teachers that any minute worse could happen, that some assault would take place, and so the school was not ignoring these signs of real trouble brewing. The mother had been contacted and said she didn't care what the school did with Olivia, it was up to them.

Olivia fitted the role. Julia could see how the girl could intimidate merely by her physical presence. She was large, not in the sense of height alone but all over. Square-shouldered, she had heavy-looking arms and legs, and her torso was broad though there were no visible signs of early puberty. Probably, Julia thought, Olivia was overweight but this weight did not look like flab. It looked like muscle. There was the same indication of strength in the neck, quite unlike a ten-year-old child's neck. Olivia jutted her chin out and her neck tensed. The face, though, was at odds with the body. It was surprisingly delicate, the features small, the complexion good. Pale, but with some healthy colour in the cheeks. It was as though the wrong head had been put on the body.

Julia asked Olivia if she knew why she was here. Olivia said yes, she did, and it was unfair, she'd done nothing, they were all liars, they couldn't prove anything . . . There was a lot more Olivia had to say, all of it with passion. She was going to stand up for herself, she said, and no one could stop her. Julia said no one wanted to stop her.

"I want to hear your version of what's been happening," she said. "Let's start with pouring red paint over Emily Green's exercise books. Why did you do that?"

"She deserved it," Olivia said, "after what she did to me."

"And what did she do to you?"

"I can't tell you."

"Why is that?"

"Because I don't want to. It's got nothing to do with anything."

"Oh, come on, Olivia," Julia said, "it has everything to do with why you poured the paint. You didn't just do it for fun, did you? Or did you?" Olivia smiled, a strange smile, secretive, and said nothing.

Emily Green was on record as claiming that Olivia threatened to ruin her exercise books, with all the work in them, if she did not give her one pound. Emily said she hadn't got a pound. Olivia called her a liar. She said Emily had plenty of money, and she had a mobile phone too. A pound wasn't much, she could spare it. It turned out Emily had already given Olivia a pound the week before, to prevent her cutting the sleeves of her jacket off. Olivia had been nice to her afterwards, but when Emily got home and had to explain the missing money she had cried and told her mother what had happened. Her mother wanted to go to the school and report Olivia's behaviour but Emily begged her not to, but her mother wouldn't agree.

All for one pound, one coin. Julia wondered if this modest target meant Olivia was smart, and knew it was more likely to be reached, or the amount just popped into her head, not thought out at all. Almost for fun, to see the reaction. But either way, she had carried out her threat, and the other threats, to other girls. Emily, though, was the only one to have parted with the money. There had been nothing subtle about Olivia's approach, no attempt at concealment. Three other girls saw her pick up the paint, in its plastic bottle, and deliberately squeeze it all over every page of Emily's neat writing so that the work was beyond rescue.

It seemed a small act of vandalism, but of course it was what might follow on from it that mattered. Paint poured onto a book was no great disaster. But then, later, Olivia older, what? Acid? Thrown into a face? Julia thought about this remote possibility and then put it out of her mind. A sense of proportion was needed.

"Olivia," she said, "what did you want the money for?"

"To spend," Olivia said.

"Yes, obviously, but on what? What can a pound buy that you want?"

"It's money," Olivia said. "I want some money. I haven't got any money and I just want some and Emily is spoiled, she always has new things. It isn't fair."

"No," said Julia, "it isn't, but how is it fair to pour paint over someone's book, because they won't give you money? That isn't fair, is it?"

She was only ten. What she'd done was so silly and clumsy it made Julia tired just to think about. Already, at her tender age, to feel such raw envy and sense of injustice, that she was a "have-not" surrounded by "haves". Julia hardly dared look at the notes again, didn't want reminding of Olivia's address, of her mother's record, of the rapid succession of male partners in her household. None of the details provided any justification for Olivia's pathetic attempt to extort money, but they did provide something that could be

214

said to offer an explanation. It was not fair. Life was not fair, not in any way at all. This painful realisation had to be made by the child. Life is not fair. In any way.

It was time to move again. Every five years, Julia moved house, each time getting a little nearer living where she wanted to live in the kind of house she wanted to own. It was always hard to move because she feared the inevitable sense of displacement which made her nervous and distracted and affected her work. Her colleagues never needed to be told she was in the process of moving house. All the signs were there, and they teased her about it. She was not an easy person to tease, but they persevered, and smirked when they got a result.

This time, she actually *was* moving to a house, and not to another flat. The price she was paying scared her, but thanks to careful saving and modest living, plus getting more than she dared to hope from the sale of the previous flat (sold at the top of the market in 2007) she could manage it. Without the money she'd inherited, of course, she would never have been able to buy the tiny flat that started her off nearly thirty years ago. The insurance money. The money she had never known came from insurance. She was against inherited wealth but she had accepted what her mother left her, substantially increased by her uncle's wise investment. It briefly crossed her mind to give it to Amnesty International, but only very briefly. She rationalised this decision by arguing with herself that though inherited wealth was unfair life had been unfair to herself. Taking the money balanced having first her father then her mother taken from her while she was so young. She, perhaps fortunately, was never called upon to voice all this to any other person.

Not even Andrew. She already had her first flat when she met Andrew. He didn't own any property, living as he did with two other final-year medical students. He was impressed when eventually Julia revealed she owned her one-bedroom flat in Queen's Park, near the park itself. She had a mortgage, but a light one. Andrew was delighted because he had no chance himself of being able to buy, and so moving into Julia's flat when they were married, as soon they would be, solved that problem. But it remained Julia's flat. When Andrew started working, he expected to contribute to the mortgage, and have his name on it, but Julia said no. It was her flat. She would continue to pay the mortgage herself and Andrew could pay the bills, or most of them.

It made the divorce, when it came (rather rapidly), simpler. Julia sold that flat immediately. She didn't want to live where Andrew had lived. She couldn't get out of the place quick enough, and in fact rented somewhere for six months so that she didn't have to stay there while it was up for sale. The marriage was a mistake, her mistake rather than Andrew's. He was a perfectly agreeable, good-looking, kind man, but what Julia had overlooked was his lack of interest in anyone except himself (and, of course, for a while, Julia). He became the sort of doctor who was interested in the various diseases his patients brought to his attention but not in the patients themselves. He lacked curiosity, whereas Julia seethed with it. Her own job made no sense to him. She couldn't come home to tell him about the children she saw because he had no interest in them, and was astonished that she thought all the time about whoever she was currently assessing.

Julia never shared her flat again, though she had affairs. Her flat was hers. She worried more about keeping it than about keeping lovers, which told her something. She knew this fierce protection of her property was odd, but put it down to feeling nothing belonged to her once her mother died. She was always just a lodger and hated being in that situation. It was clear to her that property represented stability. People couldn't be depended upon but property could. Again, this skewed view of life was not one she shared with other people, so it was never challenged.

This, she hoped, would be her final move, or as final as she realistically thought it would be. The house was not perfect, but perfection would always, she reckoned, be out of her reach because of the sheer cost. The house she now bought was in itself, if not the road in which it was situated, pretty well perfect: an end-of-terrace house, with good windows, so lots of light even on dark days, and a small garden facing south-west. The rooms were small but could easily be knocked through, leaving her with only two bedrooms and one living room/kitchen, which was fine. Even though it was a Georgian house, some clever previous owner had managed to get permission to install solar panels in the roof.

The part of moving Julia hated most, unsurprisingly, was the packing up. She couldn't bring herself to hire people to do it for her, not because of the cost but because she had a rule that every time she moved she must carefully sort through all her belongings and take the opportunity to discard things she no longer needed or wanted. It was a good rule. It meant she started off in the new place uncluttered, constantly streamlining her existence. But it was time-consuming, sitting herself down to go through every drawer and cupboard, though none of these were in the state Aunt Maureen's had been.

Every time, she always found the present she'd stolen from Iris. Every time, she'd feel the same quick-changing emotions: shame, guilt, embarrassment, and then irritation with herself for experiencing these feelings. It was not that she did not know why she kept the pathetic thing. She knew only too well. It had become a symbol of defiance, reminding her how near she had been to a very different sort of life. Always she thought about returning it to Iris. Easy enough to slip it into a drawer. But it wasn't what she thought of doing. She thought about taking it to Iris and saying she was sorry she had stolen Reginald's present, and that she was also sorry she had, at one time, stolen money, and had been cruel to Elsa, and most of all that she was sorry, all these years later, that she had tipped up baby Reggie's pram and he'd bumped his head.

She wouldn't say any of that, of course. Such a confession would be an indulgence. But she did, each time she sorted out her possessions and packed them up, wonder how Iris would react if she did confess. Iris being Iris, what would she be likely to say? "Oh, don't worry, it was a long time ago"? Quite possibly. Or, Iris being Iris, and rather slow on the uptake sometimes, might just smile vaguely and say nothing at all. But there was another scenario in Julia's mind, lurking there: Iris might not react true to character. She might be appalled and furious, especially about the tipping of the pram. A new Iris might rise up, one who — but no. Julia couldn't make this work. Iris was too old now to become angry and revengeful after a lifetime of being mild and endlessly forgiving.

There was one remaining alternative response: Iris had always known. She'd known, and chosen not to know, in the sense of choosing not to acknowledge or voice her suspicions because — this would be very Iris — it would "do no good". Iris had trained herself early in life not to live in the past. She deliberately shut it out, good or bad, people and events, concentrating always on the future. Once, as a teenager, Julia had come out with phrases her history teacher had used: we are our past, it is what made us who we are, we can't know ourselves without knowing our past, etc. All of it banal, but deeply attractive to Julia then, feeling as she did that she was robbed of her own past. Iris had laughed. "Oh dear," she said, "what a nonsense. The past is gone, Julia, that's all that matters, pet."

Iris wouldn't give the time of day (one of her favourite expressions) to confessions about the past.

She believed each day was truly a clean sheet, an attitude to life which had stood her in good stead but which Julia was never able to adopt. For her, everything in her past was loaded with significance. She couldn't rid herself of it. She couldn't throw Reginald's present away nor give it to Iris. So once more she packed it into a wooden jewellery box, with other bits of jewellery. Someone — Elsa? — would find it after she was dead and never for one moment appreciate its history. They — Elsa? Fran? — would be surprised, when they saw the silver bracelet. Not Cousin Julia's thing, they would think. Never seen her wear it. It's too girlish for her taste. She wouldn't like it, wouldn't have bought it herself, so who gave it to her?

One of the girls might keep it, perhaps wear it, though they were a bit old for such a delicate ripple of silver. Their daughters, then, if either of them had daughters. Pointless to speculate which one might take it, but speculate she did.

There were two moves: one personal, the move from flat to house; one for work, because the centre was being relocated (that was the term used in the official letter — "we are to be relocated"). Julia imagined a giant crane lifting up the whole building with everyone inside it, then swinging dangerously in the air until a site was decided upon. The spot chosen for this relocation seemed to her a bad one. Housed in its previous premises, the centre had looked modestly attractive, with a little bit of grass in front of it, and flower tubs lined up along the side wall, and a white-painted entrance hall. No child coming to it could possibly be frightened or intimidated. Great efforts were made to make the place welcoming and informal and not at all clinical, with lots of colourful posters on the walls and a cheerful brightly patterned rug on the floor of the waiting room, where there were two comfortable old sofas and a table with comics as well as magazines scattered over it.

But these premises had never been owned. They were rented, and as the rent rose the council couldn't afford them. There was space in a building it did own, and the decision was made to move the centre there. It was the work that went on inside it that mattered, the council said, not the rooms themselves. They didn't matter. They could be freshly decorated — new paint was allowed — and would look the same as the old rooms. Wrong. Julia wasn't quite sure from the actual address what the new workplace would be like, though she had her suspicions, but when she arrived there, together with her colleagues, the week before the relocation, she was quite shocked. The centre was now sandwiched between a bank, with flats above it, and a carpet warehouse, also with flats above. The centre itself was on the third floor of the block it was in, with a jobcentre beneath it. The stone steps from the street door up to the other floors were clean, the walls too, but there was very little light after the first turn of the stairs so that anyone approaching the third floor did so in an atmosphere of gloom. They were all appalled, but the best had to be made of it. Once inside, things improved slightly. The council had kept its word. Every room was newly painted, in the colours chosen, and the furniture from the old place had been brought over, with some new cushions added.

The problem, though, was always going to be getting children through that doorway and up those stairs without depressing and worrying them from the start. They would come, with their parents or social worker, along the thundering high road, and stare up at the vast Edwardian buildings and feel at once overwhelmed. It could be argued that children don't notice architecture, but they do notice size and draw conclusions from it. Imposing buildings, their exterior face none too clean, could strike some children dumb. And children were highly susceptible to atmosphere. Hearing their shoes ring out on the stone stairs would scare some of them. They would arrive tense and nervous even if they had been neither to begin with, and precious time would have to be spent making them relax. Then there was the additional problem of who else used the street door. The jobcentre was busy, with a constant stream, mainly of men, coming and going.

They all, the people who were going to work here, knew this, so there was little discussion. It was suggested that maybe there could be some sort of partition put up in the entrance hall so that the entry to the centre was separate from the jobcentre's, but even if that were agreed to by the council it still left the problem of the gloomy stairs, and little could be done about that. Julia went into the room allocated to her and closed the door.

* * *

Carlo took her to the appointment, not Iris. He wore his best suit and a pristine white shirt with a dark blue tie. Julia had been told to wear her school uniform, and to make sure her shoes were clean. Nobody told her who exactly this appointment was with, what sort of person he was, just that he was "a sort of doctor". "I'm not ill," Julia said, "I don't need to see a doctor," to which the reply was that this doctor was not that sort of doctor, not a medical doctor, just someone who would talk to her, and help her. "I don't need help," Julia said, "and I'm not going."

She had burned holes in the wooden surround of the fire-place. There was a real fire in the fireplace, and she'd been sitting in front of it, staring at the flames, and poking the logs with a poker. Everyone was out, which ought to have made her happy but she was not happy. She should have been with Caroline, going to see a film, but Carlo had been so furious with her that he'd said she couldn't go anywhere the whole weekend. He'd said she was getting out of control. "Out of control" meant staying out later than ten o'clock, banging doors so hard he said she'd damaged the hinges, swearing, looking a mess, and terrorising Elsa. She'd laughed at that last feeble accusation — "terrorise" indeed! It was ridiculous. All she'd done was send Elsa anonymous cards picturing evil-faced men with a balloon coming out of their mouths saying "Coming to get you". Just an obvious joke.

The poker was a long metal one, with a brass handle. Idly, Julia watched the tip of it turn red hot in the fire, and then she lifted it high, admiring the strong, fierce glow. Then, slowly, she swung the poker to the left and let it hover near the wood. She let it touch the wood. The sizzling was deeply satisfying, and so was the smoking black hole that emerged. She did another hole below, and then more, reheating the poker each time, and soon she had the letter E branded on the wood, scarring it irrevocably. Then she went to bed, half laughing, in a gasping sort of way at what she'd done, and half appalled. She'd been going to brand the whole of Elsa's name there but it would have taken too long.

Now there she was, in the car, on the way to the mysterious appointment with Carlo, who kept clearing his throat, as though in preparation for making an announcement that never came. Julia had decided not to speak to him. He'd forced her to come, but he couldn't force her to talk. She kept her eyes focused on the road ahead and ignored every attempt made by Carlo to chat. After ten minutes, he lapsed into silence and more throat-clearing, and then, when they were nearly at their destination, he said, "This is for your own good, Julia. You need to see someone. Someone needs to find out what's causing all this behaviour, and sort it out." Julia was tempted to ask what he meant by "this behaviour", but she wasn't going to weaken and talk, and argue about it. They had already had the row about the burning of the wood, and she'd apologised.

Carlo parked in the car park in front of the building. Julia thought about refusing to get out but then decided that kind of obstinacy might lead to him pulling her out forcefully. There was a tension in his attitude to her that made her wary, though she had never felt wary of Carlo before. He led the way, but it soon turned out that he didn't know where he was going. He stood in the entrance hall, looking about him, adjusting his tie nervously, and in the end had to knock on a door labelled "Reception". The door opened suddenly and a woman stood there. "Yes?" she said, sounding annoyed to be interrupted. Carlo said he had an appointment for Julia — he gestured towards her — and named a Mr Someone. "Up the stairs," the woman said, "first floor, second door on the right."

Again, Julia contemplated refusing to obey. The woman receptionist was still standing in the doorway, looking at her. It didn't seem worth the fuss there would surely be if she refused to go up the stairs. Carlo was already climbing them, in a hurry to keep the appointment, and clearly not wanting to remain under the scrutiny of this unfriendly, staring woman. Julia went as slowly as she could, plod, plod, head down. The stairs were wooden, uncarpeted, and the noise of Carlo's shoes was loud. She went up on tiptoe herself, holding on to the iron banister rail which was immensely cold to her touch. Carlo was at the first floor quickly, and stood waiting for her. "There's nothing to be frightened of," he whispered. Julia smiled, a great broad smile, lips clamped together, to show him it was laughable for him to imagine she was in the least frightened — resentful, yes; embarrassed, yes; but frightened, no. She hoped he got the message.

Another closed door, with a card fitted into a slot above the doorknob. This time, when Carlo knocked, a man's voice, a deep voice, shouted, "Come in!" They went in. A man, quite an old man, Julia reckoned, got up from behind a desk and held his hand out. "John Messenger," he said. Carlo shook his hand, seeming surprised, Julia thought, to be offered it. She wondered if her own hand was going to be shaken too. It felt hot and sweaty at this thought. But she got a smile instead. "Hello, Julia," John Messenger said, and she said hello back but didn't smile.

They were told to sit down on the chairs to the right of the desk, which Julia thought odd. They were obliged to turn to look at John Messenger. She'd rather have been facing him directly. He asked Carlo some questions, all of them factual, and Julia could tell he knew the answers anyway. He had a sheet of paper in front of him, and kept looking at it, as Carlo talked, nodding his head. Julia stopped turning to look at him. She studied the picture on the wall opposite. It was of fields, yellow and green fields, with hills in the background. She thought it was a watercolour but couldn't be sure. Then she studied the floor. It was linoleum of some sort, a beige colour, quite cracked in some places. It looked as though it could do with a good scrub. She imagined being on her knees, scrubbing it, a pail of hot, soapy water at her side, and a scrubbing brush in her hand. A metal pail . . .

Carlo was standing up. He shook hands with this John Messenger again, and patted Julia on the shoulder as he said, "See you in a minute," and left the room. Julia felt herself stiffen. She waited. John Messenger waited. The silence extended itself until it began to

226

seem like a test. Who would break it first? Not I, thought Julia, not I, said the sparrow. She hoped she would be asked what she was thinking of and she could say a sparrow.

"Well, Julia," John Messenger said, "do you have anything you'd like to tell me?"

Julia shook her head.

"Nothing at all?"

She shook it again.

"How about," John Messenger said, "telling me what you can remember about your father?"

"I don't remember anything," Julia said quickly. Too quickly. She sensed immediately that John Messenger now had the advantage.

"You were — let me see — almost five when he died, and you're sixteen now, so it's only eleven years ago."

Julia did not react. She'd made one mistake, and was not going to make another.

"No memories at all? No fleeting impressions? The sound of his voice, perhaps? No little things? You've blanked him out, perhaps?"

"No," Julia said, before she could stop herself.

"He has just disappeared from your memory then?"

"Yes," Julia said.

John Messenger wrote something down. "Do you think of Carlo as a stepfather?" he asked, his tone of voice gentle, as though the very words might be offensive to her.

"No," Julia said.

"How do you think of him then?"

"He's Iris's husband," she said.

"Quite important in your life, for the last few years." John Messenger's tone of voice was not so carefully gentle.

She didn't think this needed an answer. It was a fact. He was stating a fact.

"What about Iris?" he asked. "How do you think of her?"

"She's my cousin."

"So?"

"So what?" She didn't say it rudely, but the words sounded rude.

"So," John Messenger repeated, "so, do you think of Iris as a sort of mother?"

"No," said Julia, "she's my cousin. My mother is dead."

There was another silence. Her heart was pounding and the fields were all merging into each other. She blinked, and blinked again, and they settled down. She wanted to get out of the room and away from this man asking his questions, hating his detached air, the way he could ask about her father and her mother in that kind of way. "I need to go to the toilet," she said, and stood up.

John Messenger nodded. "First door on the left at the end of this corridor," he said. "Can you find your way there and back OK?"

Julia nodded and left the room hurriedly without replying. She had no intention of returning. That man, John Messenger, was stupid. She thought how much cleverer her own questions would have been, if she'd been in his position. She'd seen exactly what he was after, and she'd successfully foiled his clumsy attempts. It made her think she'd be good at his job, but she wanted to be a scientist, though she didn't know what sort. Something solid and practical, nothing to do with thoughts or feelings, the sort that filled her brain till she felt it might burst.

There seemed to be far more school visits than there used to be. Sometimes, the school would surprise Julia, proving far more agreeable than she'd anticipated, but most, in London, were daunting in their size and architectural ugliness. The playgrounds were bleak areas of tarmac and concrete, with never a bit of grass or a shrub or tree to relieve the dreariness, and once inside the buildings the worn nature of paintwork and floor coverings increased the feeling of gloom. Efforts were made, she could see that, with artwork covering the battered walls, but it was a losing battle with the general decrepitude of most schools. The head teacher's room was often an oasis of comfort and brightness among all the general drabness, with some plants on windowsills and desks, and maybe a few choice prints on the walls, which themselves would be clean, and almost always painted magnolia, and a comfortable chair or two with patterned cushions carefully arranged upon them. Julia was glad to reach these rooms, and perfectly happy, if necessary, to sit there and wait.

Head teachers liked to keep her waiting. It showed that they were busy people who barely had time to see Julia, whose function they distrusted. She was ready for the doubt and anxiety, if it lingered in the air, and knew how to deal with it. She disarmed with her direct approach, her plain speech devoid of jargon, and her quick summarising of what she already knew about the problem. Head teachers, on the whole, became quite friendly. "Best to try to deal with any difficulties as soon as they arise," Julia would say. The head teachers were relieved to agree. "We don't want things to escalate," they said, and Julia nodded sagely. She knew how sensitive these people were ever since the riots of 2011, when it was widely reported that the lawlessness on display had started in the schools, where allegedly there was no longer any discipline, or punishment for misdemeanours, where standards of right and wrong had been eroded, and where a so-called "feral" underclass was not taught how to be civilised — all the fault of schools.

Julia was their ally. She was with the teachers in wanting to prove this accusation mistaken. The council was trying, the school was trying, and Julia was trying — they were all trying to help the children. But this was a particularly tricky case. The head teacher wanted to exclude a pupil, a girl of twelve. There were a rising number of exclusions and it was Julia's job, or part of it, to find ways of troublesome children being kept in school.

"Let's go over what happened," Julia said, "from the beginning."

CHAPTER
NINE

Julia went to Caroline's wedding after all, but she didn't join in the hen night the week before. It embarrassed her even to contemplate such an event, the horror of women, in their late forties mostly, dressing up in berets and striped jumpers in an attempt to look French. Why had Caroline allowed it? Why did she have anything to do with such a plan? "It'll be a laugh," the bridegroom's sister, who was organising the evening, had said when she rang Julia. "Will Caroline think it a laugh?" she asked, restraining herself from adding that it was hard to believe, unless the Caroline she knew had changed dramatically.

But maybe she had. The old Caroline would not have got married in a church. The old Caroline would not have worn a long white dress. And the old Caroline would never have married Simon Carr, who struck Julia at once as brash, loud and full of himself. "So this is the famous Julia," he said, when Julia was introduced to him as his bride-to-be's oldest friend. "The wicked Julia," he added, roaring with laughter, "a law unto herself, eh?" Julia smiled. She knew the smile was stiff, but the alternative was to tell him not to be so silly. What, she wondered, had Caroline been telling him, so that the ridiculous remark about being "wicked" could be made? But now she was being silly herself, reacting to an inane comment like that, so she unstiffened her smile and made it genuine, and told Simon he was a very fortunate man. "Oh, I know," he said, and slapped Caroline on the back as though she were a prize horse.

There really was not much to talk about. Julia asked polite questions, which Simon answered in great detail. He didn't ask Julia any questions except what was her favourite food. Julia said she loved a good green salad. Simon, roaring with laughter again, said was she joking. No, Julia said, she wasn't.

The wedding reception itself was an affair so lavish and glittery she could hardly believe it. The table settings alone seemed to her ridiculous and vulgar — large, twisted stem glasses filled with blue lights and beads and blue decorative grass — but they were being widely admired. In front of her, when she sat down, was a tiny silver bucket. Looking down the table, she saw that everyone had a tiny silver bucket in front of them, even the male guests. Nervously, Julia picked hers up. Inside was a bottle of nail varnish with the label Butterfly Kisses on it. It was a lurid purple. She saw that the men's buckets contained a miniature bottle of Jack Daniel's whiskey. But nobody was laughing, or shooting mocking glances at each other. Suddenly Julia longed for her mother to be there, or even Aunt Maureen.

Caroline, though, seemed unfazed by all this glitz. She appeared to be enjoying herself, as a bride should. Her dress had been chosen for her by the same sister-in-law who had organised the hen night. She worked for a firm called Bridal Dreams and had got it "at cost". Julia thought that if the sister-in-law had tried she couldn't have come up with a dress less suited to Caroline. It was made of ivory satin, and had heavily embellished beading to the bust. Caroline's bust was very large and the beading, to Julia, had the appearance of chain mail. She had a veil too, waist-length, scattered with crystals. The bridesmaids' dresses, strapless and full-length, were red, and they too had crystals all over the skirt. Julia was glad she had declined the honour of being one of them.

She didn't stay long after the meal — which was very good — and the speeches. Simon's was surprisingly witty, but then Caroline had said he had a real sense of humour, once you got to know him and could appreciate it. And his family, she'd added, though a bit overwhelming en masse, was individually kind and welcoming.

"They're all thrilled Simon is getting married at last, so that's in my favour."

"I should think there's a lot in your favour," Julia said.

"Well," Caroline sighed, "I'm too old to have children, so that's not in my favour. But they have six grandchildren already, his parents, so it isn't too much of a fault."

"A *fault*?" echoed Julia.

"Well," said Caroline, "some people would think so."

Julia wondered how soon she could leave the reception. She tried hard to circulate and talk to other guests, but not counting Caroline's mother and her brother, there was no one else she knew, and it was exhausting introducing herself and establishing how all the other people were connected to Caroline and Simon. Caroline's mother was the only one the least bit interested in her. She knew exactly what Julia did, and had also heard from Caroline that she'd become a magistrate. "Who'd have thought it, Julia?" she said. "Not that I'm being insulting, but just remembering what you were like as a teenager, you've turned out so well, you're so steady and stable and successful, a real credit to yourself."

Each word seemed not only misplaced but deadly. Why did Caroline's mother think she was steady and stable, never mind successful? What had Caroline been saying to her? It made Julia think of other descriptions recently applied to her: serious, trustworthy, efficient, reliable . . . all somehow not only wrong but an insult.

She didn't want these labels attached to her. They bothered her.

Julia had booked the Quiet Coach for the train journey home. It was empty when she boarded the train and gratefully settled herself, assured of peace and quiet for the next few hours. But just before the train left the station four young women got on, laughing and calling out to each other to come on, let's sit here, at a table, and then there was a great flurry of activity as their bags were deposited in the luggage space at the end of the carriage and the rest of their belongings piled around them. There wasn't the faintest hint that they were aware they were in a Quiet Coach. I must speak up, Julia thought, but as she rose to go across to them one of the women answered her mobile. "We've been put in the Quiet Coach," she yelled down her phone, "so look for coach D, not E. E was full, there were no seats, so they've put us here, OK?" Julia was by then standing, looking towards the group, unsure whether to issue a reminder that this was still a Quiet Coach, but she saw one of the women nudge the others, nodding and smiling in Julia's direction, and reckoned the message had been received and understood.

For the first half-hour, the young women tried to respect the implied rules of the coach. They spoke in whispers, and shushed each other when any of them giggled. But they were clearly in high spirits, and gradually their voices rose and Julia was obliged to hear, in snatches, what they were saying. They were going to a wedding where they would be bridesmaids. All of them disliked their dresses, but they had been paid for by the bride, who it seemed had never had much taste. "Pink!" Julia heard. "At our age, my God." Another member of the quartet said consolingly that the pink was more of a lilac, and at least the design of the dresses wasn't fussy. The response to this was a long and loud bout of laughter which was so puzzling that Julia assumed there was either some private joke in the word "fussy" or she'd missed some vital other words. The bride was pulled to bits. None of her bridesmaids, it appeared, had ever really been close to her. None of them could understand why she had been asked to be a bridesmaid, and it was only hearing the names of the other three that had persuaded each of them to accept. That, and the location: London. "Have you met him?" one of them asked (meaning, Julia assumed, the bridegroom). Two of the others had. "Balding, short, specs," said one. More hoots of laughter. "But devoted," said another, "he adores her." There was a short silence after this statement, which Julia found interesting but couldn't quite interpret. Did it indicate respect? Or doubt? Or possibly envy? Immediately afterwards one of their phones went off, and then the drinks and sandwiches trolley came round, and the ticket inspector, and it was a while before general conversation among the four was begun again.

"It's not my idea of true love," one of them said, her intonation conveying that she was using the words "true love" satirically. "They're settling for each other, that's all." There was some mild objection to this judgement by the other three. One of them asked the speaker how she could tell. "How can anyone tell what true love looks like?" she asked. "It isn't something you can see, is it?" There was then mention of some names which meant little to Julia, but she picked up that some famous celebrity couples were being talked about, couples held up as supremely romantic, the embodiment of true love, but who had recently parted, their love not being true after all. "What a lot of cynics we are," one girl said. "No," said another, "we're just realists, that's all." A bottle of wine was opened at this point and once it had been drunk — frighteningly quickly, it seemed to Julia — there was a lull in the noise level. Then the announcement came that Euston was approaching and there was a general gathering up of their stuff by the group.

Julia was in no hurry to get off the train, so she waited until everyone else had gone. She had a good view of the girls as they walked along the platform. They were such a picture of vitality, all of them, hair shining, skin glowing, long-legged and confident. In their way, moving as a group, they were overpowering, almost intimidating. They made her shrink back in her seat feeling withered and tired. She frowned as she began to leave the train, trying to remember if she had ever been like those young women. Had she had her day, in that respect, and not known it? But she had never been part of that kind of group. She'd had friends, but she'd never functioned as part of a little gang. It had been one of the things Andrew had liked about her, that she wasn't a girly "girl".

She thought of her own wedding, as the young women disappeared from view, carrying hat boxes, as well as trundling cases behind them. Julia hadn't seen a hat box since she'd left Manchester all those years ago. Aunt Maureen and Iris both had several, containing magnificent confections of silk and tulle. By not inviting them to her wedding she'd denied them the chance once more to travel with a hat box, but then her wedding had not, in the true sense of the word, been a wedding. She and Andrew married in a registry office with two friends as witnesses and then they all went to a restaurant in Charlotte Street for a meal. She hadn't even told Aunt Maureen and the Annovazzis that she was getting married, though afterwards she sent them a card. When they wrote back to her, in astonished and aggrieved tones, the worst of the hurts she seemed to have inflicted was that of denying Elsa and Fran the opportunity to be bridesmaids. Carlo also added a note, saying he would have been happy to give Julia away, if he'd been asked, and to provide the wedding breakfast.

Why on earth he bothered to write this Julia couldn't imagine. She deduced it was a kind of showing off, Carlo being proud of bearing her no resentment.

Julia, in her last month with the Annovazzis, became expert at writing anonymous letters. She bought several pens, each with a different type of nib, and collected various pads of writing paper, stealing them from W.H. Smith. She'd discovered she could shoplift almost anything, finding it so easy she wondered why anyone ever actually paid for goods. Everything she stole was cheap, and from chain stores, only a fool risked stealing from small shops.

She studied the handwriting of teachers at school, the comments written on her own exercise books when the work in them was marked, surprised to find so much variation. Hardly any of them had good, clear, plain handwriting, even though they were teachers. It was initially hard to copy any of the writing but with lots of practice she perfected two or three samples. Her own handwriting was neat and small, and upright, so she concentrated on sloping writing, as different from her own as possible. She used tracing paper at first, to get the individual letters absolutely accurate, and then she launched into a bold, free hand. It gave her more than satisfaction to be able to execute what amounted to a forgery.

The first letter she dared to send to Carlo was just a trial, a piece of fun. She chose a lilac paper, slightly scented, very feminine, and wrote with a broad-nib pen, using dark blue Quink ink. "Darling," she wrote, "I can't meet you as arranged. Something has come up. Will meet you tomorrow, same time, same place. If you are not there, I'll understand, and wait to hear from you — but do *not* phone. Leave a message in the usual box. All my love, R." Julia hesitated over whether to put two or three kisses, but didn't. She posted this letter from Piccadilly on a Friday afternoon, using the post office near to Carlo's latest addition to his chain of coffee shops. He had six by then, and was proudest of this central one.

The letter arrived on Saturday morning, as she knew it would. She'd deliberately posted it on Friday so that it would arrive on a morning when they were all at home. Elsa picked the letters up and brought them into the kitchen, where everyone was at different stages of eating breakfast. "One for you, Dad," Elsa said, and handed over the pale lilac-coloured envelope. Carlo frowned, and took it, then tore it open carelessly. Julia carefully turned her back on the table where he and the girls were eating toast, but she was watching him through the mirror which hung over the sink where she was slowly rinsing her own cup and plate. She thought maybe he would laugh, and read the note aloud, and wonder how this mistake could have happened, but he didn't. Instead, he tore it up, got to his feet, and put the pieces of paper in the bin, already almost full of rubbish. "I'll take this out now, on my way out," he said, tying the bag up and lifting it out of the bin. No one asked who the torn-up letter had been from. Iris, who had been scrambling eggs for herself and the girls, hadn't even registered that Carlo had received a mysterious letter.

Julia found herself smiling at her own reflection. "You look happy," Iris said, smiling herself.

Julia did not exactly run away. There was no running. Her departure from the Annovazzi household was sedate. No drama, no farewell speeches, no accusations. She began to plan it carefully, starting the day after she walked out on John Messenger. Carlo was in the car, waiting. When she appeared, he thought Messenger had finished with her. "That was quick," he said. All she had to do was nod. It wasn't until they got home (in silence) that Iris said there had been a phone call, that Mr Messenger had rung to say Julia had walked out and was she with them.

Carlo was furious. Such trouble had been gone to, he ranted, to get Julia that appointment with the child psychologist — on and on he went, calling her ungrateful and selfish and rude. He didn't know what they were going to do with her, he shuddered to think what might happen next. Julia could have told him, but she didn't. What was going to happen next was that she was going to leave. Nothing childish, no dashing out of the house in a storm of tears and then obliged to crawl

240

back because she had no money and nowhere to go and no plan. That would not do. She needed time to work out how to get hold of some money and how to find somewhere to live where she would be safe and could still carry on at school till she'd done her exams. Oh, there was nothing impetuous or short-sighted about Julia.

Hardest of all was finding out the legal position. She didn't know what legally Iris and Carlo could do if she left their home. Could they force her to return? She went to the library, but though there were plenty of law books she didn't know where to start. Then she remembered that when her mother died Aunt Maureen told her that she and Uncle Tom had been made her guardians in her mother's will but that they thought it better she should live with the Annovazzis. So, Julia deduced, Iris and Carlo had no legal authority over her. Only Aunt Maureen, now that Uncle Tom was dead, had that.

But she knew she couldn't go and live with Aunt Maureen. Any appeal to her would be wasted. She'd say she was too old to have a teenager in her house, she couldn't be doing with it. No good promising to be very quiet and helpful. It wouldn't work. Where could she go, then? Briefly, she thought of asking Caroline's mother if she could live with their family but then thought better of it. That wouldn't work either. Then she wondered if she could go into a hostel, but how would she find a hostel, and who would pay for it? It did cross her mind to allege that she was being ill-treated, maybe confiding in a teacher, which might get her taken into care, but she dismissed that idea fairly quickly. There would be an investigation and any fool would be able to see Iris and Carlo were nothing but kind and generous.

But living with them became more and more unbearable even though she didn't know exactly why she felt so stifled in that house, or why she was now so constantly rebellious, unable to fit into the Annovazzi family at all. She hardly spoke to any of them, not even Fran, who minded her silence the most. "Talk to me, Julia," Fran would plead, "don't 'nore me, Julia, please." "Nothing to say," she would mutter, feeling mean, and when Fran tried to get her to respond to her chatter she moved away. Elsa reacted differently. If Julia was not going to have a normal conversation with her, then Elsa would give her the same treatment. It made the atmosphere in the house tense and awkward, all this lack of communication.

Caroline thought she was only harming herself with her behaviour (relayed to her with some relish by Julia). "What is the point?" she asked, exasperated. "What have they done to you to make you so horrible to them?"

Julia shrugged. "I'm supposed to be grateful," she said, "and I'm tired of being grateful."

"That's sick," Caroline said.

Julia shrugged again. She knew she hadn't explained herself well. If she couldn't explain how she felt, to her best friend, then she couldn't explain to anyone else. It hurt her that Caroline was lacking in sympathy and, as Julia saw it, took Carlo and Iris's side.

242

"Sometimes," Caroline said, "I don't know how they put up with you. You're poisoning their life, you're like a cuckoo in their nest."

"Well," Julia said, not at all displeased with this analogy, "cuckoos migrate eventually, and I will. Soon."

"You don't know how lucky you are," Caroline said.

"Oh, not you too," said Julia.

From then on, she never confided in Caroline again.

Jasmine came with her foster-mother, a neat-looking middle-aged woman who kept her coat on, buttoned up at the neck, even though it was hot in Julia's room and she had been invited to take it off. "They haven't adjusted the heating yet," Julia apologised. "We've just moved in here and the council are still seeing to it." But Mrs McClusky said she liked it warm, she was quite comfortable, thank you. Jasmine took her jacket off, though. It was a thick-looking red fleece, zipped up to the neck. She unzipped it in one swift movement which somehow sounded dramatic. Mrs McClusky frowned, as though the noise pained her, but said nothing. Underneath the fleece Jasmine was wearing a white T-shirt with "New York" written in red across it.

Julia smiled at her. Jasmine didn't smile back. She just looked a little to the left of Julia, though not so far left that it would appear she was trying to avoid her gaze. Her expression was not sullen. It was bored, world-weary. Julia recognised how tedious the girl was finding this, how she resented having to come here with Mrs McClusky, and decided to be brisk. No point in asking Jasmine why she was truanting so regularly.

Better to talk to Mrs McClusky, who would be bound to irritate Jasmine with whatever she said, however she said it, and out of the irritation might come some small enlightenment. It was interesting that when Jasmine slipped out of school, usually at the morning break, she went back to Mrs McClusky's. Most truants wandered the streets or shopping centres till it was normal going-home time, but Jasmine didn't. She had a key, and let herself in (Mrs McClusky had a cleaning job three weekdays) and watched television. When Mrs McClusky came home, with another younger foster-child she'd picked up from school, there Jasmine would be, sitting perfectly still in front of the television.

"It's weird," said Mrs McClusky, "she don't say nothing, not a hello or anything. I didn't even know she weren't at school till the teacher rang. I never know whether she's been at school or not. That's the truth."

"Mrs McClusky," Julia began, "does Jasmine help around the house?"

Mrs McClusky looked faintly alarmed. "Well," she said, "she has her jobs like I give them all, soon as they're able." Then a thought seemed to occur to her that made her pause and look surprised. "She cleans the bathroom regular," she said. "Very nice job she makes of it, the bath, the shower, the taps."

Julia smiled at Jasmine, without saying anything, and the girl frowned and blushed slightly. But Mrs McClusky was now busy enumerating other housewifely virtues of Jasmine's, ending by saying that from "that point of view" she had no complaints. It was just the truanting, and coming home, and just sitting there.

"It's a compliment, Mrs McClusky," Julia said, "see it as a compliment. Jasmine likes your house. She likes coming back to it. It's quiet during the day, and it pleases her when she's helped to make everything neat and tidy. It gives her the kind of satisfaction school can't give. She needs it."

"That's as may be," said Mrs McClusky, "but she has to go to school and stay there, it's the law, and I'm the one gets rung up. She don't care."

All this time, Jasmine hadn't said a word. Julia hadn't asked her anything and she hadn't volunteered any comment, but now Julia said, "I think you do care, Jasmine. I think you want to stay with Mrs McClusky. You like her house, and how she keeps it. But if you keep walking out of school the authorities will have to do something about it and you might end up being moved on. You can see that, can't you?"

Julia thought the girl was going to continue not to say a word, but after a long stare, and an even deeper frown, she said, "I hate school. I don't see why I have to put up with it. I can read and write, and all that. There's no point to it. I can learn what I want from the telly."

"The fact remains," Julia said gently, "it is the law that all children must be educated from the age of five to sixteen and you are only thirteen. You've three years to get through, so we have to think of some way of making them bearable. So, is it *all* schools you hate, or this particular school?"

"All schools."

"Mind you," Mrs McClusky suddenly said, "it's a rough place her school."

"Well," said Julia, "let's see if we can find you a school you'll be able to tolerate better, OK, Jasmine?"

Jasmine looked doubtful, but nodded.

When they'd gone Julia looked at all the schools within reach of Mrs McClusky's house. There were a surprising number, though she knew catchment areas varied from year to year and you had to live very near the good ones to have a chance of getting in. But Jasmine was "special needs" category, not through any disability but because of her history. Social workers had a file a foot thick on the girl's experiences from the age of two, when she had been found in a shed on an allotment locked in and so distressed she'd badly hurt herself throwing herself at the door in an attempt to escape. It was astounding that she had survived not just this abandonment but, afterwards, a whole series of accidents. Julia told herself she ought to be used to reading these sorts of histories but she wasn't. Most of the children who were referred to the centre had problems which, in comparison to what Jasmine had endured, were not hard to do something about. Her one bit of good luck was to be now with Mrs McClusky who gave her the sort of stability she'd never had. School, on the other hand, destabilised her all over again.

Julia wondered if home schooling might be a possibility, a tutor coming to Mrs McClusky's. Madness. Of course it wasn't even a remote possibility in the current climate. A school had to be found, and

Jasmine persuaded that it was worth attending it to avoid getting her foster-mother into trouble and herself moved on.

Before she wrote the second letter, Julia visited each of Carlo's shops in turn. She chose times when she knew he would not be there, and was careful not to attract attention to herself in any way. All she did was buy a cup of coffee, just so that she could observe who was working there. They were all young women, two behind the counter selling the beans and ground coffee, two serving cups of coffee at the bar running round the room. They wore uniforms Carlo had designed himself, bright red waistcoats worn over black polo-necked sweaters and short black skirts, showing plenty of leg. You had to have good legs to work in Carlo's shops. Each assistant had a name tag worn on her waistcoat, so Julia didn't need to find out their names. It was a problem to decide who to choose. Not, she thought, the most obviously attractive or the youngest. Finally, she settled on Ramola. She'd signed the first letter with an R, after all.

She wanted Iris to be aware of this letter, which again would be timed to arrive on a Saturday morning. This meant Julia herself would have to collect any post and bring it into the kitchen and hand it to Iris first. If Elsa picked it up, she'd hand the important letter to her father, and Carlo could once more rip it up before Iris registered its significance. It gave Julia a headache, trying to work out how she could contrive to be the one who was nearest the mat upon which letters would land that Saturday morning, but finally she resorted to sitting on the bottom step of the stairs, apparently absorbed in threading new laces into her trainers.

This time, she'd chosen ordinary white paper and a white envelope. Anything lilac would immediately alert Carlo, whereas most of the bills, etc., he received arrived in innocuous white or buff-coloured envelopes. His reaction to the first letter had, Julia reckoned, shown him to be guilty of something, only she didn't know what. He might be having a fling with someone who had nothing to do with his shops, or he might not be having a fling at all but merely be on the brink of having one. The clever bit was that the chances of him ever having seen the handwriting of anyone who worked for him were slim. He couldn't be sure that a letter was not from Ramola. The test would be to see what he would do about it. Confront her? Tell Iris? Or act on it?

Julia wrote a dozen versions before she felt she'd got the tone of the letter right. Keep it simple, keep it short, she told herself. In the end, all she wrote was one sentence: "I love you too, and will be there, Ramola." It was silly, but might, she hoped, have a devastating effect, though if it did, she might never know about it.

Elsa rang. Elsa hardly ever rang. Elsa hardly ever contacted Julia these days, and when she did it was always for some specific reason, as it was this time.

"It's Dad," Elsa said straight away, no preliminaries, no pleasantries first. "He's in hospital, he's had a stroke. Mum thought you'd want to know."

"Oh," Julia said, "I'm sorry, how worrying."

Elsa said nothing. She seemed to be expecting Julia to say something else. Finally, the pause having gone on an uncomfortably long time, Julia said, "How bad is this stroke?"

"He can't speak," Elsa said, "and he can't move his left arm or leg, and they say the next forty-eight hours will be crucial."

Another pause.

"How awful," Julia said, all the time thinking why did Iris want her to know that Carlo had had a stroke.

Immediately, she was ashamed. Of course Iris would want her to know. What she also wanted, naturally, was some show of support, some evidence of concern. But did Iris, did Elsa, imagine she was going to leap on a train to Manchester and rush to Iris's side in the hospital? She hoped not.

Carefully, she asked Elsa a few obvious questions about Carlo's condition, and then a couple about how Iris was coping, and whether Elsa and Fran were with her, and then she said, "Well, Elsa, thank you for letting me know. You will keep me in touch with how things develop, won't you? And I'll ring Iris, I'll try to catch her at home."

There were a few seconds of silence, then Elsa burst out, "Is that all? After everything they did for you? That's disgusting." Then the phone was hung up.

Julia got the last train to Manchester that day, and took a taxi to Iris's house, perfectly prepared to find nobody in. She made the taxi wait, just in case, but she could see from the lights that someone was probably in. Standing on the door-step ringing the bell she felt as she had always felt when about to enter this house: uncertain of her welcome, reluctant to go inside, stifled already by the overwhelming feeling of obligation. The life, her life, inside this house was what she had cast off at the age of eighteen. But at least Carlo would not answer the door. Iris opened it, after a long interval during which Julia could hear an internal door opening and shutting, and another light appeared in the hall.

"Julia," Iris said, seeming unsurprised, but neither pleased nor displeased. "Come in, I'm just back from the hospital."

They went into the sitting room, where Iris sat in the middle of the sofa and Julia faced her, perched on an armchair.

The room was lit only by one small lamp, though in the kitchen, which they'd gone past, all the lights blazed, as they did in the bedrooms above. There were no curtains closed anywhere, which was a break with Iris's usual habits. Curtains had always been closed in the Annovazzis' household at dusk, long before real darkness began, and even in summer all of them would be closed at nine o'clock, however light it was on a June or July evening. Julia had hated this. She never wanted the outside shut out. She'd sworn to herself that when she had her own house there would be no curtains. If people wanted to look in, they could look in. She would have nothing to hide. But then, when she was young, she was afraid of nothing.

250

Iris waited. She was listless, but composed, showing no signs of the grief Julia had expected.

"How is he?" Julia asked.

"The same," Iris said.

She offered nothing more, which again was not what Julia had expected. She'd braced herself, in the taxi, for a torrent of detail about how Carlo's stroke had come about, a minute by minute account which she would have been relieved to listen to patiently. When none of this came, and Iris went on sitting there silently, staring not quite at Julia but in her general direction — it was hard to tell exactly what she was looking at because the lighting was so dim — Julia said: "And how are you, Iris?" It was an obvious but a silly question. If she had replied, "How do you think I am?" Julia felt Iris would have been within her rights. But Iris said, "Fine. I'm fine. I think he's going to die. I think that's what they seem to be thinking will happen."

Julia wondered if she should move to the sofa and sit beside Iris, and perhaps take her hand, or put an arm round her shoulder, but something about Iris's extreme stillness made her decide such a gesture would not be welcome, so she stayed where she was and said, "Can I make you something to eat or drink, Iris? Have you eaten?"

"Yes," Iris said, "Elsa made me something earlier. An omelette, I think, with salad. I don't think I ate the salad."

"Well," Julia said lamely, "eggs are full of protein." She felt her face grow hot, and struggled to rescue herself from such a banal comment.

Just as she was about to make another attempt to show concern, Iris said, "I wanted you to come. Do you know why I wanted you to come?"

Julia shook her head, then said, "I thought . . . I thought probably it was because you needed . . ." and then her voice trailed off.

"Needed?" prompted Iris.

". . . family around you."

"Family," Iris repeated thoughtfully. "I suppose that would make sense. You are family. Not like Elsa and Fran, of course, but still. Family."

They sat there for what seemed, to Julia, an eternity, but out of the corner of her eye she could see the clock on the mantelpiece and its hands barely moved. The air in the room felt dangerous, as though it might ignite with a word. She suddenly realised that Iris was not motionless because she was relaxed or because exhaustion had made her so, but because she was deliberately holding herself in this posture. There was a tension in the tight-together knees and the shoulders pushed back against the sofa cushions which Julia had not seen at first. Her heart began to pound. She must do something, get away from Iris before a disaster she could not imagine, but could sense, overwhelmed them both. She stood up.

"Iris," she said, "it's late. You're tired, I'm tired. I think we should both go to bed, don't you? Get some rest?"

"No," Iris said, "I don't think we should. Not yet. I haven't told you why I wanted you to come."

There was nothing to do but sit down again and wait. Waiting, in these circumstances, in this atmosphere, was agony, but there was no alternative. If Iris chose to sit there all night, then that was how it must be.

"I wanted you to come before Carlo dies," Iris at last began, "so that you can say sorry to him. Tomorrow. They say tomorrow might be the last day, so far as they can tell. Of course, if he dies in the night, it will be too late, I'll have brought you here for nothing, but I hope not."

Julia's throat was dry, her tongue stuck to the roof of her mouth. She tried to moisten her lips but could not get her tongue to respond.

"Iris," she managed at last to croak, and then she couldn't go on, she couldn't manage to say what she wanted to say, which was that she didn't know what she had to say sorry to Carlo for, something apparently so important and perhaps terrible that a dying man had to hear it. There was some mistake being made, she was being suspected of some crime she had not committed, or if not a crime then some offence so serious Iris was prepared to drag an apology from her at her dying husband's bedside.

"Iris," she said again, "you'll have to explain. I'm sorry, but I think . . . I mean, truly, I don't . . ." and she couldn't get any more words out of her dry mouth.

"Elsa told me," Iris said, "years ago. I didn't believe her. I didn't believe you would do that. So I said nothing. What's the point? I said to myself. She's leaving soon, she'll be out of our lives. I never said anything to Carlo, not ever. Things went on as usual. I

253

knew you were a liar, a cheat, a thief, but I told myself you were a disturbed child. Isn't that what they call them, children like you, disturbed? I thought being disturbed excused everything. I thought being part of our loving family would settle you. But it didn't, did it? And before you left, you did that to Carlo. He'd done nothing but treat you as his own, with true kindness, never hesitated a moment about taking you in, and you did that to him. So I want you to say sorry."

The post didn't arrive that Saturday morning. Some sort of strike involving the sorting office, it seemed. Julia sat for a long time on the bottom of the stairs, long enough to fit laces into fifty pairs of shoes. She didn't want to leave the house until the post arrived, but by ten o'clock Carlo had gone, and Iris was on her way to the supermarket, taking Fran with her. Only Elsa was left, getting ready to go to her friend's house where she was going to spend the day. It wasn't until almost midday that Julia realised there wasn't going to be any post, that something must have happened to prevent deliveries.

The letter arrived on Tuesday. It was wasted. Julia knew that the post didn't come on other weekdays until around ten o'clock, and by then the house was empty except for Iris. She tried to be heavily casual about asking if there had been any post, pretending she was expecting brochures from the universities she was applying to, and when, on Tuesday, Iris said yes, the strike was over, it had only been a twenty-four-hour stoppage, but there had been nothing for Julia, Julia

254

couldn't go on to ask if there had been post for anyone else. Iris didn't mention any letter to Carlo. She didn't mention at all what had arrived, leaving Julia in an agony of uncertainty. Carlo, when he came home that day, seemed normal, betraying no anxiety or unusual behaviour, but of course, as Julia realised, he had not yet been given the letter. Where was it? Where had Iris put it? There was nothing on the hall table, nothing on the dining-room dresser, both places where letters were put when they arrived.

She began to think that Iris might have opened her husband's letter, and had either destroyed it or was waiting to confront him with the contents. But no. Iris was too serene, and quite incapable of any kind of deception. Then, as they were all sitting down to eat, Iris said, "Oh, Elsa, I put a letter to your dad down on top of the washing machine, I forgot. Can you go and get it, and the other envelopes, two I think?" A long, rambling account of how she'd come to put the post on the washing machine in the utility room followed, but Julia didn't take in a word. She waited, tense and excited, for Elsa to reappear with the letters. But when she did, handing them to Carlo, he said he'd look at them later, he was in a hurry to get to golf. Iris protested that he had to eat, but Carlo said to save him something, he'd eat later.

"Shall I open them, Dad?" Elsa said, as Carlo went to get his jacket, "Tell you what they are?"

"OK," Carlo shouted back.

Julia watched, helpless, mesmerised, as Elsa opened the two bills and called out what they were for, and then the letter allegedly from Ramola. Her face took on an expression of bewilderment, a frown appearing, her mouth hanging open a little in a pantomime of astonishment, but instead of reading the letter out she said, "I can't read the writing on this one, Dad."

"Oh, give it here," Carlo said, and shoved it, with the bills, into his pocket as he rushed out of the door.

Elsa said nothing. Maybe she hadn't been able to read the handwriting. Or maybe she had, and in spite of her youth had realised she must not read the message out. It was impossible to know.

Julia went to bed leaving Iris still sitting there. She said nothing as she got up from the armchair, as quietly as possible, aware that she must not make any gesture which might antagonise Iris further. She must appear contrite even if she resented having to do so. Iris didn't move. Carefully, Julia tiptoed up the stairs, without putting the light on, and then hesitated. Which room to take? Was Elsa in one? Fran in the other? She hadn't asked if they were here. The door of what had once been her room, then Elsa's, was slightly open. She peered round it and saw, in the gloom, a single bed and nobody in it. She lay down on the bed, fully dressed, and closed her eyes. She didn't imagine she would sleep, but she had to lie down. Her mind was seething but her body exhausted, and her mind would win but at least her body would be rested.

There was any number of lies Elsa could have told. An expert in lies herself, Julia thought she knew them all but knew, too, that this was impossible. There would always be some twist, some wild piece of invention, which she hadn't thought of. She set herself to imagine what would have been likely to occur to Elsa, all those years ago, if she had wanted to make her mother hate Julia. But that wouldn't have worked. Making Iris hate anyone was too much a perversion of her character for Elsa to have managed. So Julia reckoned she would have had to have been accused of, in some way, casting Carlo in a bad light, without Carlo being responsible for whatever was alleged to have happened. What could she have done to Carlo that Iris refused to believe, but now, with him lying in hospital dying, she had decided to believe, and why? Why, at this late stage (in every sense), change her mind?

By dawn, the light creeping greyly through the window, Julia had come to a decision. It was possible, she'd decided, in these extreme circumstances, to say sorry for an unknown, undivulged, act or word of hers which Iris believed she had committed or said. Sorry was an easy word. Short. What would it cost her to have to say "Sorry, Carlo"? Quickly done. Satisfying to Iris. Perhaps satisfying to Elsa, though maybe Elsa would prefer Julia to refuse to apologise until she'd been told what for, and then there would be the scene she wanted. What would Elsa do, if she said sorry to Carlo? Would she then tell? Iris, of course, would assume that she, Julia, had said sorry because she was acknowledging, without needing to say it, whatever Elsa said she had done to Carlo some thirty years ago.

Iris, Julia told herself, was in a dreadful state of grief. She could not be held responsible for her own

257

behaviour. Afterwards, later, when Carlo died, if he died, she could attempt to find out what Iris thought she had to apologise to Carlo for. If Carlo lived, the same applied, though investigating the truth might take longer. The important thing, the kind thing, was simply to do it: say sorry. And then see what happened. It could be done. In a curious way, the longer she practised saying Sorry, Carlo, in her head, the more it appealed to her. So easy. And there were plenty of trivial things she could apologise for. Her teenage years had been full of irritating and maligning Carlo, of driving him mad with her sulkiness and obduracy insulting him in childish ways, making him the object of her scorn, mocking him mercilessly.

She could say Sorry, Carlo, and mean it. Julia began almost to look forward to saying it, defeating whatever plan Elsa had had by doing so.

Julia wrote no more letters to Carlo. It was too risky. She never discovered whether Elsa had read the last one and understood its meaning, or whether she had asked her father about it. Somehow, she thought this unlikely. But had Carlo mentioned the contents of the letter to her? That seemed unlikely too. It would be best to drop the whole game. Elsa was still very young. She would forget about the letter even if she had after all read it and guessed at its significance.

Not long after, Julia was ready to leave her cousin and her family. She had a place at University College London, and a grant to enable her to take it up. She intended never to return. In the vacations, she'd get a job, as a waitress or something, and stay in London. Later, much later, when she'd graduated and had a proper job (though she didn't know what as) and was settled in her own home, the ultimate ambition, she'd return in a car of her own, she hoped, and collect the little table and the rug and the pictures which had been her mother's.

Elsa watched her pack. She stood in the doorway of the room, which would now become hers, her arms folded across her flat chest, one leg crossed awkwardly over the other. Julia ignored her.

"You think you're so smart, so clever," Elsa suddenly said.

Julia didn't say anything, just finished zipping up the second holdall. She looked round the room one last time. It worried her that Elsa might scratch the surface of the table, or spill something sticky on the rug. She wished she'd asked Iris if she could put these few belongings of her mother's in the attic. Too late now.

"Can you get out of the way?" she said to Elsa, who was almost blocking the door.

"Good riddance," Elsa said.

"Get out of the way," Julia said, "or I'll have to push you."

"Push!" said Elsa.

Julia promptly picked up one of her bags and swung it at Elsa's knees. It was a blow hard enough to unbalance her, and she fell backwards onto the landing, then turned quickly onto all fours and stuck a foot out to trip Julia up. The bags and Julia both fell beside her.

They both lay there in a heap, with one of the bags now beginning to roll down the stairs.

"You little cow," Julia said, "I don't know what you're think you're doing, but I don't care."

The doorbell went.

"That's my taxi," Julia said.

Iris opened the front door and shouted, sounding astonished, that it was a taxi.

"Coming," Julia shouted back. They were both on their feet again.

"I'm going to tell Mum the moment you're gone," Elsa said.

Julia didn't bother replying. There was nothing to tell. If Elsa made up lies, she didn't care. She'd made plenty up herself and didn't care about those either. The only thing that mattered was getting away. She dragged one bag down the stairs and picked up the other which had fallen almost to the bottom.

"Oh, Julia," Iris said, "I wish you hadn't ordered a taxi, I wish you'd let Carlo take you to the station, you know he wanted to. This doesn't seem right."

Julia said she was fine, she didn't want to bother Carlo.

"Give me a hug," Iris said.

Julia was horrified to see tears in her cousin's eyes. She made the hug as perfunctory as possible, and muttered goodbye and thanks.

"Ring when you get there," Iris said, "or I'll worry."

Then, when Julia was finally out of the house and putting her bags on the back seat of the cab, Fran came hurtling out, shouting her goodbyes, and there was another delay.

As the cab moved off, Julia saw Elsa appearing behind Iris and Fran, both of whom were still waving. She took hold of her mother's shoulders and turned them towards her.

When Julia went downstairs, she saw that the lamp in the sitting room was still on, and there, still sitting on the sofa, in exactly the same position, was Iris, asleep, her head lolling forward. She was snoring slightly, more of a wheeze than a snore, and this emphasised the pathos. Iris would be mortified to be found snoring. Women, in her opinion, didn't snore, only men. Julia went into the kitchen and wondered if she dared to boil the kettle or would it waken Iris? She wanted Iris kept asleep for as long as possible, giving her time to make some tea and leave the house. She couldn't leave without a hot drink and some toast.

Of *course* she was not going to go to the hospital and say sorry to Carlo. How she could have imagined in the early hours of the morning she'd do such a thing she didn't know. The idea was ridiculous. She made tea, and took a slice of bread from the bread bin and popped it into the toaster. When it was ready, she stood nibbling it and sipping the tea, her hands round the comforting warmth of the mug. She should make Iris some tea and toast and take them through to her. Her fear of the night before had gone. She felt such a sudden tenderness for Iris. Another mug filled with tea (she remembered Iris liked milk and one sugar) and

261

another slice of bread toasted; she carried them through to the sitting room, wondering how best to waken her.

But she was now awake, the small noises of kettle and toaster in the next room bringing her out of her sleep. She looked startled, as Julia entered, giving a little "Oh!" of surprise. "I've made you some tea," Julia said, in a whisper, and held the mug out. Iris took it, her hand quite shaky, but she managed to drink a little. Julia didn't sit down. She was standing there, about to say she was going to leave now, and dreading Iris's reaction whatever it might be, when the telephone rang. Iris turned her head and looked at it in apparent astonishment, as though she had never heard a phone ring before. It went on ringing but she seemed paralysed. "Shall I?" Julia said, and moved towards the table where the phone rested. But suddenly Iris stood up, slopping some of the tea from her still full mug, and moved stiffly to the table, putting the mug down carefully before lifting the receiver. Her back was now to Julia, who quietly left the room and put on her coat, which she'd left the night before on the peg behind the door, and picked up her bag from the foot of the stairs. She hesitated only a moment at the front door, straining to hear Iris's voice so that she might interpret from it whether this was a call from the hospital or from Elsa or Fran. Whoever was calling, Iris was speaking to them in an even tone, not saying much at all except yes, OK, I'm sure, no, I don't think so, or at least this was all Julia could hear. No panic, anyway, no cry of anguish. Good.

She hoped the bus stop hadn't changed. It was a good distance away but she remembered how to get to it and knew there was a bus, or there used to be, that went to the station. No chance of flagging down a taxi. Taxis didn't cruise round this suburb, and she hadn't wanted to order a minicab. She walked briskly, glad to have left her cousin's house without any scene, without encountering Elsa or Fran. They would all think less of her, for sneaking away, but she didn't care what they thought. If Carlo was dead, Julia would be wiped out of Iris's mind; if he were still alive, then Julia had escaped and she would know she couldn't be brought back. Julia hoped this reasoning was correct.

London suited Julia. Other girls from the North might find the city intimidating but she did not. She thought it was exciting. Walking down the Mall towards Buckingham Palace thrilled her, making her feel part of all the events she'd seen in films and on television featuring the location. Much of her free time was spent simply walking from park to park, and along the river, and she never grew tired of trawling the city. Manchester and the Annovazzi family began to recede quite alarmingly in her memory.

"Alarmingly" because she'd spent so many years of her life there, a time when everything went wrong, or so it seemed to her in retrospect. It scared her to think of all the wrong turnings she'd almost taken. Well, no, some of which she had taken, only she'd got out of them in time. The letters to Carlo episode particularly bothered her, and so did not knowing the effect the second silly letter had had. It made her blush with shame to recall what she'd written, dragging that shop assistant Ramola into her plot. Would she have got into trouble? Would Carlo have approached her, accused her, sacked her? Julia was glad to be in London, far away from any possible consequences of her foolishness.

Iris wrote to her throughout her years as a student, sweet little notes wondering how she was getting on, and telling her what Elsa and Fran were doing, a predictably boring list of swimming triumphs and school concerts and details of who had had a tooth filled or her hair cut short. Sometimes she mentioned Carlo, but not often. His business was doing well, but he was finding managing it tiring and was thinking of appointing a general manager. Iris always ended by saying how often she thought of Julia, and how they all missed her and hoped she wasn't feeling lost in the big city, or lonely. That last bit made Julia laugh — as if! Where she'd felt lost and lonely was in Manchester, living with the Annovazzis, being utterly out of place, desperate to be free.

She replied only once to Iris, a few weeks after she arrived, telling her how happy she was, how settled, and then that she was going to be working very hard and wouldn't have time to write very often. She didn't go "home" (what Iris called "home") for the first Christmas, which upset Iris, because (she wrote) Christmas was a family time. Not to Julia it wasn't. She worked on the post and in the evenings in a bar and managed to save enough money to join a trip to

Austria, skiing. They drove there in a van, four of them, and stayed in a hostel and she had the best Christmas she'd ever had.

When she graduated, Julia hesitated over whether to give Iris the address of the flat she was going to be sharing with three other friends. She didn't want to be tracked down, but on the other hand she didn't think it wise to disappear entirely or Iris might have one of her fits of anxiety and report her missing, so, reluctantly, she sent a card with her new address, telling Iris that she was training to be a chemistry teacher. Immediately, a letter came from Iris, saying how relieved she was to hear Julia was alive and well because she'd begun to dread something awful had happened, and she felt so responsible for her welfare, and had done ever since Julia came to live with them. The letter was thick with reproach, and all of it was justified, but, as ever, it only deepened Julia's rage that she should be made to feel guilty and ungrateful. She didn't acknowledge this letter at all.

Then, four years later, by which time Julia was no longer teaching, Iris wrote asking if Elsa could come and stay for one night the following week. She could sleep on a sofa, or even on the floor, and would be no trouble. She was coming for an interview at Goldsmiths Training College, though Iris would much prefer her to have applied to a college in Manchester and didn't know why it had to be London. Julia wrote back swiftly saying she was very sorry but she wouldn't be at home that day and neither would her flatmates, so it wouldn't be possible to have Elsa to stay. She wished her good luck with the interview. There was, to her relief, no response, though she was pretty sure Iris, and certainly Elsa, would have seen through her excuse.

But Elsa turned up, not on the night her mother had asked if she could stay but the night before. Julia didn't recognise her, which was hardly surprising given the fact that Elsa had been only ten when she last saw her and was now seventeen. The spectacles had gone, and so had the gawkiness. Her height was now in proportion, and she was trendily dressed. Completely self-assured, she said, "Hi, Julia," and when Julia didn't react, "I'm Elsa." She stepped inside, taking off her rucksack and putting it on the ground. "Nice to see you too," she said, smiling, perfectly at ease, as Julia still just stood there. "Took ages to find this street," Elsa said. "I got lost twice, there are so many Victoria Streets."

No one else was home that night, so there were plenty of beds. Julia found clean sheets and made a business of putting them on, and then she offered Elsa some bread and cheese, which was all she had. Elsa sprawled on the sofa and munched away and Julia felt more and more that she was the interloper. "Mum misses you," Elsa said, "she's always going on about you." Then, with a pause, "Drives us all mad. She's never taken the hint, has she?" Julia didn't ask what hint. She was concentrating on being civil but distinctly frosty. If there were any hints to be taken Elsa was staring them in the face. Elsa, she reasoned, must have come with a purpose, even if it were one as obvious as merely to annoy her and catch her out, force her into giving the hospitality she'd been determined not to offer. "Mum's quite hurt that you don't come to see us or keep in touch. Dad tells her not to be so touchy. He says they did their best for you and it's not their fault if you reject them."

When Julia didn't respond to this either, Elsa put her head on one side and studied Julia. "It's funny," she said, "I don't really remember your mum, but somehow I think you look like her now. Do you? Do you think you look like her?"

"Why have you come here, Elsa?" Julia said. "Not just to wonder if I look like my mother, I'm sure."

"No," Elsa said, "that's true. I needed a bed for the night, but I could have afforded a hotel, couldn't I? Instead of trailing all this way here. So why did I bother eh? Well, curiosity, of course. To see what you looked like now. I haven't got very good memories of you when you lived with us, but then I don't suppose you've got good memories of me."

"No," said Julia, "I haven't."

"But you'll have them of my mum, I'm sure? She was always kind, wasn't she?"

Julia nodded.

"And my dad? Wasn't he kind too?"

Again, Julia nodded. She was about to say something, about to ask Elsa to stop fooling about, and to say whatever she was bursting to say, but Elsa carried on.

"You caused my dad a lot of trouble," she said, "I wonder if you remember that? I've always wondered why you were so horrible to him. It didn't seem to make sense. Was it because you were jealous of me? Jealous, because you didn't have a father? Was that it?"

"I think we should both go to bed," Julia said, and got up and left the room. It was the point at which she wilfully rejected the opportunity she'd been given, and it never came again. In the morning, when she came down, Elsa had gone, leaving her worried and uneasy.

CHAPTER
TEN

There was a funeral, of course, but Julia didn't go to this one. She didn't send a wreath, or flowers, either. But a week later she wrote to Iris, a careful letter, saying that she had been sorry to hear about Carlo's death but that she had thought she would not be welcome at the funeral. She was grateful, she wrote, for everything Iris and Carlo had done for her, and she was sorry if she had not always been as appreciative as she should have been. She made no reference to having been asked to apologise to Carlo for something Elsa had apparently accused her of. A generalised apology was, she reckoned, enough.

She didn't expect to hear from Iris ever again.

The feeling of guilt was stronger than it had ever been. She was never going to see Iris again, but Julia thought about her cousin constantly, going over and over their history, starting with being her bridesmaid and ending with the scene in her house the night Carlo died. She'd carried this guilt, for all the wrong things she'd done, for years but it had never been so intense, never eaten away at her as it was doing now. Again and again she told herself that nothing could be done about it that had not already been done. Guilt had to be admitted and accepted and then absorbed. Who, after all, was not guilty of something less than admirable in their life?

But in her own case, the list was long. Guilt had shaped her life. It had made her, she was sure, a closed-up creature, always wary, suspicious that she might be found out long after there was anything to find out. She had never allowed anyone to get too close in case she let slip any of her grubby little secrets. She'd been a child when she failed to confess that she'd tipped the baby's pram, and her silence could be explained by fear of the consequences, if she told the truth, not only for herself but for her mother. But later? What was the excuse then? She told herself, comfortingly, that she couldn't really remember exactly what had happened. Maybe the baby's head hadn't been knocked at all. Maybe she hadn't really stolen money, nor done any of the other things she was ashamed of. Who could be sure of anything in their childhood?

On many different occasions, she'd thought of walking into a police station and saying that when she was eight she might have caused the death of a baby. What would the police do? Pull out a file on the case? But it would have in it, if it existed at all, the coroner's verdict which (though she didn't know exactly what this was) absolved anyone from blame. She would be an embarrassment, and, as ever, the refrain "what good would it do?" ran in her head. It would only distress Iris, and it was Julia's conviction that Iris's life had not been blighted irrevocably by her son's death. She never

270

mentioned it, and when her mother had sometimes done so Iris had said firmly that it was in the past and she didn't want it mentioned. Once, when Elsa had seen a photograph of her mother with a baby, at her grandmother's house, she had asked Iris if it was herself. "No," Iris had said, in Julia's hearing, "it was another baby, before you were born." She had shown no emotion, was brisk and matter-of-fact (it was nine years afterwards) though Julia, listening, had felt afraid.

Guilt, she'd discovered as she grew up, could be lived with. She even, at one stage, convinced herself that she'd been brave, bearing the guilt, keeping it to herself, though she'd disabused herself of this notion later. The guilt about the other lesser acts of dishonesty was easier to deal with. They were familiar in her work where she repeatedly saw the lying and cheating and general nastiness exhibited by some children. Her own behaviour in the past fitted a pattern. Where she was lucky was in not having her various deceits exposed. She'd been given the chance to leave them behind, label them to herself as a phase in her development, whereas other children were not so fortunate. And she, unlike so many of them, had been treated kindly. The guilt about how she'd reacted to this kindness was the hardest and most complicated guilt to absorb.

Everything, in every person's life, led back to childhood, a truism which she'd found could not be stressed enough. Childhoods did not explain or justify all subsequent behaviour, of course not, but they were the obvious starting point for any understanding. She'd thought long and hard about her own childhood experiences, searching for key moments and influences, and discovered how difficult it was to be sure of them. Again and again she came back to the secrecy surrounding her father, how she'd known so little, and how her mother had been determined that she should know nothing. The lesson she reckoned she'd picked up was that hiding information was not just permissible but *a good thing*. It had to be done. *Not* concealing things was weak, if the revelation might damage you. There was, in fact, no need to call the habit one of concealment. It could be called a policy of self-protection.

It was a filthy, wet morning, the sky a sullen grey, the pavements dark with rain. Getting up had been hard, the house so cold that Julia shivered making herself coffee. The central heating system had failed the day before and there'd been no chance to call someone to come and put it right.

The bus that took her to the magistrates' court was packed to more than capacity but the driver had let extra passengers on, out of pity for their drowned state, at the last bus stop. A double buggy jammed the exit doors, the young woman holding the handle looked defiantly at a man sighing pointedly as he tried to make a space for himself to the right of it. Another buggy blocked the aisle, the area allowed for buggies already full. Julia closed her eyes. She thought of all the bus rides to school in Manchester on mornings like this, and how she'd endured them by fantasising about her life after school, a life which would be full of sun and warmth and light and fun. Once she'd wished that there existed a means of looking into the future, so that she could see herself in that happy place, but now she was grateful it did not exist. She wouldn't have wanted to see herself on this bus, clad in a black raincoat not dissimilar to her old school raincoat, and black boots, on her way to a magistrates' court, there to be depressed even more by what would pass before her.

She arrived late. This was good. It cut out the biscuits and chat. The other two magistrates were waiting for her in the corridor, relieved that the session didn't have to be cancelled because she hadn't turned up. She had time only to hang up her dripping wet coat and then they were straight into court and onto the first case. In contrast to herself, Julia felt the woman glowed with energy and optimism. She was dressed in an alarming collection of colourful garments, a dizzying array from her hat down to her socks and multicoloured shoes. It hurt the eyes to look at her. At first, it all looked a mess, a jumble, some sort of sartorial disaster, but gradually Julia realised there was a degree of coordination. The colours were in the same spectrum, violent pink deepening to dark purple, a magenta merging into lilac. It must have taken hours to put together. The charge was a serious one. This flamboyantly but well-dressed woman, aged forty, hitherto a respectable shop assistant in a department store, had stolen a baby. She had taken the fifteen-month-old girl, asleep in her buggy, and wheeled her out of the supermarket while the mother was struggling to control her other child, a three-year-old boy, who was pulling boxes of cereal from the shelves. The buggy had been at the end of the aisle, the brake on, a wire basket, half full, laid down beside it, while the mother ran down to stop the boy and followed him when he raced round the corner to the next aisle. It had taken perhaps three minutes for the boy to be hauled back to where the buggy and the mother's wire basket had been parked, but in that time the accused was out of the car park and halfway down the street outside and lost in a crowd.

The shop had been crowded. No one had seen the accused take the baby out, though plenty had seen the mother battling with the destructive three-year-old. CCTV cameras showed the accused walking at a leisurely pace out of the shop and across the car park into the street beyond. After that, there was no trace of her, but the last image showed her about to turn left. Left led to the high street. It took five minutes for the alarm to be raised in the supermarket and another five for the supermarket to be thoroughly searched. The police were then called, and they arrived eight minutes later. Descriptions of the child were taken from the mother, who was incoherent with distress. First she said the little girl had been wearing a blue jacket and then that the jacket was red. She couldn't remember what make the buggy was, but thought it was a Maclaren or maybe a Mothercare. The only distinguishing feature she came up with was that the child was wearing a white hat with ear flaps, bought the day before, brand new, made of faux fur.

274

A police car toured the high street looking for the child but, though there were plenty of children in buggies being trundled about by mothers, and several were stopped, none contained the missing child. An appeal went out on local radio, emphasis laid on the white hat, and it was this which brought the response leading to the discovery of the child in the accused woman's flat. The accused, known to have no children, had been noticed wheeling a buggy into the lift of her block. The police had retrieved the child and arrested the accused. Only two hours ten minutes had passed. The child was still asleep and oblivious to what had happened.

There were medical reports to consider. The accused had a history of miscarriages and of one cot death the year before. This had led to separation from her partner and a three-month period of sick leave. There were no previous charges against the accused, who professed herself deeply sorry and claimed not to know what had come over her. She couldn't remember taking the child. She couldn't remember being in the supermarket. All she could remember was finding herself at home, and the buggy with the sleeping child in it, parked in her living room. She claimed that she had been about to ring the police when they arrived.

The chairman was gentle with her, as Julia had known he would be. She'd sat on the bench with him several times and admired his handling of some tricky cases. In a case like this, what was at issue was whether the accused had, or had not, known what she was doing. Had she experienced a mental blackout, explained by the extreme recent stress she'd been under? Or was this merely a pretence and in reality she deliberately stole the child? Looking at the accused, Julia could not make her own mind up, and listened intently both to the chairman's questions and the accused's replies. The woman seemed so extremely calm and collected. Her manner was polite, her answers short, clear, direct. There was no sign of any trauma, but then of course the incident was over days ago. But there was something about her apology for what she had done that struck Julia as false. She did not seem truly contrite, prefacing her "very sorry" with "of course", in a matter-of-fact way, almost briskly.

They withdrew to confer. No harm had been done, but nevertheless a serious crime had been committed and the case must be referred to the Crown Court, so their discussion was short, merely going over the obvious points. When they went back into the court, and before the chairman could speak, the accused's solicitor said there was something his client would like to say to the bench before hearing what was to happen to her. The chairman agreed to hear her, and she was once more brought in. She had changed. Gone was the composed demeanour, the confident manner. She seemed to wilt in the box when previously she had stood there straight-backed, head held high. Her voice had altered too. It was suddenly a barely audible whisper which was a strain to catch. "I have something to confess," she began, and then stopped. The chairman waited a minute or two, and when she failed to continue asked if what she felt the need to confess had any relevance to the taking of the child, because unless she was sure that it had, there was no need, or reason, to make a confession. The woman replied, in a slightly stronger voice: "It has, it has, it was the start."

They waited.

Julia didn't go on to work. She called in, saying she felt ill and was going home to bed, which she did. Once home, she lay down on her bed for a while, without undressing or getting under the duvet, looking out at the branches of the gigantic plane tree, now bare of leaves and its stark black limbs revealing a crow's nest in the highest fork. The sky behind, showing through the branches, was almost white, any colour bleached out by the cold, or so she fancied. Soothed, she got up and went to her desk and took out a pen, a proper fountain pen she had had since she was a schoolgirl, and now rarely used. She would have to write. She was not up to telephoning. The conversation would be too difficult. Her voice would fail her. And a visit was impossible, the thought of a confrontation unbearable.

The letter took her most of the rest of the day. She told Iris everything, every little detail, trying to explain, without attempting to justify, her behaviour as a child. She badly wanted to tell her about the woman who had made her bizarre confession in court that day, and the effect it had on her, but she held back. To do so, to tell Iris how this confession acted as a catalyst, would only complicate matters, and she wanted to be direct and simple. The hardest part of the letter was the last bit, where she felt Iris had to be made to believe how she had suffered, that she had not got off scot-free. But saying that, however she said it, however she tried to phrase the truth of what she was saying made her sound self-pitying: poor me, I did wrong but oh how I have been punished by my conscience. She would be burdening Iris, as she had always vowed she would not. To stoop to such a thing was to be despicable.

She copied out her final version, feeling that once posted she might so wish to blot out what she had written that she would forget it, and she did not want to do so. This was her "clean breast" and she needed evidence that it had been made. Unlike the woman in court that morning, one wrong-doing had not ultimately led to crime. She had been lucky she had managed to turn herself away from lying, stealing, forging and all the other misdemeanours in her young life. For years now she had never even been tempted. She was a good person, law-abiding and dutiful. But the letter to Iris reminded her of what she could have become. She could have been any one of a number of women who had appeared before the bench she sat upon. She felt she had redeemed herself but this redemption was not complete until she unburdened herself to Iris and, at last, accepted the consequences, something she had struggled successfully for so long to persuade herself was not necessary.

What these consequences would be she could not imagine. It was too frightening.

Elsa turned up at seven one morning, unannounced, a week after Julia sent her letter to Iris. When Julia

278

opened the door, still in her dressing gown, Elsa said: "I thought I'd catch you at this time," as though she had just popped in from a few doors down the street, maybe to borrow something. "What time do you leave for work?" she asked as she stepped inside and took off her heavy black coat, hanging it in a familiar way on the hook behind the door.

"About nine," Julia said.

"Very civilised," Elsa said, and then, "Plenty of time for a chat, then. Coffee?"

Julia felt as though Elsa was offering coffee, not requesting it, but she nodded and said she would just pull on some clothes first. There was something formidable about Elsa now, something threatening that hadn't been there before. She'd nothing of her mother about her but plenty of her father's confidence without his charm. Julia tried to remember what she did, what her job was, whether she was married and had children, all of which information Iris would definitely have told her in the letters she'd gone on writing even though they were never answered. A manager, that was it, a manager of a firm that made kitchenware of some sort. And she didn't have children, nor was she married, but she had a partner who Carlo hadn't liked.

She dressed distractedly, barely noticing what she was choosing to put on, and then went straight to the kitchen and made coffee. Elsa was in the living room, examining the bookshelves.

"Heavy stuff," she said, "not much light reading, is there?"

Julia didn't reply. She set the coffee down, and gestured that Elsa should help herself to milk or sugar.

"Good coffee," Elsa said, after the first sip. "Dad would approve. Do you remember how —"

But Julia stopped her. "Elsa," she said, "you haven't come here to discuss coffee. You've come about the letter I wrote to your mother, haven't you? So shall we get straight to the point, whatever it is? Then you can go home and I can go to work."

Elsa drank some more coffee, then replaced her cup on the table in front of her. "The point," she said. "That's very you, Julia. Not 'How are you, Elsa?' but wanting to go straight to the point. Wanting there to be something as simple as a point." Then she reached into the bag she had with her and drew out a letter. Julia could see her own handwriting on the envelope. Elsa put the letter beside the coffee cup.

There was an absolute silence between them. Julia's face felt hot, her hands, holding her own cup of coffee, sweaty. This was a game Elsa was enjoying, but the nature of the game was mysterious. Julia realised she was meant to feel uncomfortable. Well, she did. But why should she feel this, merely confronted with her own letter? She cleared her throat, and then said, "I see that's the letter I wrote to Iris. Presumably she gave it to you to read."

"No," Elsa said, "she didn't. She's never seen it, never read it."

"So you open your mother's letters?" Julia said.

"At her request," Elsa said. "She has cataracts in both eyes and can't make out any print. She's due to

280

have them done next week. Privately. Expensively But she's nervous, and wanted the best person. You'll remember how timid she can be."

It was hopeless. Julia felt suddenly faint, baffled by Elsa's attitude, weakened by her obvious strength. Elsa was waiting for a reaction now, but she couldn't summon one up. She felt humiliated, embarrassed. Then she tried to shake off these feelings, to become more herself, assertive and calm.

"Elsa," she said, pleased that her voice had regained its normal level, "obviously, you've read the letter and, obviously, you've come here to say something about it, so can you just say it, and then go? The letter wasn't intended for anyone except Iris, and I'm sorry you had to read it."

"Oh, don't be sorry," Elsa said, "I'm glad I've read it. It explains a lot. I always knew you were a nasty bit of work and now I have the proof."

Julia stood up. "You've said your bit," she said to Elsa, "so well done, that's enough."

"It isn't enough," Elsa snapped, "so you just sit down again. My mother, when she can read again, is never going to be shown your disgusting letter, the letter you're so proud of, full of your own virtue. It would cause her the most awful distress, not that you'd care about that."

"Of course I'd care," Julia interrupted, "I do care, how can you think I don't? That was what the letter was about, how much I —"

"What your letter was about," said Elsa, "was *you*. That's all. How *you'd* suffered, how you'd had to endure all this guilt, how unlucky, unfortunate, all the rest, you'd been, and how brilliantly you'd risen above all this 'suffering', how well you'd done to come through it and make something of your life when you could so easily have slipped into a life of crime. That's what your letter is about. You never once, in it, try to put yourself in my mum's place. Do you think she ever wanted to take you into her family? Do you? Can't you see how my grandmother bullied her? How *she* couldn't face it, knowing what you were like, so she forced my mum and dad to have you? Your mother was nothing but trouble and you were the same, so don't give me all this how you suffered."

Elsa was quite breathless with fury. Julia kept silent, waited again. It was no good attempting to defend herself, or to pick on the outrageous accusation that her own mother had been "nothing but trouble". Her professional self took over, and she waited, doing nothing to provoke Elsa further. At some stage, Elsa would have to go. It was just a question of how long this would take, and of whether Elsa had more to say. Was venting her rage enough? Or did she want something? Julia couldn't decide. She told herself she didn't have to. All the cards were in Elsa's hands, and held very close still to her chest.

"I'm not stupid," Elsa suddenly said, "I may not be as clever as you think you are, but I'm not stupid. I know there's nothing I can do about what's in this letter, all the admissions in it. Is admissions the right word? Probably not. But you know what I mean, I'm sure. There were suspicions, at the time, about you, did

282

you know that? No, you didn't. Mum never told me, or Fran, about her baby boy dying, but Grandma did. You were the last person to touch the baby, everyone knew that. You'd said yourself that you tucked him in when he was asleep. No one knew you'd taken him for the walk you describe in your letter, but they knew you'd touched the pram. Grandma went over and over it, how she wouldn't have put anything past you. But there was no proof. There still isn't. It's all maybe a possibility on that score. Mum doesn't need to know about that walk and you tipping the pram, but you haven't the wit to see it, what it would do, for all your training. Just keep your mouth shut. That's the least you can do." Then Elsa leaned forward and tore the letter into tiny pieces. "That's what I think of your wretched letter," she said, and stood up. "Feel guilty some more," she said. "Feel guilty till the day you die. You deserve to. It isn't so easy to offload, it sticks, it will go on sticking."

Elsa stood up and went in search of her coat. Julia felt obliged to follow her, feeling as she did so like a little whipped dog. She watched Elsa put her coat on and button it up, and then she was out of the front door without any goodbye, slamming it behind her.

Weeks it took, to recover from Elsa's dramatic visit. Again and again, Julia shifted her opinion of what had been said, first seeing it was a mindless rant and then realising it had been no such thing and that there were elements within it she would be unwise to ignore. She wished, of course, that she had never written to Iris. It was a stupid thing to have done, as she had always known it would be if she gave in to the temptation to do it. Exactly why she had succumbed to the need to write such a letter she couldn't understand, except that it had had a lot to do with the confession made by the woman in the dock that morning. Julia had watched her closely as she listed a whole string of familiar minor crimes in astonishing detail. Going back over two decades, she had itemised every article she had successfully stolen, able to name the shops, the prices, and the dates the thefts took place. She had smuggled drugs into the country several times (small amounts) without being detected and sold them afterwards. The admissions went on and on, though both her own horrified solicitor and the chairman tried to call a halt. Finally silenced, in the middle of recalling ludicrously trivial motoring offences, the woman had smiled, and sighed, and looked hugely relieved.

Julia, leaving the courtroom later that morning, carried in her mind a picture of this woman's excitement during her confession. She was, if not mentally unbalanced, certainly not in possession of all her faculties. But, as the chairman pointed out afterwards, there was an element of conscious boasting in what she'd insisted on telling them. She wanted people to know how clever she'd been, how easy she'd proved it was to steal and cheat. This boasting, though, was also masochistic. She craved punishment, the chairman thought. This last suggestion stuck with Julia. She wondered if she herself perhaps had always craved punishment. Had she? No, that was absurd. Forgiveness, then? Possibly. Nothing she'd done to Iris was so very terrible. Iris would tell her this. For heaven's sake, Julia pet, she would surely say, how can you be dragging all this stuff up, as if it matters now?

So she'd given in to the impulse she'd suppressed for so long, never imagining Elsa would be the reader of her letter and not Iris. But then she ought to have foreseen that Iris might very well anyway have shown the letter to her daughters, to share its contents with them and consult them over what to say in reply. It would have been natural. I was a coward, Julia thought, and cowards get their comeuppance. Elsa had been right in what she'd come to say, and now the situation was worse than it had ever been, nothing gained, everything lost, peace of mind unobtainable, unless she did what she should have done in the first place, if she was going to do anything at all.

"Julia!" Iris said. "Well, this is a surprise, goodness it is, I can't believe it." She stood at the open door staring at Julia, checking her out, her eyes going from head to feet and back again, while Julia stayed still, not daring to venture inside without an invitation. I must look, she thought, like the penitent I am.

Iris had aged, or perhaps it was the recent cataract operations that made her seem much frailer, her walk a little unsteady. She led the way straight into her kitchen, saying she must have a cup of tea immediately to get over the shock. Once the tea was made, and the two of them were seated at the familiar table, she seemed more like her old self. Her expression, though, was not the kindly one that Julia remembered. Instead, it was searching, the eyes quite sharp and she was not smiling.

"Been a long time, Julia," she said, "a very long time."

"I know," Julia said, "I'm sorry."

"You didn't come to the funeral," Iris said, "you didn't pay your respects."

"No," said Julia. "I should have done, I know."

"Why not?" Iris said. "Why cut us off like that? Not a word from you all this time. What did we do wrong?"

"Nothing," Julia said. "I am the one who's done wrong, and I'm ashamed."

"Well then," Iris said, "we'll forget it, and start again, shall we?"

"Not yet," Julia said. "I wrote you a letter. Elsa read it when you couldn't read, but she didn't tell you. It was about the past, all the mean things I did, and —"

"Oh," Iris said, "the past is past, why rake it up?"

"I have to," Julia said, "it won't let me go."

"Well then," Iris said, "get it over with and then we can get on."

It wasn't as difficult as she had imagined it would be and Iris's response wasn't as emotional as she had thought it would be. She didn't, in fact, seem distressed at all, only puzzled that Julia was, as she put it, "making a meal" of describing her past faults. The tipping of baby Reggie's pram she brushed aside. "Nonsense," she said, "you've got it all wrong. He didn't die of a blow to the head at all. Why did you think that? Little Miss Big Ears, that was you, always listening to grown-ups and getting everything wrong. It was a respiratory failure that killed him. You can see the coroner's report if you like. I've got it somewhere. All that torturing of yourself, Julia, that's you all over. You've never grown out of it, all drama when there was none there."

All the other things got the same dismissive treatment from Iris except for the matter of the letters to Carlo. "Now, that," Iris said, "was naughty, that caused a lot of trouble. The girl — can't remember her name — denied ever sending them but Carlo sacked her all the same. He didn't believe her. Elsa guessed it was you, though. You'd have to ask her how she knew, but she did. Her dad didn't believe her either. He thought she was just making trouble for you. She was jealous of you, Julia. You knew that, I'm sure. She resented you being taken into our family, that was it. And you were mean to her, just as you've said. But none of all that really upsets me. It's how you behaved later, once you'd left our house. That hurt, Julia. Cutting yourself off, not keeping any contact, that hurt. And you being what you are, it didn't make sense. You should have seen it would hurt, when you'd been with us all those years, part of our family, and then never a word. How could you be any kind of psychologist, or whatever it is you are, and do that to us? That's what I want to know. The rest doesn't matter."

Sitting listening with her head bowed, unable to meet Iris's eyes, Julia found herself in one part of her brain noting her cousin's unexpected strength and being surprised by it. She'd never suspected that Iris had it within her to be so frank and direct: Iris, who was always so mild-mannered, eager to please, forever shying away from confrontation or unpleasantness. And she was right. Julia knew she was right. How could she not have known Iris would be hurt and bewildered at the way she had cut herself off? But, of course, she had known Iris would be hurt. She'd known this perfectly well. It was obvious. What was worse was that, knowing this, she had allowed herself to ignore it. She'd just wanted out of that family at all costs. Understanding what she was doing hadn't meant she was going to change.

"Well, Julia, what are we going to do about all this, eh?" Iris was saying. "A storm in a teacup, all water under the bridge, and here we are, sitting across from each other again. You think I've a lot to forgive you for. Well, it's forgiven. Now tell me about yourself. What's happened to you all these years? Oh, not the career, I know about that, roughly, but the rest, what about your personal life, Julia? Are you happy single? Did you never meet anyone else after your divorce? Am I prying? But family can ask, can't they? Tell me about yourself, Julia. I've a lot to catch up on."

Julia left Iris's house two hours later, exhausted. Iris's appetite for trivia was extraordinary. She'd wanted every detail of a "personal" life that hadn't much detail in it. All Julia could do was broad sweeps and that didn't satisfy Iris. She tried to talk about her work, and about being a magistrate, but Iris wasn't interested. It was no good saying that her work *was* her. Iris wouldn't have it. She insisted that there must be what she called "affairs of the heart". "You're not made of stone, Julia," she said, "you're flesh and blood, you have feelings. They must have come to the fore sometimes. Now tell me, I'm broad-minded."

Lamely, Julia dragged up a couple of affairs she had had but said nothing about her failed marriage. When Iris asked her point-blank if she had ever thought about having children she lied and said no, never.

The girl was called Precious. She was aged eleven, and in foster care. The carers, however, were relatives, an "aunt" and an "uncle". But they were both unknown to Precious when she arrived in this country from Ethiopia. How exactly she had arrived was unclear. The aunt and uncle maintained that she had simply arrived on their doorstep one September morning the year before carrying a bag and a piece of paper with their address and telephone number on it. There was no passport in her possession so whoever had brought her into the country had either kept it or had somehow smuggled her in without one. Precious had been with these relatives (though their exact relationship to her was another thing shrouded in mystery) for almost a year. She spoke no English, beyond please and thank you, when she arrived but was now fluent and doing well at school. But she was said to be a liar and a cheat and was causing more and more trouble in the family. No one could understand her behaviour. The aunt and uncle were bewildered and upset. They had taken Precious in, though they had three children of their own plus an elderly cousin living with them. They had treated her with love and kindness and had been as generous as their circumstances permitted. But, said the aunt, she appeared to hate them. She was becoming thoroughly nasty and the family was now afraid of her. If Julia couldn't do something they were considering passing her on to another set of relatives, if they could be persuaded to have her.

She was a strikingly beautiful girl but she bristled with hostility. Self-possessed and seemingly confident, a confidence bordering on arrogance, she sat before Julia straight-backed, head held high, everything about her a challenge. Julia didn't say anything for a long time, but Precious was not in the least perturbed by her silence. She seemed to enjoy it, holding Julia's gaze steadily, as though daring her to blink. There would be no point in questioning her about where she had come from and how her journey had been made. All that would have been gone into many times and Julia didn't think she would get a better result than had already been obtained. Precious, she was sure, expected to be asked why she behaved as she did, why was she repaying her aunt and uncle for their kindness by being so unpleasant and making herself objectionable. So Julia wouldn't ask why.

Instead, she said, "You're doing so well at school, Precious. What subject do you like best?"

"Maths," Precious said.

"Do you want to study maths later, maybe at university?"

"No," Precious said. "I want to be a lawyer. I will be a lawyer, like my father."

Julia looked at the notes. There was no mention of a father who was a lawyer. No mention of either a father or a mother. And a father who was a lawyer didn't fit with the story of Precious turning up, apparently alone. Surely such an educated and therefore presumably reasonably affluent man would not just have dispatched a daughter in such a way? Or had Precious been told by him to stay silent about how she entered the country? In which case, what was the motive?

Julia cleared her throat and said, "That's interesting, a father who is a lawyer. Do you know what kind of law he specialises in?"

"He doesn't," Precious said, "he is in prison. Before that, he helped people."

"Do you want to do the same, to help people?"

"No," said Precious.

"So what sort of lawyer do you want to be?"

"Crime," Precious said. "Murder."

"Defending people accused of murder?" Julia asked.

"No," Precious said, "prosecuting them. Then they'll hang or get beheaded."

"Not in this country," Julia said, "we don't have the death penalty. We have life imprisonment."

Precious curled her lip. "That, then," she said.

"It will mean a lot of studying," Julia said, "a lot of support from your family."

"They are not my family," Precious said. "I'm just staying with them because I have to."

"But," said Julia, "they don't have to let you go on staying with them, and if you can't get on with them better than you are doing at the moment, and you have

291

to move on, it will mean changing schools, making it harder to study, and you might not like where you're moved to either. So, Precious, that's a lot to think about. Maybe you should decide to make the best of it. It won't be forever. You aren't being ill-treated. You are doing the ill-treating."

Precious stood up. "You don't know what it's like," she said, "I'm not ill-treating anyone. It's silly saying that. They don't like me, they don't want me, and I don't like them and I don't want to be with them. They want me to thank them all the time. They keep telling me how grateful I should be. I'm not grateful. I don't see why I should be."

"Lots of reasons," Julia said. "Sit down, and I'll run through them, then maybe we can come to some compromise. I'm here to help you, Precious."

Again and again, all year, she had been reminded of the dangerous road only just not taken, the tempting road that all the children she saw reminded her of, and which she went on trying to bar them from. Help, at the vital moment, that was what was needed. Help that she had lacked.

Isa & May

Margaret Forster

The curiously named Isamay is trying to write a coherent thesis about grandmothers in history — from Sarah Bernhardt and George San to the matriarchal Queen Victoria and other influential grannies — while constantly ambushed by the secrets of her own family. An only child, she is named after her grandmothers, Isa and May, who have formed and influenced her in very different ways. Jealous of each other, they both want to be first in their granddaughter's affections. Isa has an edge, in that young Isamay looks like her. May, on the other hand, is indomitable and opinionated, and from her Isamay inherits her stubborn determination.

Now Isamay, almost 30, begins to want a child of her own, but her live-in lover, Ian (always mysterious about his own family history) is sure that he does not want children. And soon Isamay has her heart set on the idea.

ISBN 978-0-7531-8700-5 (hb)
ISBN 978-0-7531-8701-2 (pb)

Over

Margaret Forster

Louise, a mother and primary school teacher, is trying to hold herself together after her teenage daughter dies in mysterious circumstances. She's trying to get on with life, trying to understand not "what happened", but what is happening to them all in the wake of the accident, and why.

Don, her husband, cannot accept that his child's death might have been an accident. He wants someone to blame, becoming obsessive in his quest for a reason, travelling restlessly, neglecting work and family in pursuit of the "truth". Their other children handle the tragedy better than their parents. What they can't deal with is the way their parents are tearing each other and the family apart.

ISBN 978-0-7531-7894-2 (hb)
ISBN 978-0-7531-7895-9 (pb)

The Battle for Christabel

Margaret Forster

A heart-rending tale of the legal and emotional battle for an orphaned child.

When the single mother of a young child is tragically killed in a climbing accident, the battle lines are drawn. On one side are Christabel's indomitable Scottish grandmother and Isobel, a friend of the family. On the other, are Betty, the foster mother, and the social workers. Everyone suffers, but the main casualty is the child.

ISBN 978-0-7531-7393-0 (hb)
ISBN 978-0-7531-7394-7 (pb)

Home

Toni Morrison

An angry and self-loathing veteran of the Korean War, Frank Money finds himself back in racist America after enduring trauma on the front lines that left him with more than just physical scars. His home — and himself in it — may no longer be as he remembers it, but Frank is shocked out of his crippling apathy by the need to rescue his medically abused younger sister and take her back to the small Georgia town they come from, which he's hated all his life.

As Frank revisits the memories from childhood and the war that leaves him questioning his sense of self, he discovers a profound courage he thought he would never possess again.

ISBN 978-0-7531-9170-5 (hb)
ISBN 978-0-7531-9171-2 (pb)

I Should Be So Lucky

Judy Astley

Viola hasn't had much luck with men. Her first husband, Marco, companion of her youth and father of her only child, left her when he realised he was gay. Her second, Rhys, ended his high-octane, fame-filled life by driving his Porsche into a wall. No wonder her family always believes she needs "Looking After", and her friends think she really shouldn't be allowed out on her own . . .

Which is why, at the age of 39, she finds herself shamefully back at home, living with Mum.

Viola knows she has to take charge; she needs to get a life, and fast. With a stroppy teenage daughter, a demanding mother, and siblings who want to control her life for her, where is she going to turn?

ISBN 978-0-7531-9082-1 (hb)
ISBN 978-0-7531-9083-8 (pb)

ISIS publish a wide range of books in large print, from fiction to biography. Any suggestions for books you would like to see in large print or audio are always welcome. Please send to the Editorial Department at:

ISIS Publishing Limited
7 Centremead
Osney Mead
Oxford OX2 0ES

A full list of titles is available free of charge from:

Ulverscroft Large Print Books Limited

(UK)
The Green
Bradgate Road, Anstey
Leicester LE7 7FU
Tel: (0116) 236 4325

(Australia)
P.O. Box 314
St Leonards
NSW 1590
Tel: (02) 9436 2622

(USA)
P.O. Box 1230
West Seneca
N.Y. 14224-1230
Tel: (716) 674 4270

(Canada)
P.O. Box 80038
Burlington
Ontario L7L 6B1
Tel: (905) 637 8734

(New Zealand)
P.O. Box 456
Feilding
Tel: (06) 323 6828

Details of **ISIS** complete and unabridged audio books are also available from these offices. Alternatively, contact your local library for details of their collection of **ISIS** large print and unabridged audio books.